Reunited

God help her, she was tempted. She wanted to know what had put those lines on his face and those shadows in his eyes. There had been a time when she would have tried to make them go away. But she'd already settled her accounts with Kalen. Awkwardly she pushed his arm away. "Go now."

"I need your help."

"You need the help of an AWOL army officer?" She clucked her tongue. "That would violate at least a dozen regs. I'm shocked, General. What happened to that highly polished, everything-by-the-book attitude of yours?"

"No one knows you were CID." He ignored the disgusted sound she made. "You know how the Chinese operate. I need an insider to infiltrate the tong, someone who won't raise any suspicions. You're it."

"So you came all the way to Paris to—what? *Persuade* me to come back to work for you?" She laughed.

His mouth flattened, and a muscle ticked in his jaw. "You served your country once."

That was the wrong thing to say to her. "My *country* left me to die in China."

For my friend Sarah Jane Elliott—
who flirts with danger,
dreams of dolphins,
and spins imaginings into stories.
Raven would have no other namesake.

THE
STEEL
CARESS

Jessica Hall

A SIGNET BOOK

SIGNET
Published by New American Library, a division of
Penguin Group (USA) Inc., 375 Hudson Street,
New York, New York 10014, U.S.A.
Penguin Books Ltd, 80 Strand,
London WC2R 0RL, England
Penguin Books Australia Ltd, 250 Camberwell Road,
Camberwell, Victoria 3124, Australia
Penguin Books Canada Ltd, 10 Alcorn Avenue,
Toronto, Ontario, Canada M4V 3B2
Penguin Books (N.Z.) Ltd, Cnr Rosedale and Airborne Roads,
Albany, Auckland 1310, New Zealand

Penguin Books Ltd, Registered Offices:
80 Strand, London WC2R 0RL, England

First published by Signet, an imprint of New American Library,
a division of Penguin Group (USA) Inc.

First Printing, May 2003
10 9 8 7 6 5 4 3 2 1

Ⓟ REGISTERED TRADEMARK—MARCA REGISTRADA

Printed in the United States of America

and utterly boring. D.C. politicians eyed their attractive young mistresses from across the room while they remained coldly sober and ushered about their older, not-so-beautiful wives. Foreign dignitaries, having the advantage of interpreters to cover any faux pas, imbibed more freely. Debutante daughters and sons being groomed for great things strayed to corners to ridicule their parents in whispers and plot future, wilder gatherings.

Then there were the single career girls on the prowl, like the two young women at the Japanese ambassador's table. They made the rounds for other than social reasons—some to show off for the married men who would otherwise be escorting them, others looking for more serious prey—the kind who would assure they wouldn't spend the rest of their youth typing letters and answering phones.

Hey, I should get a raise, Sarah's ghost whispered inside General Kalen Grady's head. *After all, I sleep with the boss.*

She'd said that eight years ago, curled up at his side, her fingers drawing little circles on his bare chest. Sarah had loved to tease him.

And I gave her so little in return, Kalen thought. *Plenty of sex but no promises, no dreams.* It had cost him nearly everything—including her.

The secretary's voice climbed an octave. "What about that red-haired guy standing near your boss? The one in the gray suit—now he looks appetizing."

Although he stood across the room, Kalen Grady didn't have to turn to see the speculative looks. He'd bugged the table to gather evidence against the senator, who was rumored to be in bed with a couple of major Japanese automakers. So far, all he had was the polite small talk over dinner and a sub-

Chapter 1

"Everyone calls her the Dragon Lady," the senator's assistant murmured to her companion, a junior secretary at the Department of Transportation. "Not very original, but in this case, the name fits."

"Poor Mr. Tanaga." The secretary watched the Japanese ambassador as he dutifully introduced his wife to one of the Australian delegates. "He seems like such a nice man, too. So why *do* they call her the Dragon Lady?"

"What else would you call a cold-blooded, thick-skinned, fire-breathing snake?"

Both women giggled. Both were also completely unaware of the tiny microphone hidden in the floral centerpiece on the senator's table, or the man standing on the other side of the room who was using it to listen to their conversation.

"Oh, but Tanaga is a sweetheart, honey, he really is." The older woman's voice dropped to a mere whisper, but the sensitive mike still picked up every word. "You know, if you show him a little TLC, you might just snag yourself a weekend at his house on Martha's Vineyard."

Like all Washington political soirees, the Japanese Embassy's Spring Ball was exclusive, well attended, sequent seventeen minutes of surreptitious feminine scheming.

"Is he gay?" the secretary wanted to know.

Inside his head, the ghost laughed with delight. *If you don't stop sneaking around with me, someone's going to think you're gay or something.*

Conor Perry, Kalen's point man in the surveillance van outside the Japanese embassy, cut in on the transmission. "Uh, want me to kill that mike, boss? Doesn't sound like we're going to get anything . . . productive tonight."

Kalen touched the flag pin on his lapel, which concealed his own transmitter. "No, thanks, Con." He had tired of listening to ghosts and harpies, however, and performed a one-eighty scan of the crowded room.

Where is he?

Fujiko Tanaga, the Japanese ambassador, had promised to put Kalen in contact with Dai Gangi, son and heir apparent of the Dai tong, but so far he hadn't delivered. That was why Kalen was roaming through clusters of diplomats, making polite noises and wondering how much longer he would have to nurse the expensive and incredibly bad Sauvignon in his glass.

"He's straight, but he's a walking target," the senator's assistant was saying. "They say he got his last girlfriend killed."

That's your problem, babe, the ghost whispered. *You've ticked off so many bad guys out there, anyone who marries you will have to wear a Kevlar vest under her wedding gown.*

But Sarah would have married him anyway. Sweet, open, trusting Sarah, who would have gone to her death for him, had loved him without reservation.

Sarah, who hadn't died, but had come back to haunt him anyway.

"General Grady," the secretary of commerce, a stern-faced older woman, beckoned to him. "What do you have to say about these new Chinese laws regulating Internet access and censoring Web content?"

"I'd say America Online is going to be a tough sell in Beijing, Madame Secretary," Kalen said, and handed his half-full wineglass to a passing waiter. "If you'll excuse me, I need to have a word with our host."

"Tell Tanaga I expect more leeway on the transmeta technology exchange, or he can tell Toshiba to cut production fifty percent next year," the lady warned. Although she wasn't joking, the group around her produced polite chuckles.

"Yes, ma'am." Kalen inclined his head and slipped away. Tanaga had not in fact been waving at him, and more than likely had been avoiding him. Kalen's gut told him it was because Dai had pulled a disappearing act.

Time to remind the ambassador who pulled his daughter out of that cyber café drug scandal last summer and kept the media from driving him back in disgrace to Tokyo.

Yet when he caught up with the Japanese politician, the shorter man looked almost relieved. "General."

"Ambassador." Kalen inspected the conversation clusters around them. "Has Dai canceled?"

"No, as it happens, Gangi and his escort arrived a short time ago. Regrettably, I have been unable to locate them since. My security guards at the entrance tell me they have not left the mansion." He covered his nervousness with a polite laugh. "I know our gatherings are large, but I believe this is the first time I have actually misplaced two guests."

Guests didn't disappear at Washington soirees. Not when they were there to see and be seen. "Who was Dai with?"

"A Caucasian woman wearing the most astonishing green dress." Tanaga sounded faintly scandalized. "My wife tells me she has only one name—Portia."

Kalen's polite smile stayed in place, but he didn't have to flip through his mental files. He knew exactly who Portia Santiago was—a sultry South American mestiza whose incredible genetic luck had propelled her out of Brazilian poverty and onto magazine covers around the globe. Although the fiery brunette was considered one of the ten most beautiful models in the world, she had yet to challenge the woman who had held the number one spot for five years straight.

Raven.

"Give me a moment, Ambassador." Kalen stepped away, and touched his flag pin again. "Conor, we've lost track of Dai and his girlfriend," he said in a low murmur. "Look for a Chinese American male in a tux and a tall, dark knockout in green designer rags."

"We'll check it out, boss," Conor replied over the earpiece. "Can we keep the knockout if we find her?"

"Not tonight."

The team, who were mixed in with the normal caterers and waiters, went immediately but discreetly into action. Kalen did a three-sixty, looking at dress and skin colors to sort out the guests quickly.

"What other rooms are open to guests?" he asked Tanaga.

"My offices are secured, as are the family quarters." The amabassador took out a silk handkerchief and used it to wipe his hands, which were sweating. "That leaves the rest of the house accessible to our guests."

Kalen thought for a moment. Gangi was rumored to be quite the ladies' man. "Where would a couple of youngsters go to have a private moment?"

"The rock garden, perhaps, or the reflecting pool." The ambassador turned to one of his men and relayed orders in rapid Japanese. The man took off. "If they are out there, he will return and inform us."

The sound of muttering above their heads made Kalen turn and look up. On the second floor, a maid carrying an armload of coats and furs was trying to open a door, with no success.

"Should that door be locked?" he asked Tanaga, who shook his head. His instincts went on full alert. "Excuse me, Ambassador."

By the time he reached the maid, the ambassador's wife was already there, trying to get in. Madam Tanaga, aka the Dragon Lady, appeared practically swamped in the heavy black fabric of her satin skirts, but they weren't holding her back from vigorously jiggling the doorknob and scolding her servant.

"Ah, General, do you wish to leave? Forgive me. This *baku* girl has somehow jammed this door." Madam Tanaga went to hand Kalen the glass of champagne she held, then thought better of it and gave him a pretty smile instead. "Perhaps a man's strength would solve the problem."

Kalen tried the doorknob, which had to be locked from the inside. "Have you tried knocking?"

"Yes, but no one should be in there." The ambassador's wife looked peeved. "It is only a coatroom."

"Perhaps they only meant a brief visit." The thin,

flexible metal strip he took from his pocket slid easily behind the door catch. With a hook and a tug, he pushed it back, allowing him to pull open the door.

"It must be one of the upstairs maids. Let me handle this, General. *Kore wa nan desuka . . .*" Madam Tanaga moved past him, then came to an abrupt halt and stumbled away. The crystal glass fell from her fingers and smashed on the floor, sending a spray of champagne across the white marble floor. She opened her mouth, dragged in a breath, and screamed.

The maid immediately dropped all the coats and furs on top of the puddle of champagne and shattered crystal as her hands flew up to cover her face. She began to shriek in harmony with the ambassador's wife.

Kalen had his gun out and shielded both women before they'd made the first peep, but a glance inside the coatroom made him holster the weapon and close the door.

"Take them both downstairs," he told another, horrified servant, pushing Tanaga's wife and the semi-hysterical maid at him. "Post security at the bottom of the stairs, and keep the rest of the guests away from here."

Once the women had been led away, he stepped into the room.

Dai Gangi occupied it, as well as his beautiful companion. They were holding each other like lovers embracing. Swatches of black electrical tape covered their mouths, and a length of heavy chain had been wrapped around their bodies. Someone had hung them from one of the overhead coatrack bars, but the chain binding them together wasn't what had killed them.

The long, sharp sword that the killer had thrust through both of their chests had done the job perfectly.

"You've been quoted as saying what gives someone pleasure helps them cultivate style," the Parisian reporter read from her notes before producing a distinctly cynical smile. "If that's true, then anyone could look like you."

"Anyone can cultivate personal style," Raven said as her dresser finished spritzing the back of her head. "To look like me, you'd have to go talk to those cloning people."

"No one will ever look as beautiful as my Raven," Honore Etienne said from the doorway. "Lise, you have had your fifteen-minute interview, now go out and get a table before the rest of Paris drinks up my champagne."

As the reporter left, Raven stood up and stretched her long, lean body. She was so tall that her fingertips nearly touched the ceiling of the dressing room.

"Did you stay up all night watching Humpty Bogart movies again?" the fashion designer demanded as she shut the door.

"Humphrey Bogart, and no, I didn't." Raven shed her street clothes as the dresser opened a long golden box and removed the contents. "Why, are there bags under my eyes?"

"I would beat you if there were." The Frenchwoman paced around her. "Take off your bra. You can't wear that with my dress. And change your G-string. Those ties will show through the skirt."

Raven eyed the handful of blue silk and white lace that the dresser was patiently holding. "Looks like everything will show through that skirt."

"A mere illusion of nakedness, *cherie.*" Honore flipped up the outer, gauzy layer of the dress to reveal a flesh-colored layer of fabric beneath. "Only to tease the eye, not to satisfy the curiosity."

"Good, because you know how much curiosity there is about the birthmark on my butt." Raven changed her G-string to one without ties, then stepped into the dress. "Geez, Ray, this feels like tissue paper."

"Burmese silk," Honore corrected, and watched as the dresser tugged the sleeves into place. "Ah, you look *enchanté, ma petite.*"

"I feel like disenchanted old pâté." Raven turned to the right and measured the line of the ghostly, weightless silk as it dipped below her waist in the back. "Lise should have stuck around; this outfit has real style."

"*Merci beaucoup, cherie.*"

She adjusted the fabric, which barely covered the top of her buttocks. "And if I bend over far enough, that style is going to show everyone that my dimples aren't on my face."

"That is why you are wearing the show closer, and not Charise," Honore said as she smoothed a faint wrinkle from one fitted sleeve. "You never bend far enough. Come, we have many eyes waiting to be dazzled."

Raven followed the designer out to the cramped passage behind the stage. All around them, dressers and fitters bustled, adding the final touches to the sixteen models hired by the House of Etienne to debut its spring collection. Voices jabbered in five languages as hands tugged at fabric and brushes whisked over cheekbones. Eyes rolled, lips formed obscenities, fingers clenched. Perfection had to be achieved in these last moments before the music began and the cameras began flashing, and everyone was feeling the stress.

Everyone but Raven, who had walked so many runways she could do it in her sleep. And lately had felt the same about everything—that she was merely performing on automatic pilot.

I'm tired. Everyone gets tired once in a while. That's all it is. She pressed a hand to her churning stomach. *And hungry. But, then, I'm always hungry.*

She borrowed a cell phone from one of the assistants, and dialed a number. "After this shindig is over," she said to Honore as she listened to it ring, "want to run out and grab a cheeseburger with me?"

"What is this cheeseburger? I hire three chefs from Le Duc for the party at my villa tonight." The designer made a rude sound. "You know Alain make his capons Marseilles especially for you."

"Do I get a side of fries with it?" Raven heard a voice answer and said into the phone, "Fael? Raven. Where are my motherboards?" She listened to her supplier for a moment before cutting him off. "No, not the damn AK31s, they don't have on-board RAID controllers and the integrated audio sucks. I'll take the AK35GTRs if I have to. And get me another cube while you're at it. You still want me to do that retrofit on your mainframe, don't you?" She chuckled as Fael instantly agreed to deliver everything. "Thanks."

"Enough computer talking." Honore took the phone from Raven's hand, switched it off, then shook it under her nose. "And if I see you with so much as a ring of onion tonight, I kill you with my bare hands."

"An onion ring." Raven suppressed a grin as she peered in the vanity mirror and sketched a line of silver gloss along the full curve of her lower lip. "You're such a food snob, Ray."

"After the last time you made me eat—what were they? Chips of Soy?"

"Chips Ahoy. American cookies." Sent special delivery from New Orleans in a care package from Val, her friend and Jian-Shan's new wife. *Bless her maternal little heart.*

"American junk food." Honore shook her head and shuddered. "Yes, that make me food snob for life."

"Madam Etienne!" One of the designer's frantic assistants rushed over. "The press, they are delighted, they are calling for you, they are demanding to know what the new line is to be named."

"Lacroix has his mermaids, Cadente has her ballerinas, and Laroche has his angels." Honore waved one of her clever, bejeweled hands at the waiting models. "I have my mistrals." She shot a mischievous grin at Raven. "The winds of change, eh, *cherie*?"

"We'll definitely blow them away." She gave the designer a wink and sauntered over to take her position with the other models as the fast, frantic beat of hip-hop rolled back from the stage. "If I don't faint from hunger first."

A stagehand pulled back the curtain, and the runway procession began. Each model, dressed in a color and style to complement her shape, skin, and hair tones, moved with energy and grace out onto the stage. As she watched them, Raven was reminded again of what a talented designer her friend was. Each garment had been tailored not only to flatter the body wearing it but seemingly to touch and grasp the essence of the woman within. *Honore really is a genius*, she thought, and glanced back over her shoulder.

The older woman blew her a kiss and mouthed two words. *You're beautiful.*

Some of Raven's pleasure faded as she turned back toward the waiting stage. It was true, she was beautiful—dramatic, symmetrical features; flawless skin; and a thick, silky mane of dark chestnut hair. The Swiss surgeon responsible for all of that had followed her directions to the letter.

Make me unforgettable.

Before the year in Switzerland, she hadn't been anything more than healthy and average. She'd been Sarah Jane Ravenowitz, who had been called "nice" and occasionally described as "the girl next door," but never "beautiful" and only occasionally "attractive." Not even Kalen—

No, she wouldn't go there again. Not to thoughts of him. Bad enough that she constantly dreamed of her former boss and lover. He had broken her heart. He had ruined her life. He had sent her to China—and no matter what he said about his involvement in the ambush, he'd left her there. To die. For all intents and purposes, General Kalen Grady had killed Sarah Jane Ravenowitz.

But I rose out of the ashes. Raven's lip curled. *Maybe I should have called myself Phoenix.*

Honore's collection of barely there spring dresses caught everyone by surprise. Exclamations of delight rang out as each model emerged, whirling in saucy half-circles that flared opaque skirts and ruffled feathery, unconstructed sleeves. Gloved hands removed oversized straw hats and tossed them at the surprised audience, and elaborate cascades of curls bounced to frame the models' smiling faces. The House of Etienne had taken the popular return-to-romance trend and pushed it to a sexy new height, and from the sound of the audience, Paris had fallen instantly in love.

"Miss Raven?" one of the stagehands whispered frantically, pulling her out of her tangled thoughts. "It's time."

A hush fell over the room as the sixteen models lined the runway, poised like young acolytes, and the snappy music segued into a lush, melodic ballad. Raven took a deep breath and climbed the steps.

That's right. Look at the body, look at the face. Take your photographs. I want him to see what he made out of me. What I made out of what he abandoned.

"You're beautiful," the stagehand murmured. "Just beautiful."

That she was.

Kalen had spent the previous thirty-six hours pulling together the people, resources, and paperwork required to initiate the Dai operation, and three of the last four hours on the Concorde justifying the expenditures and his own involvement to everyone from the chief of accounting to his own boss.

Everything was in place, except for the bait.

Even knowing there was no other woman suitable for the job, he'd argued with himself. *You agreed to stay away from her. She agreed to stay in Europe. After that night in New Orleans—*

He could justify breaking his word to her—what had happened between them last fall didn't matter now. The violence was spreading daily, erupting in formerly peaceful neighborhoods as the tongs took their war to the streets. He had no choice but to recruit the last woman on earth he wanted involved in one of his operations. And to add insult to injury, the only way he could contact her was by staking out a goddamn fashion show.

So far sixteen stunning young women had strolled out onto the stage, wearing what looked like fancy negligees. All of them were magnificent, like young sirens out to lure any man to his doom. Not one of them was the woman he needed.

Kalen was beginning to wonder if she would show when silence fell over the room, and a woman wrapped in mist stepped onto the stage.

"Le Corbeau," a reporter beside him said in a reverent whisper before bringing his camera up and focusing. "Le Bon Corbeau."

The Raven.

For a moment, he saw a haunting image superimposed over the elegant, veiled form walking down the runway. The ghost was just as tall and lean, but wore her mouse-brown hair in a ponytail. Her face was average, ordinary, nothing special. She had bright, dark eyes, and a saucy mouth, but otherwise a totally forgettable face.

Which was why she'd been such an effective agent.

Captain Ravenowitz, reporting for duty, sir, the ghost had said, the first time they met. She'd been straight-faced and standing at attention, her expression pure business—and still he'd seen trouble written all over her.

Slim fingers reached up to tug the veil back, and the ghost vanished.

There were reasons a woman became a legend. Some said Raven had the most perfectly proportioned face ever captured by the camera—utterly faultless from the graceful wings of her dark brows to the balanced perfection of her full lips.

Sarah's mouth had been a little crooked on one

side, he recalled, and she suffered with chapped lips
every time the temperature changed.

Other critics, baffled by Raven's instant and endur-
ing popularity, blamed her slightly slanted, mink
brown eyes—"as deep and mysterious as the mist-
shrouded moors of Ireland," one wrote, trying to pin
down the elusive star quality.

*How can I look tough when I have these puppy dog
eyes?* Sarah would say, pointing at her reflection.
When Kalen had told her she resembled a dog as
much as he resembled a jackass, she laughed, then
demanded, *Okay, wise guy, what else do you call it when
they droop at the corners like this?*

Dozens of cosmetics manufacturers fought for contracts to use her smooth alabaster skin as a showcase
for their products. Raven, it was rumored, had her
own special face cream made for her in some remote
village in the Alps. She'd been offered several for-
tunes for the formula, but had always denied that
the cream even existed.

Kalen saw the ghost again—a ghost with freckles
scattered across her too long nose and a small, vel-
vety mole under her right eye.

*If you want Mata Hari, Colonel, you'd better transfer
me back to Armament Division,* the ghost had said to
him once. *But if you want someone who knows how to
plant a tracer, tail a target, or blow up a bridge without
getting caught, well, then, I'm your girl.*

Raven's body shouldn't have matched the perfection of her face, but it, too, seemed to have been
sculpted by the gods. Gods who defied the anorexic
standards of fashion and created tall women with
taut, toned muscles, high, full breasts, and incredibly
long, shapely legs.

Kalen knew *Playboy* had offered Raven a million

dollars to pose nude for a special anniversary issue, and she had turned them down flat. He often wondered why she drew the line at outright nudity— she'd already paraded everything else she possessed before the entire world, had taken a dozen celebrity lovers, and did exactly as she pleased.

An ugly heat surged inside him as he thought of her many public affairs. *That was to rub my nose in it. Like everything else.*

Raven let the filmy fabric float from her hand and continued her walk down the runway. She ignored the snapping lights and the voices that swelled with every step she took. Her movements were so liquid and effortless she seemed to glide through the air. By the time she reached the end of the runway, every man and woman in the room was standing, calling her name. She paused, scanned the room as if inspecting the audience for flaws, then allowed her legendary smile to slowly appear.

The face and hair and mouth had changed, but the smile hadn't. It was warm, generous, and contagious—just as it had been eight years ago, when he'd sent her off on her last mission.

I love you, Kalen. I want a house, and a ring, and you, naked, on my grandmother's quilt, waiting for me when I get back.

He kissed her good-bye. *When you get back, we'll talk about it.*

And that not only stuck the knife in his ribs, but twisted it. A small shred of Sarah Jane still existed behind that gorgeous, stranger's face, and he saw it in every smile she sent to the camera.

Raven's gaze swept past him, then darted back and locked on his face.

She shouldn't have recognized him. He'd grown

out his hair and beard, then bleached them. He wore contacts that concealed the vivid color of his eyes. And still her lips parted and soundlessly shaped his name.

Kalen.

He nodded.

Her gaze went flat, and her expression iced over as she mouthed another word. *No.*

He had only a couple of seconds before she would stroll offstage and disappear, and the mission would be over before it ever got off the ground. Kalen couldn't allow that to happen. He pushed forward to the edge of the stage, moving rapidly, willing her to keep her eyes on him. *That's it—keep watching me. Don't run away yet.*

As if she'd guessed his intent, she pivoted on her heel.

He planted a hand, vaulted onto the stage before a nearby security guard could react, and caught her by the arms from behind.

"Hello, Raven." Then he lifted his hand and pushed the pressure dart concealed in his palm against her jugular vein. The drug inside the dart entered her bloodstream at once and efficiently went to work.

She whirled, her eyes wide. "You . . ." Her hands came up against his chest, then she abruptly went limp.

Pretending it was all part of the planned finale, Kalen swept her up in his arms and carried her back down the runway, amid laughter and cheers from the thrilled crowd.

Chapter 2

"Watch for the designer," Raven heard a cold voice say. "She's sharp enough to guess where I brought her."

Whatever drug he'd stuck her with was new, she realized as strong arms lowered her. It had knocked her out temporarily, but now she felt wide awake—and yet still unable to move. She opened her eyes to see her own living room ceiling, and the man standing over her. He had radically altered his appearance, but she'd have known him anywhere.

"General." To her surprise, her voice worked fine. "You look like Spike from *Buffy*."

He lifted a bleached brow. "I didn't think you'd know it was me."

"You're wearing the leather jacket I gave you for our birthday in '94," she said, reminding him of the very first thing that they'd discovered they shared—the same date of birth, December 30. She looked around, tried to see if there were any agents with him. "What's the matter, all the five-star hotels booked up for the weekend?"

His once green, now blue eyes narrowed. "We need to talk."

The colored contacts and radical dye job meant

Kalen was operating undercover. And that wasn't all that had changed—he looked as if he'd aged ten years overnight. Shadows had joined the lines of experience around his eyes and nose, turning what had been a tough, handsome face into an edgy stone mask.

She'd seen him look like this only once, after a rescue plane went down over Kosovo, killing five agents and seven civilians. Two of them had been young children. In the weeks after the accident, he'd been unable to sleep for more than an hour at a time. She knew because she had lain in his bed and held him, and had woken up to find him staring at the ceiling, night after night.

Her initial shock gave way to anger. *Never again. After New Orleans, I swore I'd never let him do this to me again.*

"Honore." She felt the effects of the drug thinning and struggled to sit up. "She's probably called out the French Air Force by now." She had to get to the gun hidden under the table beside the chaise.

"Your friend will keep." Kalen glanced around her apartment. "This looks different from the last one."

She'd been forced to abandon that apartment after Kalen and his men had broken in, looking for her. She'd hired a Swedish designer to furnish her new place, and his stark, minimalist style had suited her perpetually bleak mood of late.

"Less stuff for me to dust." While his back was turned, she groped under the table.

"Looking for this?" Without turning, he held up the gun.

Damn. "Don't you have any of your own to play with?"

"You're going to listen to me for fifteen minutes."

He came over, sat down on the chaise, and kept her still by placing an arm over her abdomen. "It's important."

"Nobody flies across an ocean just to *talk* for fifteen minutes." She made a *tsk*ing sound, ignoring the wonderful way he smelled. "Can't the army budget a telephone for you? Have they spent it all on hammers and toilet seats again?"

"One phone call from me and you'd disappear, and we both know it. I can't spend the next week chasing you up and down every back alley in Paris." He watched her face. "Listen to what I have to say, Raven, then I'll go."

God help her, she was tempted. She wanted to know what had put those lines on his face and those shadows in his eyes. There had been a time when she would have tried to make them go away. But she'd already settled her accounts with Kalen—*all* the accounts. Awkwardly she pushed his arm away. "Go now."

"A friend of yours was murdered in Washington two days ago." He stood up. "She's connected with a case we're working on."

She didn't have so many friends that she could afford not to know. "Who?"

"Portia Santiago."

Portia? That wasn't possible. Portia had made it, she'd already hit the top of their profession. Chanel had been rabidly courting her agent for months, trying to sign her to rep their new fragrance line.

She was also a tough kid. Fighting her way out of the slums of Rio had included learning to use a knife like a seasoned dockworker. They'd worked out together whenever Portia was in Paris, and Raven had picked up some new tricks from the younger girl.

"Bullshit." Even as the harsh word exploded from her lips, she saw him remove an envelope from his jacket pocket—an envelope with photos. "How? Christ, *why*?"

"Her boyfriend, Dai Gangi." He removed a photograph and handed it to her, then helped her sit up. "We're pretty sure it was a tong hit."

Her hands felt numb, but she held on to the photo and studied the ghastly image. During her years with the Army Central Intelligence Division, she'd seen many horrific murders, but never one as sadistically brutal as the sight of her friend and the Chinese man skewered together on the long, bloody blade. Her stomach surged. "Why use a sword?"

"To send a message to me." He rubbed his eyes. "Gangi asked to meet me at the embassy. He was going to give up the White Tiger swords to us."

Now Kalen's presence made sense. The White Tiger swords were not only a priceless collection of ancient Asian blades, but the symbol of power for Shandian, a criminal Chinese tong. She had helped T'ang Jian-Shan, the tong leader's renegade son, steal the blades, then smuggle them into the United States, but they'd since disappeared.

Kalen was after the swords, not her.

"Does Jian-Shan know about this?" He nodded, and she handed the photo back to him. "Tell me the rest."

Kalen brought her up to date on the investigation, which had yet to recover the priceless swords, and the tong wars currently being fought and escalating in the streets of three different U.S. cities. At the end, he added, "We're moving in an undercover team to infiltrate the Dai family. The younger son, Zhihan, was close to Gangi. He may have a line on the White Tiger."

"And you want the swords." She swung her legs over the side of the chaise. Her apartment suddenly looked too small with Kalen standing in the middle of it. She'd forgotten how big he was, how much space he encompassed. "Thanks for telling me about Portia. You can go now."

He didn't move. "I need your help."

"You need the help of an AWOL army officer?" She clucked her tongue. "That would violate at least a dozen regs. I'm shocked, General. What happened to that highly polished, everything-by-the-book attitude of yours?"

"As Portia's friend, you could attend the funeral without your presence being questioned. Zhihan will be there out of respect for Gangi. No one knows you were CID." He ignored the disgusted sound she made. "You know how the Chinese operate. I need an insider to infiltrate the tong, someone who won't raise any suspicions. You're it."

"So you came all the way to Paris to—what? *Persuade* me to come back to work for you?" She laughed, tried to stand, then sat back down. "Or do you just intend to keep me drugged and send me to infiltrate them via wheelchair? Are you partnering me with a ventriloquist?"

His mouth flattened, and a muscle ticked in his jaw. "You served your country once."

That was the wrong thing to say to her. "My *country* left me to die in China."

"You volunteered for intelligence duty; you knew the risks." When he saw that didn't impress her, he added, "This girl was your friend. You can help me bring her killer to justice."

She produced a gentle smile. "I hate to dent your ego, Kal, but I don't need you or the CID or my country to do that."

He nodded. "You need me to clear the charges against you with the army. After the mission is completed, I'll have them dismissed. You'll be able to come home again."

Home. She'd lived in exile long enough for it to be an excellent bribe. To be able to live in America again, free of the past, surrounded by people who spoke the same language and shared the same history. All she had to do was give up her pride, her self-respect, her personal freedom, a good portion of her sanity, and possibly her life.

It was almost worth it, too. "You're still good at dangling carrots, General. Does that come from working with so many jackasses? I've always wondered."

"Look at the rest of the photos." He dropped the envelope in her lap, and the photos spilled out. His voice went deep and soft. "She was twenty years old. Just a kid."

Sudden, ferocious anger welled up in her. "Don't you try to play me, Kalen. Don't you dare."

She grabbed the photos to toss them in his face, then saw something that made her go still. Carefully she fanned them out, and stared at one that showed Portia's body stretched out on an expensive carpet. The sword had punched through her heart, so there wasn't a lot of blood. The slim brown fingers of one hand rested against the wound in her breast. The other hand lay on the carpet, next to a crumpled mink coat.

It was the white flower on the lapel of the mink coat that made Raven stare until her eyes burned. A white flower with large, pink-tipped petals. What rare-flower experts called a blushing lotus.

Dunhill had shouted at her, just before the shooting started. *Major, there's a sniper up there—*

Seven years ago, she'd led an operation into Shalal Xiudaoyuan, the abandoned monastery where they'd planned to surprise a pair of tech smugglers reported to be hiding guidance chips in the sacred scrolls of the temple. She'd gone in with four well-armed, highly trained agents and had been the only one to get out alive.

Barely alive, with a blushing lotus clutched in her bloodied hand.

"All right." Her stiff lips made it hard to form the words. "What do you want me to do?"

Whiskey, former U.S. Army colonel Sean Delaney decided, was truly God's gift to the Irish—and every other fool on the earth. Whiskey let a man forget his troubles and eased him down the path to damnation without a lot of weeping and moaning along the way. And at that moment Sean would have cheerfully handed over his own soul to the devil himself for a full glass and a dark, quiet place to drink it in.

Tonight was not for drinking, though. He dragged a hand through his silver hair, pushing it out of his eyes. Tonight he was on the job.

From what he could see through his binoculars, Kalen Grady was merely talking to Raven, doubtless handing her the usual patriotic speech—Sean had heard every variation of it so many times he had them all memorized.

It's a matter of national security.

Soldiers serve their country, whatever it takes.

You're the only man for the job.

"That's the way, boyo, flatter her—tell her she's the only one you can trust to do it right." Sean fully expected Raven to react by kicking the general's ass, something he would personally enjoy observing. Then he saw her expression waver, just for an instant. "Bullocks, girl, don't *listen* to him. He's only coddin' you."

But after a few minutes, Raven got up slowly and went into the bedroom, and Kalen pulled out his cell phone and made a call. Sean dropped the binoculars. "If that don't beat all."

Tipped off by a call from a customs agent he used to monitor activity at the airport, he'd tailed Kalen since the moment he arrived in France. The general was traveling under one of the aliases Sean had listed with his agent, hoping Grady would come looking for him. But the general hadn't even bothered to check out the Irishman's usual haunts, heading instead for the Etienne spring fashion show.

Not even worth extraditing, am I?

He took his cell phone from his jacket pocket and dialed Raven's private line. Through the binoculars, he watched her pick up the bedroom extension.

"Ray?" She sounded shaky.

"It's Sean, darlin'. What are you doing there with himself the general?" He watched her sit down on the edge of the bed. "Hasn't he reefed you enough, girl?"

"Can I have that in English?"

"It's like yelling 'God bless the Queen' in the middle of a Dublin bar. That kind of reefing."

"I love it when you get Irish on me, old man." Raven turned to look out the window at him on the roof of the building opposite her own. "Any particular reason you're staking me out?"

"Him, darlin', not you." He saw Kalen move toward the bedroom door. "He's coming. Here." He gave her his mobile number, then added, "Be a wise girl, Raven, and tell him to get stuffed."

As he ended the call and settled back with his binoculars, Sean thought about whiskey again. Nothing warmed his soul anymore, not even when he got drunk and stayed that way. And he couldn't look at a woman, any woman, without thinking of her. It didn't matter what they looked like, all the women he saw reminded him of her.

T'ang Kuei-fei.

She'd been T'ang Po's mistress, until he'd sold her to his nephew, Yin. She was a survivor in every sense of the word—and Sean had been counting on that when he'd recruited her.

All you have to do is contact your son, Jian-Shan, and convince him to work with us.

He didn't know at the time that Kuei-fei had used him solely to get to her son, and had never intended to persuade him to work with the CID.

Kuei-fei had played him like a naive rookie, and he'd fallen for it. Not once, but twice.

He'd gone after her in Paris, shadowing her, telling himself he was keeping her safe. But as he watched her, he'd fallen a little in love with her. She wasn't like any woman he'd ever known. She was quiet and thoughtful, and had more strength in her than ten combat veterans.

When she had tried to sell Grady out to T'ang Po, Sean had stopped her in time. Then he realized how desperate she was underneath that serene, beautiful face of hers. How she would fight to find and protect her son. He'd made her more promises, and told himself he could keep them.

The road to hell wasn't paved with good intentions. It was littered with them.

He and Kuei-fei had gone from Paris to New Orleans together, still chasing her son. Kalen Grady had kept Sean out of the loop, so he hadn't known the general's plans to use Jian-Shan to lure T'ang Po into the open. Determined to safeguard her son and granddaughter, Kuei-fei had ditched Sean, and run right into the middle of the final standoff. She'd stepped in front of T'ang Po's sword to save her son, and had died in Jian-Shan'shis arms. The brave, noble lady had sacrificed herself, when all she had ever wanted was to see the son they'd taken from her. T'ang Po had died, too, and that had touched off the current war between all the major tongs.

He knew he would suffer for it every day for the rest of his life. That was his punishment for failing her. But there was Kalen, who could have prevented it all. Sean had saved the general, and lost Kuei-fei in the process.

And for that the general had to pay.

"Who called you on the phone back at your place?"

"A friend." Raven stared at Paris disappearing beneath them as the Concorde turned west toward the ocean. At this time of night, Paris looked like a tangle of jeweled necklaces tossed onto black velvet by a careless hand. She rose a little from her seat to look at all the empty rows. "Why did you buy out the entire flight?"

"We need to go over the operation." He nodded toward the only attendant on the flight, who instantly produced a tray with an assortment of beverages and snacks. "You want something?"

Her stomach rolled at the thought of food. "Just water, thanks."

Kalen accepted a cup of black coffee, then waited for the attendant to depart before he opened his briefcase and pulled out a slim file. "We're fairly cer-

tain the Dai will show up at Portia's funeral to pay
their respects, and that's where you'll make first contact." He reached across the aisle and handed her a
mug shot of a young Asian man. "This is Dai Zhihan,
Gangi's brother and our prime suspect in the
murders."

She kicked off her shoes as she studied the man's
face. Someone had split his lip, and his bruised, flat
eyes glared at the camera. "Looks like he resisted
arrest."

"Gang fight. He ran with the Yu Dawn for a couple
of years. Charged with assault and attempted murder
three times, no convictions." Kalen lifted a page. "All
the witnesses against him developed spontaneous
amnesia."

"Hmmmm." That wasn't unusual in Asian com-
munities, where codes of silence were viciously en-
forced. "Why would he kill his own brother?"

"With Gangi dead, he now takes over as heir to
the tong." Kalen removed another photo, that of an
older man. "This is the current head of the Dai
tong—Ruiban, Zhihan and Gangi's father. He rarely
makes public appearances, but he's the man who will
ultimately control the swords."

She committed both faces to memory before handing the photos back to him and taking a sip of water.
"How are you working backup?"

"My team will be posing as your professional entourage. Photographer, makeup artist, and publicist."

She nearly snorted water through her nose. "Excuse me?"

"I'd have Conor pose as your latest boyfriend, but
that would defeat the purpose of having you on the
op." He shut his briefcase with a small slam. "That,
and we need a minimum of four people working

undercover to handle the surveillance and data transfers."

"I see." She set her water aside. "General—"

"Use Kalen."

"Right. Kalen." Even with the aisle between them, Raven wished she could move to another row. "I don't have an 'entourage.'"

"Now you do."

She rolled her eyes. "It's not that simple. Anyone who has worked with me knows I only use the best hairdressers and makeup artists. And the best are *French*."

"As far as your adoring public is concerned, you've never been to the U.S." He put the file away. "You can say your agency provided us as part of the perks."

"I don't work for an agency." She stared at his nearly white hair for a moment before it sank in. *Us.* "Oh, no. No. You're not thinking of—Kalen, you know absolutely nothing about the fashion industry."

He rubbed his eyelids carefully, as if the colored contacts he wore were bothering him. "I learn fast."

It was bad enough that he made her this jumpy, just sharing space on an empty plane. If Kalen was in her back pocket for the rest of the operation, she would definitely screw it up. She also couldn't tell him that. *Wouldn't* tell him that.

"Don't you think you're getting a little old to play Danger Ranger?" Raven hooked a leg over the arm of her seat and let her bare foot swing. "You haven't worked as a regular field agent since you put on your first star."

"I've kept my hand in."

"Sure you have. Kalen, the last time you were in the field, we were putting out U.N. fires in Kosovo."

She didn't mention Siberia, or the mission during which they had become lovers. "Times have changed. A *lot*."

"I'll manage."

He would, too, Raven realized. Physically Kalen was in as good if not better shape as when he had been in the field. He'd been supervising the army's covert intelligence agents for more than a decade, but not always from behind a desk. Rumor had it that he had personally led a number of missions against Chinese crime families operating in the United States and Europe.

It didn't matter how much experience he had—she would work for him, but she wouldn't work with him. Having Kalen anywhere near her for any length of time would only ruin her concentration, and potentially blow her cover.

There was another way, of course—as soon as they arrived, she could carry out the operation by herself. She had a number of stateside contacts, and the Irishman would put her in touch with whoever else she needed. She could do this her own way, keep a low profile, not let anyone know she was back. Just like the last time.

She glanced at Kalen, who was engrossed in some official-looking document. According to her watch, she had three and a half hours to plan it—more than enough time.

Thanks for the ride, General, but New York is definitely where we part ways.

"She shouldn't be here. She belongs in prison."

The firm conviction in Brooke Oliver's voice made Conor Perry turn and look over his seat. "The boss wouldn't bring her in unless we needed her."

"Why *do* we need some walking clothes rack on this mission?" Hyatt Smith asked as he parked the van in the special area reserved for official transports. "We slap enough makeup on you, Captain, you could pass as a reasonably attractive airhead bimbo."

"Oh, bite me, Smith." Brooke grabbed her jacket and opened the sliding passenger door to jump out. She automatically scanned the garage, then frowned. "What's the media doing here? U-2 flying in for a concert?"

The sight of all the TV news vans made Conor wince. "I hate to say it, but Raven's about as famous as U-2. And she's a hell of a lot better-looking than Bono."

Brooke spun around as Hyatt emerged from the van. "You didn't send out that bogus press release already, did you?"

" 'Fraid so." The computer programmer gave her a sheepish grin. "Boss called me this morning from Paris, said to get the ball rolling. Guess he didn't want to leave her an out."

Brooke muttered what she thought of that under her breath.

Conor pulled on his favorite Redskins cap. "We'd better head inside, scope out how bad it is."

They'd barely passed through Terminal 4's main entrance when they spotted the first television reporter giving a live update via remote camera. The smiling black man in a beautifully tailored suit was gesturing toward the gates and pointing to the overhead monitors.

"In just ten minutes, Raven will be landing," Conor heard the man saying to the camera. "Some of the fans here have been waiting for nearly four hours to catch a glimpse of the elusive beauty—"

"'Elusive beauty.'" Brooke snorted. "Please."

A few feet away, another reporter was busy interviewing a group of excited teenage girls bearing copies of _Vogue, Cosmopolitan,_ and _Vanity Fair._ All of the magazines featured Raven on the cover.

"—and she's so badass, you know," one of the girls gushed as the three agents passed by. "I read her Weblog like, every single _day._"

"What's a Weblog?" Conor asked Hyatt.

"It's like a diary, only you keep it online and open to the public," Hyatt told him. "It's the latest rage among the techno geeks." He skirted around a couple wearing matching T-shirts with large, stylized black birds on them and checked the gate schedules scrolling on an overhead monitor. "They're coming in at Gate 7-B."

Brooke walked over to the bank of windows overlooking the runway. "There must be five thousand people out there. Perfect."

Conor chuckled. "They didn't teach me this one in classified op school."

"Sure they did," the blond captain told him. "It's the one that always got fubar."

Outside the terminal, airport security had sectioned off an area for fans and reporters, which was now densely packed. Many of those waiting there carried banners that read NYC ♥ RAVEN and RAVING FOR RAVEN. As the sun set, teenagers were already raving—the new fad of spinning small multicolored glow sticks on strings in intricate patterns—and the whirling lights added to the sense of barely controlled chaos.

The three agents exchanged glances.

Brooke's lips were white. "We need to check this now."

"I'll see if I can get someone from security to change the gate designation," Conor said. "Maybe we can get the flight diverted to another airport."

Hyatt shook his head and pointed at the silhouette of a descending SST. "Too late."

When the Concorde rolled to a stop, Kalen unfastened his seat belt and looked over at Raven. He was pleased that she'd slept through most of the flight; it had given him time to catch up on his paperwork without distraction. Now she was staring through the window again. "Ready to go?"

She cleared her throat. "Kalen, did you tell the press that I was coming to the U.S.?"

"I had my people put out a standard release—why?"

She tapped the window. "That's why."

He leaned over and saw the mob waiting outside the terminal. "What the hell is that?"

"That"—she got up and brushed past him—"would be my public. Who seem remarkably well informed about my arrival."

He caught her arm. "You're kidding."

"Just when did you send out the press release? This morning, before you kidnapped me?" When he nodded, she heaved a sigh. "That means I was on the news at noon."

"And?"

"Kalen, this entire airport is crawling with reporters by now. As for the civilians, I have thirty-seven fan clubs in the United States alone." She ducked her head to look out the window again. "And it looks like thirty-six of them are out there."

He swore. "I'll have the pilot taxi to another gate."

"Great." She sat back down. "Tell the pilot to take

off and fly us to another airport that can accommodate a supersonic transport jet. I believe Dulles is the
closest; maybe he won't even have to refuel."

For a moment, he toyed with the idea of flying to
Washington. However, in the aftermath of the tragic
events of September 11, such a move would only
bring more unwelcome attention and speculation
from the media.

"No, that won't work." He pulled her out of the
seat and gave her a small push toward the front exit.
"We'll deal with it."

"Look at it this way: you wanted to be part of my
entourage," she reminded him, and walked toward
the forward baggage compartment. She retrieved the
small black case she'd brought on board with her,
placed it on a seat, and popped open the locks. "Now
you'll get your chance."

He watched her pull out a black leather jacket and
a matching baseball cap with the word ELLE embroidered in silver letters. "What are you doing?"

She glanced at him as she shrugged into her jacket,
which had the silhouette of a crow worked in fine,
silvery stitches across the back. "Dressing for the
media and my fans."

He slammed the case shut and locked it before
pulling it off the seat. "Let's get this over with."

The moment Raven stepped out of the plane, several thousand people began to cheer and applaud.
Lights flashed madly as she descended the stairs,
smiling and waving to the cameras. Kalen followed,
scanning the area and catching a glimpse of Conor
and his team waiting at the end of the walkway to
the terminal. As soon as they got within a hundred
yards of the crowd, reporters began shouting out
questions.

"Raven, how long will you be in New York?"

"Is Bill Blass stealing you away from the House of Etienne?"

"Vera Wang's show is this month. Will you be modeling for her?"

"Will you be at the memorial service for Portia?"

At the last question Raven's smile faded, and she paused to speak into a reporter's microphone. "I'm here to pay my respects to my friend, Portia Santiago. She was a lovely person, and I am devastated by her loss."

The crowd fell silent for a moment.

Kalen saw tears sparkling in her eyes, and leaned forward, making his action appear like a comforting gesture. Against her ear he murmured, "Keep walking."

"Give me a minute," she said through her smile.

"I'm feelin' you, Raven," a teenage boy nearby called out in a heavy Hispanic accent.

"Yeah, keep your head, boo," another said.

Raven gave the two boys one of her megawatt smiles. "Thanks, guys."

One produced a chain of glow sticks. "Rave one for Portia!"

Hundreds of voices yelled in agreement and admiration as the two boys reached over the barrier and began whirling the glow stick chains. Dozens of hands lifted similar chains over their heads to do the same. Someone switched on a portable stereo and hip-hop spilled out into the air.

"What are they doing?" Kalen asked her.

"You need to get out more, Kalen. It's called raving." Raven deftly caught a string thrown to her by one of the teens and began spinning it between her hands.

Kalen recognized the moves as adapted forms of martial arts that she'd mastered while working for him. He should have put a stop to the nonsense, but like her fans and the reporters, he was mesmerized.

At last, Raven turned in a circle and flipped the chain high into the air. Shrieks of delight came from the crowd as they lifted their gazes to follow the whirling circle of light. Kalen watched the glow sticks fall into the crowd, where dozens of teenagers scrambled to grab them. Realizing the time was right to made a quick exit, he reached out to haul her toward the terminal.

Only Raven wasn't there anymore.

You are getting old, General.

Slipping behind a nearby baggage cart, Raven ripped off her jacket and turned it inside out to expose the reversible plaid lining, then pulled it back on. She exchanged her cap for a short, curly blond wig from her pocket before darting into one of the service doors marked BAGGAGE CARTS.

As she ran down the empty corridor, she yanked the wig over her dark brown hair and stuffed her ponytail up under the back. A pair of oversized, pink-tinted glasses completed her disguise as she edged out into the terminal and around the crowd waiting to see her. She hunched over to reduce her height as she strode toward the terminal entrance, and hoped it would be enough to get her past Kalen's agents.

Where are they? Ah, there. The two men and one woman were already back from the gate, and she recognized the pattern they moved in. *Kalen needs to change his training techniques.*

Her decision to renege on her promise and slip away from Kalen hadn't been a hasty one; she'd thought it through during the entire trip from France. She could get money, supplies, and accommodations with a few phone calls. A twinge of guilt struck her, but she told herself it was better for her to investigate the murders on her own, away from the general's rules and regulations.

Besides, we'd drive each other crazy inside of a day.

Her mouth twitched as she recalled the last time she'd tried to give Kalen Grady the slip at an airport. At least this time she would get away with it—

"Going somewhere?" A hard arm encircled her waist and clamped her to the side of a tough, tense body. Kalen glared down at her, and she could almost see the green fire burning behind the blue contacts.

Oops.

"It was worth a shot." Her wig was perfect, the jacket looked totally different, so how had he spotted her so fast? "What did I screw up?"

"The perfume."

She'd forgotten that Kalen had a nose like a bloodhound. And suddenly she felt exhausted again, as if the weight of the world pressed down on her. "Look, you know I'll find another chance, and I'll go. Make it easy on yourself and let me do it now."

He leaned in. "If you walk on me again, I will hunt you down and toss you to the MPs. I'll see to it that you do at least twenty years, hard time. Are we clear on that?"

"Crystal." She looked over her shoulder at the three agents catching up to them. The blond woman looked particularly disgruntled. "Here come your reinforcements, Fearless Leader. Are you performing the introductions here, or do we go directly to Pott-sylvania Central?"

"Quiet." As a reporter and her camera crew walked by, he pulled her against him and pressed her face against his chest to make it appear they were hugging. In a low voice, he said, "We have to go. Now. No more stunts."

Being in his arms made Raven tense, but she quickly relaxed against him. He already had enough weapons to use against her, and she would get another chance to slip away.

"This feels nice." She let her head fall back and brushed his bearded chin with her lips. It was a small surprise to discover that the bleached beard was real. "We look like twins now, don't we? Maybe I'll go blond."

"Don't be an idiot."

Kalen's hands spread over her back, and his touch gentled. Seven years of separation dissolved into nothing as they stared at each other. Everything else abruptly went away, too—the airport, the people around them, the rest of the world.

How does he do this to me? Raven wondered. *He looks at me as if I have no other purpose than to be here, for him.* Behind them, a man coughed politely, and she closed her eyes for an instant. *I'm not Sarah. I can't let him take over my life again. He has no right.*

"Boss?"

The intensity faded from his eyes, replaced by weariness and something darker.

"Let's go." Kalen kept one arm around her as he guided her through the main entrance. The trio of agents trailed after them. "Where's the van?" he asked one of the men.

"We're over there." The man wearing glasses pointed to a reserved section of the parking garage across the terminal road.

At least the army had upgraded their surveillance vehicles, Raven thought as she climbed into the van. This one was fitted out to double as a utility repair truck, right down to the coils of fiber-optic cable and the orange work-zone cones clipped to the back end.

Inside, however, it was a different story. Sophisticated computers and other electronic monitoring equipment lined both sides of the interior, along with a mini satellite dish and a backup transmitter. Enough power and hardware, she realized, to listen in on a conversation miles away.

This is some serious tech. What isn't he telling me?

"Sit." Kalen pushed her toward one of the console seats, then dropped down beside her. The man with the glasses slid in behind the wheel, while the other man and the woman took seats beside the opposite console. "This is Conor Perry, my point man, and Brooke Oliver, our unit cryptographer. The one driving this rig is our computer expert, Hyatt Smith. Conor, Brooke, Hyatt, this is Sarah Ravenowitz—"

"Call me Raven," she said as she pulled off the wig and shook out her hair. "Damn, I don't know how Dolly Parton can stand it."

"She needs the counterweight," Perry said, understanding her perfectly.

Something itched in her memory, until she placed him. They'd worked together during one of her last missions. "I remember you—Suriname, back in '90, wasn't it?"

Conor grinned. "I wondered if you'd know me without all the camouflage paint."

"I never forget a handsome guy, especially one

who doesn't blow me up when I'm setting detonators in plastic explosive." She stuffed the wig in her pocket and felt rather than saw Kalen watching her. _However much I want to._

She turned to the woman, who still appeared irritated. "How many brands of Chinese do you speak, Brooke?"

"Thirty-two separate dialects." The blonde seemed to have a permanent mortally offended expression. "And if you don't mind, it's captain."

"That's going to sound a little strange—me calling my makeup artist 'captain'." Raven stretched, and yawned, then propped her feet up on the nearest empty seat. "So, how good are you at plucking eyebrows?"

Kalen, who was already on the phone with someone, cupped a hand over the receiver. "We'll discuss all this later."

"Good idea." Lately everything seemed to wear her out, but happily Raven was able to catnap under almost any conditions. And she needed to do that now. "Wake me when we get to spy headquarters, will you?"

She closed her eyes and promptly fell asleep.

Chapter 3

"Don't you understand English? I'd like something simple but classic. Timeless but sophisticated. My goodness, I expected to find a much better quality of design from someone like you."

Kameko Sayura opened one of the lower display cases and removed a chain with a sapphire pendant that wouldn't emphasize the customer's rather pudgy neck. "Perhaps something like this?"

The woman from Beverly Hills scrunched up her short nose. "No, that's too small. No one will even realize I'm wearing it."

"Where do you plan to wear the necklace, madam?"

The customer sniffed. "Jacob and I will be seated with the Spielbergs at the Oscars this year. Kate always wears her Winstons, you know."

It was the size and price tag, not the design, that the woman was concerned with. Meko nodded and reached under the counter for her special portfolio. "Then perhaps I can interest you in a more exclusive design?"

The necklaces on the page were photographed individually, worn by the celebrities Meko had made them for.

"Oh, my." The customer's jaw sagged an inch before she recovered and pointed to Demi Moore's photo. "Something like that would be darling."

And would pay off the last of her mortgage, Meko thought, smiling. "These pieces are in a different price range, of course."

"It isn't a question of money, dear."

Not when your husband was a senior studio producer, apparently. "Of course. Let me prepare some sketches for you, madam. The piece should be unique, unlike any other I've made. Designed just for you."

The customer was so delighted she didn't mind making a significant deposit, and promised to return for a private appointment at the end of the week.

As the woman left, Meko tucked the check into her bank bag and saw her assistant smirking. "What is so funny?"

"The way you played her," Tara Jones said, and laughed. "She came in here determined to hate everything, and in five minutes not only did you have her eating out of your hand, but you had her writing you a check. You do that to everybody."

"You were the same way when you came in the shop for the first time," she pointed out to her young employee. "And I wasn't able to sell you anything."

"You didn't try with me. You were too busy talking me out of getting my navel pierced. Which I still might do, for the summer."

The tall redheaded teenager laughed at her expression. "You know I'm just kidding."

"I know." She gave Tara a fond smile. "Let's close up the shop, and I'll give you a ride home."

Tara went to get her purse from the back room, then hurried back out with a small brown envelope.

"I forgot to tell you when you got back from lunch—the postman brought this for you."

Meko went still for an instant when she saw the writing on the envelope, then she tucked it into her purse. "Thank you, Tara."

She drove her assistant to her home, an expensive mansion set in the middle of Beverly Hills. "Are your parents in town this week?"

"Nah. Dad's over in Thailand, shooting on location, and Mom is doing some charity gig in Palm Springs." Tara, who was used to being left in the care of servants, tried very hard to sound nonchalant.

Meko knew better, and her heart ached for the girl. "If you don't have any plans, why don't we go see a movie after work on Friday? Then we can have dinner and celebrate your birthday together. You're going to be how old—twenty, right?"

"Sixteen." Tara's eyes shimmered as she gave her employer a quick hug. "Thanks, Meko."

Meko drove home, waiting until she was inside the house before she removed the envelope from her bag. It bore a Chinese postmark, and she was tempted to soak it in a bucket of water before opening it.

Why now, after all these years of silence? He can't hurt me anymore.

Angry with herself for being afraid of a mere letter, she tore open one end and removed the contents. An old black-and-white photograph of a sword and a note, written by her father.

Her father, who had died six weeks ago.

She had received only one phone call after Takeshi Sayura's ghastly traffic accident in Hong Kong. Her brothers, to whom she had not spoken in more than ten years, had contacted her and demanded that she leave at once for Japan.

Our father is dead. Jiro, her obnoxious younger brother, had spoken like one of the Mugen. *You will show him respect this once, Kameko.*

Before she could tell him what she thought of him and her father, her elder brother, Ichiro, had gotten on the line. *Meko? Why are you arguing about this? Father is dead. We need you here.*

It had been hard to refuse Ichiro, the only member of her family who had not condemned her for becoming an American citizen. Her gentle brother had always taken her side with their father, even when she had left her husband and done the unthinkable by divorcing him. Still, she had found the strength to say no.

And now this letter from her father.

"I'm sorry, gentlemen, but the service for Mr. Dai is closed to the public." Harry Fong, the director of the Shan Lang Buddhist temple, made an apologetic gesture. "You may leave a card for the family, if you wish."

FBI special agents Robert Jennings and David Hessler dutifully produced their badges.

"We need to speak with with the family, sir," Jennings said. "Please stand aside."

Fong's sad smile bent at the edges, then he bowed and opened the door to the main prayer room.

"Never been in a Chink church before." Hessler scanned the interior as he replaced his badge. The curved roof, stone walls, and ornate, brightly laquered wooden posts made him uneasy—as if he'd stepped into another place and time. "You said this thing lasts forty-nine days?"

"Not the funeral. The family prays for forty-nine

days," his partner said, pausing to admire a vivid wall mural of dragons dancing among flowers that stretched the length of the room. "It's the first ceremony that's the important one—the head of the family always shows for it. That and the cremation."

Hessler snorted. "Hope they don't wait forty-nine days to toast the little shit." He noticed a pair of elderly Chinese women who had turned around to glare at him, and smirked as they quickly looked away. "You see the old man anywhere?"

"In the front, by the altar." His partner nodded toward a group of suits gathered before a large framed portrait of a smiling young man astride a gleaming motorcycle. An old man near a brazier was thumbing through a thick stack of bills. "The one with the white hair—that's him."

"What's he doing?" Hessler's eyes widened as Dai Ruiban tossed the bills into the flaming brazier. "Burning money?"

Jennings, who, unlike his partner, had worked Chinese cases before, stifled a sigh. "It's joss money. They print stuff on it that the dead person will need in the afterlife—clothes, shoes, jewelry, that kind of thing—and then they burn it to send the stuff to him."

"Counterfeit money you burn for stiffs." His partner grunted. "Now I've heard everything."

Before the agents could approach the Dai, several young Chinese men in black leather jackets converged and formed a tight circle around them.

"You in wrong place," said one with a heavy accent and a fresh knife scar on his face. "You leave now."

Jennings sighed and produced his badge again. "If we leave, we come back with lots of reinforcements. Like the NYPD and INS."

"*Poq gai*," another voice said, and the circle of tong thugs parted. A younger version of Dai Ruiban advanced into the circle. He was a head shorter than both agents, and had a grim, scarred face. "What do you want?"

"FBI." Jennings pointed toward the altar. "We need to have a word with Mr. Dai."

Black eyes narrowed. "The Dai prays now."

"He can pray later," Hessler told him, and made a shooing gesture. "So take your thug friends and run along, junior."

"My name is Dai Zhihan." Zhihan grabbed Hessler by the lapels and shoved him against a wall. "Disrespect my father again, and I cut out your fat tongue."

"Hold on there." Jennings put a hand on Zhihan's arm. "You don't want to get yourself hauled in front of a judge for assault and obstruction, do you?"

"Zhihan." The slightly stooped figure of Dai Ruiban appeared, and his son released Hessler. The old man looked at the circle of thugs, and they retreated to rejoin the other mourners. "May I help you gentlemen?"

Jennings repeated his request.

"Of course. Forgive my son. This is a time of great sadness for our family." The old man said something in a low voice to Zhihan, then gestured toward one side of the room. "If you will accompany me, please."

The Dai led the two agents to an adjoining room. Hessler kept glancing back at Zhihan, who watched them go like a hungry shark.

"This doesn't feel good, Dave," Jennings murmured. "Maybe we should call it in."

"Screw that." Hessler turned his back to a wall and looked around the room, which was filled with small statues, flowers, and a lingering scent of burning incense. "They try anything, they'll be up to their eyeballs in more feds, and they know it."

Ruiban took a seat in a chair designed like a small gilded throne. "What is so important that you must interrupt the funeral for my son?"

Jennings kept his tone respectful. "We'd like to ask you some questions regarding the Hip Sing and On Leong tongs."

"I know nothing about them." Ruiban looked mildly surprised. "Nor would my family or our friends. We are very hardworking people, gentlemen. We do not associate with such criminals."

"Then who murdered your son and his girl-friend?" Hessler demanded.

The old man's shrewd eyes widened a fraction. "I do not know. Is that not your job to discover?"

Jennings cut off his partner's blustering response. "Yes, it is. And in order to do that, Mr. Dai, we'll need to interview you and your family and find out who Gangi's friends and enemies are."

"I see." Ruiban steepled his fingers. "My son has been dead for nearly a week, and yet you chose this time to begin conducting your investigation."

Jennings had the grace to look a little uncomfortable. "It's standard procedure for our agents to attend the funeral, get a look at who shows."

Ruiban considered that for a moment, then removed a card from his jacket and silently handed it to Hessler.

"What's this for?" the agent asked as he studied the card.

"It is the name and phone number of my attorney. You may contact him and make an appointment." Ruiban rose from the chair. "You will leave now."

Hessler crumpled the card in his ham-sized fist. "Like I told your men, if we have to come back, a lot of people are going to end up in jail."

"Do what you must." Ruiban inclined his head. "Zhihan, escort these gentlemen to their car."

The younger man, who now stood inside the doorway, bowed. "Of course, Father."

Hessler fumed all the way out to the parking lot, but Jennings, the quieter of the pair, was watching Dai Zhihan's expression. There was something spooky about the way the scarred man's eyes gleamed.

"I'm sorry we upset you and your father," he felt he had to say before he climbed in the car.

The Dai's son gave him an ugly smile, then turned on his heel and stalked back into the temple.

"I say we call in the INS, the local PD, and the DEA," Hessler said later as they drove back to the city. "Shake down Dai's gang bangers, see what drops out of their leather jackets."

"I guess so." Jennings looked up at the soaring web of cables as they drove onto the Brooklyn Bridge. "Didn't that bother you—the way he smirked at us?"

"Smug little bastard. He—" Hessler broke off and swore as he fought with the steering wheel and stomped on the brakes. "Shit!"

Jennings realized why Zhihan had been smiling just before their car spun out of control and collided with a semi.

Cut the brake lines and the steering cable while we were inside.

The impact of the crash flipped the agents' car up against the mesh of the bridge suspension cables, which prevented them from hurtling over the side and into the East River. Through the blood in his eyes, Jennings saw the water below, then turned his head and screamed.

The back end of the jackknifed semi slammed into the agents' car, crushing both men inside instantly. A split second later, the ruptured fuel tank exploded.

As he listened to the report from the FBI liaison, Kalen watched Raven. She woke up as soon as they pulled into the FitzWilliam Hotel's parking garage, stretched like a lazy tabby, then sent him a drowsy smile before chatting up Conor Perry. Conor, who enjoyed friendly women as much as the beautiful ones, lit up like a radar screen over a Middle Eastern war zone.

And if he didn't check his libido, Kalen was going to send his ass off to Afghanistan tomorrow.

"We're staying here?" Raven asked as she looked around at the empty parking spaces.

Hyatt and Brooke had already gotten out and were unloading some boxes from the back of the van. Before Kalen could reply, the Bureau agent transferred him to a deputy director, who wanted some definitive answers on interdepartmental responsibility for the investigation.

"Top floor," Conor said as he offered a hand and helped her out of the van. "Let me take that case for you, Major."

"Raven." She kept her grip on her suitcase. "I can handle it." She gestured with her free hand. "The general buy this place out too?"

Conor cleared his throat. "No, ah, I believe most of it is closed for renovations."

"Is she bitching about the hotel already?" Brooke muttered, loud enough to be heard.

Instead of being offended, Raven grinned and called back, "Not at all. I'd love to stop by the Russian Tea Room while I'm here."

Kalen put the director on hold and took Raven's arm. "We'll head up to the suite."

His team stayed behind to unload the rest of their equipment and supplies while he escorted her up to the presidential suite he'd requisitioned. Two guards in street clothes stood posted outside the elevators, and by the time they arrived he'd finished debating jurisdiction with the FBI director. He exchanged a few words with the men on watch before indicating an open door down the richly carpeted hallway.

Raven ran her fingers over a highly polished rosewood foyer table before she sauntered into the suite. "This one mine?"

"Captain Oliver will be staying with you for the duration," he told her as he followed her inside.

"That would be unwise." She set her suitcase on a burled-oak coffee table and folded her arms. "You also need to lose the armed bookends out there."

He went to the wet bar and poured himself a glass of ice water. "Why? So you can ditch the operation?"

"No, I'd prefer to stay out of Leavenworth, thanks." She came over and took the glass from his hand. "However, when I bring Zhihan back to my suite, he may wonder why I need two armed guards and a baby-sitter with an attitude problem."

The thought of her using seduction to get information out of the tong leader's son made him see red. "You're not sleeping with Dai."

"Ah, no. My services don't include sex upon demand." She waited a beat. "With anyone."

"That's not what the papers say."

"Don't believe everything you read." She took a
sip and sighed. "Look, either you let me do this the
right way, Kalen, and we nail the bad guys, or you
don't, and I fly back to Paris after the funeral." She
handed the glass back to him. "Decide."

He set it on the bar. "Two FBI agents were killed
in a traffic accident out on the Brooklyn Bridge this
afternoon. It happened ten minutes after they left
Gangi's funeral."

"That's a terrible thing." She met his gaze. "So was
losing my entire team in China."

"That wasn't your fault, or mine."

"Then whose was it?" She circled around him to
the window and studied the panoramic view of the
city. "You know as well as I do, you've got a bad
leak, minimum. Maybe even a mole in your
department."

He watched her trace squares on the windowpane
with her fingers. "I know."

"I'm not staking my life on the CID again." Her
shoulders tensed, and a strange note entered her
voice. "Let me go and do this by myself."

"No."

She swiveled to face him. "I'll report in directly to
you. I give you my word."

"There's too much at stake; I can't allow you to go
in by yourself. I handpicked the team myself. They're
the best—"

"—and you trust them more than you trust me."
She kept her expression as blank as his, but he sensed
that he had wounded her in some way.

"I'll move the guards, and Oliver can stay in the
command post room. But the team stays, and *you*

stay." He was already regretting giving her that much. "I have to go. I'll have dinner sent up to you. Report to me at oh-eight-hundred for briefing."

She nodded and went back to staring at the city.

After Kalen left, Raven bolted the door, retrieved a small black box from a hidden seam in her case, and switched it on. The signal scrambler had cost her a pretty penny, but it would jam any audio or video monitoring device within a hundred-foot radius. She carried her case into the master bathroom and turned on the shower for good measure.

The things I have to do for my country.

Once she had taken her cell phone and data transmitter from the lead-lined false bottom of the case, she dialed Honore Etienne's private home number.

"Bonjour?"

"It's me, Ray." Raven held the phone away from her ear for several minutes as the Frenchwoman shouted obscenities in her native language without stopping. "I'm glad to hear your voice, too," she said when her friend paused for breath. "The mistral dress is at my place. I'll have someone deliver it to your office tomorrow."

"Pfft." Honore's voice dropped a few decibels, from furious to highly offended. "You think I care about a dress when you are stolen from us and possibly to be murdered?" More swearing, accompanied by the splashing of what Raven suspected was her friend's best cognac into a glass. "Where are you? Did you kill him?"

"I'm in New York, and no, he's still breathing."

"Why? That madman hit you over the head when he drag you from my stage? Never mind this," she added before Raven could say anything. "I will come to you, *cherie*, with Bruno and Pierre. They will break his legs, slowly—"

"Ray. *Ray*." She took a deep breath. "I'm fine. I agreed to come here with him. Now, I need you to do a couple of things for me." She recited a list of names and gave Honore the address of the hotel. "Tell them it'll be open house, all night."

"They will love it, of course, but you are insane, *cherie*. Why are you escaping?"

Her smile wobbled. "Do you remember those old photos I showed you once? The ones from Geneva?"

"*Oui*, but—"

Raven's fingers tightened on the phone. "That's why."

Honore didn't say anything for a minute. Then, "*Mon Dieu*. But what about *le generale*?"

"He was the one who kidnapped me. I'll call you in a few days. 'Bye." She hung up before the designer could curse her further, then dialed another number.

A melodic choir preceded the gruff voice that snapped, "What?"

She pressed her aching forehead against the cool tile wall. "Irish, are you still in Paris?"

Immediately Sean Delaney's tone changed. "No, darlin', I'm about six blocks from your hotel. You in trouble?"

She didn't ask how he knew where she was—the Irishman's personal resources were legendary—but she wondered what the angelic singing in the background was all about. "I need some backup. You available?"

"Can you give me your status?"

She turned on her transmitter and plugged it into the data jack on her cell phone. "What's your IM?" Sean gave her the code, and she quickly instant-messaged the basic information on the operation to him, and added a final request: *I need you to cover me at the funeral. Be there, nine* A.M.*?*

Through IM, Sean typed, *Sure. What's wrong?*

She bit her lip for a moment. The Irishman was former CID, now retired, and had worked for Kalen for years. On the other hand, she trusted Sean more than she would ever trust the general. *CID has a leak, and your boss won't let me fly solo. This Zhihan character has a bad rep. I want someone I trust at my back.*

Will do, Sean typed back. *Don't tell Grady I'm on this.*

She disconnected the data link and put the phone back up to her ear. The sound of singing was stronger, and she recognized the song as "Ave Maria." "Irish, what are you doing in church?"

Sean sighed. "Saying my prayers, darlin'. Saying my prayers."

"Jian."

The low whisper of his wife's voice against his skin stirred T'ang Jian-Shan from a deep, relaxed sleep. He opened his eyes to see hers, only a few inches away. Her red-gold hair lay tousled against her pillow, and her fallen angel's mouth was still slightly swollen from his last kiss.

"Valence." He smiled and reached for her before he was fully awake. "More?"

"Always." Her lips curled, and she held up a cordless phone between them. "But General Grady needs to speak to you first."

He glanced at the digital clock on their bedside table, then took the phone and sat up. Val snuggled up to him, rubbing her cheek against the hard, flat muscles of his chest. "It's midnight, General Grady."

"Sorry to wake you, but we need to talk."

Several minutes later, Jian-Shan walked into his office and pulled a fax from the machine by his desk. He cradled the cordless phone against his shoulder as he studied the scan of the sword Kalen had sent him, then quickly pulled a photo from his desk files. The two swords appeared to be identical. "It may be one of the Nagatoki, but I'll have to examine the blade itself. You say it was used to kill the son of a tong leader?"

"And his girlfriend."

As Kalen brought him up to date on the investigation, Val came in with steaming cups of Shikoro's mint tea. Jian-Shan smiled his thanks to his wife, then handed her the fax and the photo.

The general finished detailing the current operation, then asked, "How much progress have you and Val made on locating the collection?"

"Val has made contact with every reputable Asian weapons collector in the world. I've been in touch with less-reputable ones. Thus far, we've only heard some vague rumors on both sides of the market, nothing more."

While the men were talking, Val had taken a magnifying glass from the desk and was intently studying details of each image. She frowned, and retrieved a reference volume from the bookcase.

What she found in it made her look up at Jian-Shan, her dark eyes wide. "*Cher,* may I speak with him?"

"Just a moment, General. My wife needs a word with you." He transferred the call to his desk phone and put the general on the speaker.

"What is it, Val?"

"Kalen, this sword you have is part of the White Tiger. It has markings that are unique to Nagatoki. Do you have the scabbard?"

"No, just the blade."

"It could be one of the key swords. And there's something else." She flipped a page in the reference book. "Five of the markings I can make out from the photo aren't Japanese, they're Mandarin."

"Nagatoki made plenty of swords for the Chinese. What difference does that make?"

"Written Chinese—the pictographs that have represented the spoken language for thousands of years—didn't change until the twentieth century. That's when the Chinese government decided to simplify many of the traditional characters. These markings are modern; Nagatoki couldn't have possibly have etched them himself. Which means T'ang Po probably did."

"What do the new marks mean?"

"One of them is *bao*, which means 'treasure,' and another is *si*, which is the word for 'death.' And that's not all." Val flipped to another page in the book. "If you add two of the symbols from the Phoenix blade, and the Night Dragon blade we recovered from the museum, it spells out 'treasure of power and death over.' "

"Over what?"

"That's what I need the third sword to find out. The next symbol is fractured and incomplete. I can't know what it is until I put all three blades together and complete the code." She paused. "This sounds like a warning, not the clue to a treasure."

"We know T'ang Po hid millions away from the tong." Kalen sounded skeptical. "Enough to give anyone the power of death over anything."

"It could be," Val admitted. "Or it could mean Po hid something more lethal than what mere wealth can buy. Something with the power to destroy many, many lives."

Chapter 4

Kalen walked out of the bedroom they'd set up as the communications center and found Brooke arguing in a low voice with Conor and Hyatt. He was already tired and in no mood for more bickering. "Don't you people have some daily reports to complete?"

Brooke started to fume about something, but his point man cut her off. "Boss, uh, we've got a situation."

He thought of Raven, alone, in her suite. "What did she do now?"

Hyatt retreated to his computer console, while Brooke stalked off to work at the desk. Conor thrust his hands in his jacket pockets and rocked back on his heels. "Uh, I think you'd better go see it for yourself."

"Check out the equipment for tomorrow with Hyatt," he said as he went to the door. "I don't want any screwups at the cemetery."

The sound hit him as soon as he stepped outside the well-insulated suite—voices, laughter, the pop of a champagne bottle. All the sounds of a party in progress. All coming from the direction of Raven's suite.

She wouldn't, he told himself. *She's a professional; she knows how sensitive this operation is.*

"Hey, there," a tall blonde in a short pink beaded sheath said as she emerged from the elevator. She gave him a smoldering smile. "Could you point me toward Raven's party?"

Or not. He swept a hand toward the suite at the end of the hall.

"Thank you." She made a kissing sound in his direction and shimmied her hips all the way down to Raven's suite.

Kalen wasn't sure what pissed him off more—knowing his most crucial operative was throwing a wild party right under his nose or being obliged to wade into the middle of it to find her and demand to know why.

She'll probably say something cute, like that she was bored, and I'll put my fist through a wall.

Someone had propped open the door to Raven's suite with a chair, which was flanked by two very pale, black-clad men conversing in rapid German. Inside, reporters, photographers, and other, more exotic creatures filled the front room. Two waiters were squeezing through the press of bodies, making the rounds with silver trays of crystal flutes and fancy canapés.

Raven herself stood in the center of a huddle of reporters, and as he worked his way in to get to her, he picked up the last of what she was saying.

"—for a couple of weeks," she told a silver-haired man in salmon chinos and a pale pink shirt. "That enough of an on-the-spot interview for you, Paul? Or do you want my shoe size, too?"

"I'll take ten minutes in your closet, darling," the

reporter told her. "Five, if you'll let me bring along my cameraman."

"I wouldn't let him, Rave," an elegantly thin redhead in an acid-green leather jumpsuit advised in her incongruous Cockney accent. "He'll pinch something for his mum for sure."

"Or himself." A young black woman with caramel-colored skin and dark, feline eyes linked her arm through Raven's. Her Bali-print sarong and rich, deep voice echoed the primal colors and sounds of Africa. "Who are you chasing this season, Paul? That Italian tenor, or the Peruvian soccer player?"

The reporter sniffed. "Alake, you know I never stalk and tell."

"Spike!" Raven smiled at Kalen over the shoulder of a photographer and gave him a little roll of her hand. "Over here, darling."

At least she'd had the sense not to use his real name, Kalen thought as he moved to join her. Now all he had to do was clear the room so he could throttle her in private.

"This is my new personal assistant, Spike O'Shay," she was telling the others. "Spike, this is Paul Winter from *New York Fashion*, David Jones from *Elle*, and Howard Dickenson from *Cosmo*. And my friends, Gemma Firth, from London, and Alake, from Abuja." She gave the group a wink. "Spike's just getting into the business, so he has a lot of names to memorize."

"A fashion virgin, are you?" The British model gave him a wink. "No better way to pop your—"

"*Gemma!*" Paul pressed a narrow hand to his throat.

"—ah, get your feet wet than with the Blackbird here." Dimples appeared on Gemma's thin face.

The Nigerian model sidled up to him and trailed a dusky finger down his bearded cheek. "But if you ever grow tired of wet feet, come and see me, handsome."

A man would have to be dead from the neck down not to appreciate Alake's dark allure, Kalen thought, smiling at her. "I'll keep that in mind."

"Here, luv." Gemma giggled as she took a small satin sack from her purse and slipped it into Raven's hand. "Something you can use for on-the-job training."

He eyed the sack, then the woman he wanted to strangle. "I have a message for you, madam."

"Do you? Excuse us for minute." Raven took his arm and led him into the bedroom. As soon as she closed the door, she leaned back against it and tilted her head. "Gonna ground me for a month now?"

He gestured toward the front room. "I'd like an explanation first."

"It's just a little impromptu reception." She patted his cheek, then grimaced when he caught her wrist. "A shame you never liked parties. I'd have loved to see you dancing around the room with a lampshade on your head."

His grip tightened. "If you're trying to deliberately sabotage this mission, you're doing an excellent job."

"You're the one who sent out the press release, *Spike*." She glared. "I thought I'd get the interviews and the photo ops out of the way early. Or would you rather I deal with the media at Portia's funeral tomorrow?"

Slowly he eased the pressure on her wrist. "I hadn't thought of that." He watched her eyes. "But that doesn't explain why you invited all the clothes ponies."

Her easy smile faded. "This is a party, not a press conference. It would look weird if I didn't invite my professional colleagues. It may also interest you to know that Gemma and Alake were both good friends of Portia's. They knew Gangi, and they may know his brother. I was trying to find out when you interrupted us."

"You know what standard procedure is, and you ignored it." He leaned down until he could feel her breath on his mouth. "From now on, you clear everything with me first."

Someone pounded on the door. "Raven? What are you doing in there, chasing him around the bed?"

"I know the job, Kalen." She tossed the sack Gemma had given her on the bed, sidestepped him and opened the door. "Now let me do it."

When she slammed out of the room, he went over and picked up the sack. Inside were a pair of steel handcuffs and two keys. What had Gemma called it? *Something you can use for on-the-job training.* He'd never tied Sarah up, but Raven probably wore the handcuffs like bracelets.

Instantly he imagined what he could do to her if she were cuffed to the bed.

"Jesus." He dropped them on the bed as if they were coated with acid. "It's going to be a long night."

It was after three A.M. when Raven finally pushed the last reporter out of the suite and staggered to her bed. When the alarm she'd set went off three hours later, she opened one eye and groaned.

"No. I'm back in Paris. I can sleep until noon. Noon next Friday." She hit the snooze button, rolled over, and stared in the dark at the ceiling. "Any time now, Fairy Godmother."

No magic fairy appeared, no wish-granting wand waved.

"This sucks." Raven heaved a sigh and hauled herself out of bed. "Mrs. Peel never had to put up with this crap."

The master bathroom, which resembled a small spa, offered two separate showers and an old-fashioned claw-footed tub. Everything was gold-shot white marble. Raven decided she hated it on sight as she stripped and stepped into the first stall. Her ritual cold morning shower made her resort to a few of Honore's favorite phrases, but it did wake her up enough to drag on a robe and face the mess in the front room.

Only there wasn't a mess anymore—everything was sparkling clean.

She glanced up at the ceiling. "I apologize."

"Good morning, madam." A uniformed maid carrying out the last bag of collected guest debris appeared and gave her a timid smile. "Would you like me to start the coffeemaker for you?"

The thought of drinking anything that wasn't heavily spiked with hemlock made Raven shake her head. "No, thanks."

After the maid departed, the phone rang. It was Hyatt, and from his faintly strained tone she imagined the general was already giving him grief.

"Sorry to bother you, Major, but we're having a briefing in the Eisenhower Suite in ten minutes."

Oh, are we? "Tell Patton I'll be there in twenty."

She could hear the subsequent gulp. "I, uh . . . I don't think you want to keep him waiting. Not this morning."

"Feed him a muffin or something, Hyatt. He's always grouchy when he skips breakfast." She hung up the phone and headed back to the bathroom.

Six years of prepping for shows and shoots gave Raven the practice and speed to be ready in only a few minutes, but she took her time. When she finally looked and felt more human, she emerged to discover the maid had left her a breakfast tray on one of the side tables. Yet the prospect of attending Portia's funeral and snaring Dai Zhihan had her feeling so queasy she only picked up a slice of dry toast and carried it with her to the Eisenhower Suite.

Before she went in, she thought of that day—years ago in the temple at Shalal Xiudaoyuan—when she'd opened her eyes and seen Jian-Shan standing over her. *I don't want to do this.* He'd given her the blood-stained flower later, at the village, and told her he'd taken it from her hand. *But I have to do this.*

Taking a deep breath, she knocked once and stepped inside.

Three faces turned her way as she sauntered in. Conor's hazel eyes crinkled with appreciation, while Hyatt's myopic gaze bounced from her to Brooke and back again.

Of the trio, Captain Oliver looked more like a recruiter's poster than a covert agent. She had a polished gleam to her, like the edge of a good blade.

And she's just as much fun to play with, Raven thought as she took a bite of her toast. *I wonder if she starches her lingerie.*

"Morning, Major." Conor eyed her toast. "Bring any for us?"

"Get your own food, Perry." As she chewed, she inspected the room, in which someone had set up enough tech to support a shuttle mission. No sign of Kalen, however. "So where's the boss?"

"Brooke, I'll need an update on the Dai tong members known to be residing in Chicago," Kalen said as he came in. He'd obviously been out for a run, but hadn't bothered to shower or change yet. He draped a towel around his neck as he regarded Raven. "You're late."

"My time card got stuck." She sat down in the nearest chair. "Shall we?"

Brooke turned her back on Raven and stalked toward one of the computer terminals. "I'll pull those records for you now, General."

"You can do it later." Kalen seemed oblivious to the waves of silent outrage that followed his statement. "Let's go over today's schedule."

Raven kicked off her shoes and hitched a leg over the arm of her chair. "Will I have time to get in some shopping this afternoon? Bloomie's has a fifty-percent-off sale."

Conor, who was drinking some coffee, choked for a moment. Hyatt looked ready to do the same, minus the coffee.

"You"—Kalen pointed to her—"will shut up and listen."

She silently saluted him with her toast.

Conor tactfully stepped between them and spread out a diagram on the coffee table. "Here's the layout of the cemetery, and where Ms. Santiago's service will be held." He traced the entrance and exit routes, and predicted where the Dai contingent would enter.

"What about bodyguards?" Kalen asked, drying his face on the towel.

Raven could smell him, and shifted in her seat. *So I like the way he sweats. He can smell like dirty socks, just like every other guy on the planet after running three miles. I can live with that.*

"The Dai is always surrounded by at least four very large, very capable bone-crackers, and they'll have backup. He'll also have half a dozen more men in and around the funeral assembly, twice that walking the perimeter." Conor spread out surveillance photographs of Dai Ruiban and pointed to the different men as he spoke. "Zhihan's shown a preference for cruising alone in the past, but now that he's the crown prince of the Dai, I'll wager his father's men will be keeping an eye on him, too."

Brooke studied the photographs like a suspicious code inspector. "Why so many guards?"

"That's the front-line tong infantry." Kalen pointed to the open areas on the diagram. "They'll be out in the open, vulnerable to drive-bys or snipers. More bodies to put between them and the flying bullets."

"The Dai operate out of Chicago," Conor added. "This isn't their home turf, so the local tong might construe this appearance at the funeral as a power play."

"Ahem." Raven raised a hand. "I hate to be a wet blanket, but it's going to be kind of hard to make contact with my target if someone is shooting at him."

"I've arranged for local law enforcement to block off and police the area, so don't worry about it. Just look beautiful and useless." Kalen looked over at Hyatt. "Monitoring?"

"I've set up three bugs in floral arrangements, and one on either end of the casket." He pushed his glasses up on the thin bridge of his nose. "And then we've got the parabolic unit, the mesh unit, and the backup remote."

Raven's brows rose. "Mesh unit?"

"It just got through testing at NASA." Hyatt

grinned like a boy as he brought a case to the table and opened it. "Highly advanced, state-of-the-art audio tech." He took out a shimmering veil of what looked like silver gauze. "Wear this, and you can hear a whisper from five thousand yards away."

"How? By the way it flutters?"

He took her seriously. "The fibers are tuned to respond only to human speech patterns, so it not only tracks the right sound waves, it actually filters out background noises before it relays to the base unit."

Raven reached out and touched the mesh. "It feels like wool. Really scratchy wool."

Instead of looking offended, Hyatt nodded. "I know. We're still working on the texture—you see, the synthetic strands are a crystalline compound, made from ordinary quartz, and then—"

"Thanks, Lieutenant." Kalen held the mesh up in front of Raven's blouse. "You'll have to change your clothes, it'll show through the fabric."

"So would sackcloth, which would be more comfortable. Can I wear that instead?"

"You'll have a regular backup remote wire as well." Hyatt gestured toward her chest. "Just in case."

She rubbed the mesh against the inside of her wrist, then shook her head. "I can't wear this stuff against my skin."

"Afraid of getting a little rash?" Brooke asked in a distinctly snide tone.

"No." Raven took the mesh from Kalen. "But I'm posing for *Sports Illustrated's* swimsuit issue next month, and they have a no-rash clause in the contract." She studied it for a moment. "Hyatt, does it have to be worn flat to work?"

"No, that's the beauty of it. You can wrap it around any size torso, arm, leg—"

She took the mesh, twisted it lightly and draped it around her neck like a scarf. "Will it work like this?"

"Oh, man." Conor chuckled. "Hyatt, you gotta show that to the application team when we're through."

"All right." Kalen rose from his chair. "Brooke, you'll be with Hyatt, monitoring Raven from the van. Conor, you'll be snapping photos of her from the perimeter. I'll walk her in and watch her back. Get the remote wire."

Raven began to unbutton her blouse, but glanced up in surprise when a hard hand pulled her out of the chair. "What?"

"We'll do it in there." Kalen nodded toward the master bedroom, then turned and took the backup wire and pocket-size recorder attached to it from Hyatt. To the team, he said, "Finish your prep work. We'll leave in ten."

Raven rolled her eyes at his back, but obediently followed him into the next room.

He didn't want to wire her, but telling Brooke to do it would be like throwing a cat in cold bathwater. And he'd be damned if he'd let her undress in front of his men. "Take off the shirt."

She began unbuttoning her blouse again. "You could have asked the Snow Queen to do this, you know."

"Brooke has other things to do." Checking the wire relay to the recorder gave him an excuse not to watch her striptease. And still he watched her, from the corner of his eye, like a teenage boy wrecked on hormones. "Hurry up."

Raven's lingerie was like the rest of her wardrobe—astronomically expensive, French, and sinfully seductive. Beneath the plain white silk blouse she wore a satin bra designed to exactly match the color of her skin—and barely cover her breasts. The two triangular cups were outlined in small seed pearls and hooked together with a freshwater pearl clasp.

She looked down at herself and prodded the seams with a finger. "I don't know how much you can stuff in this without it showing. Maybe I should borrow one from the captain—she looks to be about a cup size bigger than me."

"No." He wasn't aware of how fast he moved, only that a moment later he was pushing her hand away and measuring the length of the wire against her. When he flicked open the clasp, her hands came up to hold the two halves of the bra in place.

His mouth hitched as her hands dropped down and curled into fists. "Relax. Think of it as a dry run for the swimsuit issue."

She let out a slow breath and lowered her chin so she could watch him. "Do I wear an earpiece, or has NASA developed some kind of weird hair extension for that?"

"An earpiece. Hold still." He adjusted the wire so the tiny microphone would stay hidden behind the front fastener, then bent the wire to curve around and under her breast. The soft skin his knuckles brushed felt slightly damp. He wondered if she could see the sweat trickling down his spine. "You're sweating."

"So are you."

He should have known; she had eyes like a peregrine. "Why?"

Her dark brown eyes met his as he looked up.

"My stomach's upset." Her fingers fluttered over her flat abdomen. "I don't like burying my friends."

He caught her hand, then pressed it against the wire. "Hold this while I fix it."

Kalen used a towel to dry her skin, then taped the wire against her chest and abdomen. The small strips of flesh-colored adhesive concealed the darker wire cable, making it virtually invisible beneath the blouse.

Touching her, however, made him clench his molars until his jaw ached. "Unzip your pants."

She dutifully loosened her silk trousers, and he moved around her to tape the mini-recorder against the small of her back. "Leave it loose, or it'll pop when I sit down."

He tugged at the tape, then felt her shudder as his fingertips grazed her spine. "Is it uncomfortable?"

"No. I strap recording devices to my body all the time." She sounded amused, but her back muscles tensed. "Helps me unwind after a long day of looking beautiful and useless."

He felt a small twinge of guilt. "I shouldn't have said that."

"Why not? It's what you really think. What you've always thought." When his hands left her, she moved away and fastened the front of her blouse and trousers, then surveyed her reflection in the mirror and made small adjustments. "And you're right, too. Beauty is definitely profitable, but essentially useless. And it makes an agent far too conspicuous."

He stared hard at her, trying to see Sarah again. "You were beautiful in your own way, before."

The murmured words hung between them for a moment, then she shook her head. "I was good at my job because I was unremarkable."

He didn't like the way she said that—as if she'd considered herself ugly. And there was no comment he could make about that that wouldn't propel them into a shouting match. Finally, he settled for "You were a good agent, and a team player."

"Yep. One hundred percent on the job, twenty-four seven." She picked up the mesh and draped it around her neck. "Just like you."

The tall, beautiful woman standing before the mirror was not Sarah, he reminded himself. Would never be Sarah again. "But not anymore."

"No, General." She fluffed her hair. "Not anymore."

Duty. Honor. Country.

Brooke Oliver had believed in those three words from the moment she entered West Point. She'd never wanted to be anything but an army officer, just like her father. She'd decided that on the day the veteran battalion commander had been killed fighting in the deserts of Kuwait.

She'd been too small to see the flag draped over his coffin. Her mother had lifted her up in her arms, and told her to say good-bye to her father. That was when Brooke had wrapped her small arms around her weeping mother's neck and whispered that she would be a soldier one day, so she could hunt down and shoot the men who had taken her daddy away from them. Brooke's mother had stopped weeping.

"Yes, darling," she'd whispered to the little girl. "You do that for Daddy."

Her mother had seen to it that she'd kept her promise by enrolling her in junior ROTC and other army programs. Brooke had to sacrifice a lot to follow in her father's footsteps and join the long gray line, but her mother had only to remind her of her promise to make the teenager work that much harder.

You want to make your father proud, don't you, Brooke?

So when other girls had gone to dances and proms, she'd stayed home and crammed on regs for her academy entrance exam. It had paid off, however, and she'd risen quickly to the top of her class. The honors she received at graduation included a special citation for exemplifying the academy's Cadet Honor Code: "A cadet will not lie, cheat, or steal, or tolerate those who do."

And now here she was, backing up a traitor who had done all those things, and probably more.

"I don't believe this." Brooke jammed her headset over her ears and tuned in to Raven's frequency. Two car lengths in front of the van a long black limousine maneuvered through the morning Manhattan traffic. "We're stuck in this van for the duration, while *she* gets to ride around town in a frigging air-conditioned limo."

"She's a celebrity; it goes with the territory." Conor checked the clip in his weapon, then shrugged into a dark tweed jacket. "What's your problem with Raven, anyway? She's been decent enough to you."

"She's nothing but an airheaded bimbo. Don't get me started."

Brooke listened to Kalen's voice over the headset, heard the way his tone changed as he spoke directly to the model. Her linguistic training enabled her to pick up nuances that escaped the average person. There was no doubt in her mind that the general and the bimbo knew each other very well.

You're still feeling sick. Kalen's voice dropped, became a murmur. *You're too pale.*

I think I'm getting a headache—got any aspirin on you?

No. His disapproval was plain. *You should have eaten something before we left the hotel.*

Raven laughed. *Oh, and you've been an absolute joy this morning?*

The intimacy of that laugh made Brooke grind her teeth. She tugged off the headset and tossed it aside.

Conor Perry bent over to check the console. "Problem?"

"No, I'm picking them up fine." She knew Conor had worked for the general for several years, and so she kept her voice casual as she added, "They've slept together before, haven't they?"

"Maybe." He shrugged, unconcerned. "If they did, it's no business of ours."

"She said something about him getting grumpy when he doesn't eat breakfast." Hyatt, who was driving, glanced back at Brooke. "Only one way she'd know that."

"Hell, *I* know that," Conor said, "and I've never slept with him."

"It doesn't matter." Brooke set up another blank tape in the recorder and checked the time left on the one she'd started. "Whatever it was, it's over." She saw the two men eye each other and swiveled around. "She's nothing but a convenience in for this op, and as soon as it's over, she'll head back to Paris to get her nails done."

"Sounds like wishful thinking to me." Conor holstered his weapon and checked the tiny earpiece on his sunglasses before putting them on. "You're aiming pretty high, Cap. Maybe you should join the air force."

"Stuff it, Perry." She tucked a stray piece of hair back into the tight, neat twist at the back of her head.

"Ravenowitz might have been CID once, but whatever skills she had are history. Probably from brain damage, breathing in all that French perfume."

"Hold on." As Hyatt chuckled, Conor leaned in and lowered his voice. "Look, I know you don't like her, but take a little friendly advice: lose the attitude."

She reared back. "Why should I?"

"We can't do the job unless everyone's on the same page." His tone sharpened. "We're army, remember? Teamwork."

"I'm right here, Perry." She wagged the headset at him. "Every step of the way."

"You'd better be. I don't know what's going on with the major, but she's off balance. I've worked with her before, and I can tell the difference. Kalen's been biting our heads off since she got here. You antagonize Raven, you're going to send her further off balance, piss off the boss, and put the whole mission at risk."

She'd never seen the mellow Conor Perry get angry before, and the small shock of being the cause of that snapped her self-control back into place. "You're right. Sorry."

"Good." As Hyatt parked on the road beside the cemetery, Conor buttoned his jacket. "Keep your ears on and your heads down. I'm outta here."

As she slipped the headphones back on, Brooke clamped down on another surge of fury. She would play the game for now, but she had no intention of relinquishing her goal. Kalen Grady was a brilliant man, on his way to becoming one of the Joint Chiefs. The only thing he lacked was a partner who not only understood his unique position but would do everything to support his rise to power.

And Brooke intended to be there with him, every step of the way.

"Captain, I'd better run that download now." Hyatt's glasses glittered as he left the driver's seat, sat down at one of the remote terminals, and hooked a modem line into the laptop he'd taken from Raven's suite. "What does he want me to find on here again?"

"Anything and everything." Brooke was hoping for something that would ruin Raven for good. "Just dupe all the files."

Hyatt completed the connection and began hacking into Raven's database.

Some three hundred people arrived to pay their last respects to Portia Santiago—models, photographers, designers—and nearly all of them stopped to speak with Raven. She felt Kalen watching as she pressed hands and listened to the murmured expressions of sympathy.

"Target approaching," she heard Conor say over the tiny earpiece she wore.

On the other side of the grave, two Chinese men arrived to stand in respectful silence. Bodyguards moved in to form a wall of bodies behind them. The wide, dark shades that Raven wore enabled her to study the father and son, but she made no move to draw attention to herself.

Dai Ruiban looked like an ancient, weathered statue and stood just as motionless and silent. His slitted gaze swept the assembly once, then settled on the priest who arrived to bless the grave and read the final prayers. His expression remained polite but distant.

He's only here out of duty, Raven thought. *And I'll bet he's seen a lot of people put in the ground.*

The photos Kalen had showed her of Zhihan had prepared her for his cruel face, but not for his presence. He had a spare, kickboxer's form that vibrated with tension. His dark eyes moved from face to face, and judging from the set of his jaw he was upset, even angry. Then he looked directly at her, and a chill sank into her bones.

This one has put people in the ground personally—and enjoyed it. But would he have killed his own brother?

To start the ball rolling, Raven gave Zhihan a small, respectful nod, then moved to stand with Portia's mother. "Mrs. Santiago? Are you okay?"

The heavyset Brazilian woman spoke little English, but from her moaning and her wringing hands, it was only too obvious that she was ready to crumble. Gemma Firth appeared and flanked the devastated woman, helping Raven support her as she wept throughout the brief service. At the end, the priest took over, and guided the heartbroken mother away from the grave.

"Bloody hell," Gemma muttered.

"Not for Portia." Raven shook her head. "She's in heaven, arguing with God about the latest style in wings." She stepped up to put her flower on the casket, then went still.

Kalen moved in behind her. "It was quick," he murmured.

She almost didn't hear him. Her gaze was fixed on the pair of lotuses someone had left on top of the casket.

"Awful way to go," Gemma came to stand beside her and toed the loose dirt at the edge of the grave

with her narrow stiletto-heeled shoe. "You be sure
and nail a few of those angels for me, Portia luv."
As if she couldn't bear to look at the casket, she
wandered away.

Raven kept staring at the twin white flowers. Once
might have been a coincidence, but twice was too
much. *Now would be an excellent time to pray.* But
first she was getting those damn things off her friend.

She leaned down and placed a hand against the
smooth wood, dislodging the lotuses and making it
appear as if she'd accidentally knocked them off.

Then she stepped on them and ground them into
the grass.

"Do thou guard, guide, and preserve us, Lord, always and forever. Amen." *I'm going to get who did
this to you, kiddo. To us.* "Take care, sweetie, and
safe journey."

Killing Gangi and his woman at the Japanese embassy had been exhilarating, the Lotus thought, but
too quick. There had been no time or opportunity to
linger and appreciate the beautiful patterns the blood
made on the imported tile floor.

Attending the funerals had not been part of the
contract, but it made up for the hurried nature of the
hit. And now a bonus had dropped out of nowhere—
proof that there was a living witness to one of the
Lotus's other, far older crimes.

The media loved Raven, not only for her spectacu-
lar good looks but for the air of mystery surrounding
her. Everyone knew she was an American, yet no one
knew her surname. While other models had trouble
learning to program their cell phones, she was rumored to be an expert on computer systems.

And now she sees my flowers, and knocks them off, and steps on them.

The Lotus had always been scrupulous about body counts—a strict requirement of both the profession and career planning. Yet in all the years of killing for hire, there had been only one body left unaccounted for, that of a young American intelligence operative who had been caught in a carefully arranged ambush in China.

The Lotus remembered her well. Watching the terror appear in her eyes before shooting her in the face had been completely gratifying. But then, the fear and the terror were always the best part of the kill.

Yet when the Lotus had returned to the temple, trail marks showed that the brown-eyed woman's body had been dragged out into the jungle. A thorough sweep of the area had turned up no clues as to what had happened to the corpse. It was assumed that foraging animals had done nature's work.

Raven looked nothing like that young agent, but the survivor of such a wound would have had to undergo extensive reconstructive surgery. Was it possible that she was using her current profession as a cover to continue her intelligence work? Had she come to the United States not to mourn her friend but to locate the one responsible for the murders, and her own mutilation?

The hunted thinks to become the hunter, the Lotus thought, and nearly smiled. *What a delicious thought.*

Chapter 5

"He's moving," Conor whispered over the transmitter. "Two o'clock, coming right at you, Stretch."

"Here we go." Kalen released her arm and drifted back from the grave.

"It was a good service." Alake appeared and touched her arm. "I did not know you prayed, Raven."

"Leftover habit from Catholic school." She straightened and turned to find Gemma and her target standing beside the Nigerian model. "Hello."

"This is Dai Zhihan—his brother was killed with Portia." Alake made an elegant gesture. "Zhihan, you recognize Raven, of course. She and Portia often worked together in Paris."

"Mr. Dai." Raven didn't make the mistake of offering her hand, but inclined her head. "I'm so sorry about your brother."

Zhihan gave her a measuring look, then gestured toward the casket. "As I am about your friend. She was far too young and beautiful to die this way."

That wouldn't have stopped you from sticking a sword in her, or butchering my team. Raven fought to keep her expression calm and reserved, but her blood was reaching the boiling point. *And if you did, you're going down.* "Thank you."

"I don't know about the rest of you, but I could bloody damn well use a drink." Gemma wrapped her arms around her abdomen. "What say we go find us a nice dark little tavern and share a pint or two?"

Raven shook her head and didn't have to fake the weariness in her voice. "Sorry, but I'm not exactly in the mood to bar-hop."

"We are having a small reception this afternoon for friends," Zhihan said to Gemma, but his gaze remained fixed on Raven. "You can come and drink with me."

Asians were far more reserved than most people, especially in body language, but Raven could feel the intensity of his interest. She took off her glasses for a moment and let her eyes meet his. "I don't want to intrude upon a private time."

"It would be my pleasure." Zhihan moved closer, and his thin lips curved. "And yours."

He was hooked.

She forced warmth into her voice. "I'd like that."

"Hello, light of my life."

Only one person called Kameko that. "Nick. What a surprise."

"I haven't had a chance to call you since I got back last month. Thought I'd check in," her ex-husband said, sounding genuinely concerned.

Which meant he was lying. "I'm fine." No, she wasn't. "How was your trip?"

"Tokyo is still overcrowded, dirty, and expensive, but I survived. Hold on a sec." He covered the receiver, but she could still hear the track announcer in the background. "That was some service they had for your dad at the family temple. Everyone was there."

"Everyone but me."

Paper ripped close to the phone. "Your uncles were kind of upset that you didn't show. I told 'em how you felt, but you know how the old guys are. Family is family." There was a click of a lighter, and he sucked in a breath.

"You shouldn't be smoking." She hated cigarettes, another of Nick's addictions.

"I've cut way down. So, how's the jewelry business?"

She closed her eyes. "Do you need money again?"

"No, no." He sounded offended—as if he'd never called her to beg for a loan. "I'm doing fine. Your brother's been taking real good care of me."

Meko didn't want to be reminded of how much money her ex-husband had borrowed from her relatives, either. "Then what is it, Nick?"

"Listen, Meko, did your dad send you something before he died?"

She glanced at the envelope she'd left on her desk. "Why would he? My father and I hadn't spoken to each other in years, you know that."

"Because of me." Now he sounded like a sulky child.

"Because of you," she agreed.

"I didn't file for divorce, Meko. That was all you. I'd have been happy if we'd stayed married forever." He released a ragged breath. "I loved you. I still love you."

This time, she knew he meant every word. Nick Hosyu had been a thief, a liar, a gambler, and her father's bagman, but he had genuinely loved her. He'd even been faithful to her—as faithful as a man obsessed with gambling away every cent he had could be.

After the bank repossessed the little house they'd bought with their wedding money—Nick had taken care of their finances and hadn't bothered to pay the mortgage for eight months—she'd left him. Stunned and horrified, he had followed her, begging her to take him back, making all the same old promises.

Don't do this to me, Kameko. I'll get you a bigger house. A better one.

She had refused. The little humiliations and betrayals had built up over the years, and she had felt smothered by them. Nick went to her father, as he always did in the end, and Takeshi had commanded her to return to her husband. He told her that he would make good on Nick's debts to the various loan sharks he owed, and Kameko would work harder at pleasing her husband.

It is time you and Nick had children. That will settle him down.

Being ordered to have a child was the final straw. Meko had called an attorney and started the divorce proceedings that same afternoon.

"Nick, I have to go, I have work to do," she told him, banishing the painful memories. "Take care."

"Okay, but would you call me if anything does come in from your dad?" He forced another laugh. "You know how the mail is in China. They deliver it by oxcart."

She had to ask. "What do you think he would send me?"

"Something real important, Blossom. Call me. Okay?"

She hung up the phone and picked up the envelope. She hadn't wanted to open it, from the moment she'd recognized the bold slash of her father's handwriting. The contents made no sense to her, not the photograph of the sword or the incomprehensible note he'd written.

> Use this historic evidence to identify. Good exam-
> ple rank sword, the real evidence as specified under
> research. Everyone is skeptical, guarded. Until a rep-
> resentative delivers everything, don't betray your
> dear relatives. All goodness only needs someone to
> find it.

"All goodness." She snorted and put the letter into her desk drawer so she wouldn't have to look at it. "As if you knew anything about that, Father."

The phone rang again, and she prayed it wouldn't be Nick again. "Hello?"

"Miss Sayura?" a woman's voice asked. "This is Valence St. Charles from New Orleans."

She didn't know anyone by that name. "Yes?"

"I'm sorry to bother you." The voice was pleasant, colored by a soft Southern accent. "I'm trying to recover some antique Asian weapons."

Meko frowned. "I'm sorry, I don't do that kind of restoration work."

"I meant 'recover' as in getting back what's been stolen. The White Tiger sword collection was taken from our New Orleans museum last winter, and my husband and I are trying to track it down."

The words from her father's letter burned behind her closed eyes. "I don't know anything about that, Ms. St. Charles."

For a moment the woman didn't respond. Then she said, "I was wondering if your father might have."

Meko felt like laughing—hysterically. "I would ask him, but my father is dead. Good-bye." She hung up the phone, and when it rang again, she pulled the cord out of the wall jack.

Whoever else wanted to talk to her would just have to call again later.

Something was wrong.

Kalen noticed how quiet Raven had become on the way back to the hotel from the funeral, but he hadn't mentioned it. She'd just seen a friend buried, and despite her professional experience with death, she had never learned to distance herself from it.

That, it seemed, was another small piece of Sarah that had been left behind.

Yet she stayed quiet. She barely said two words through the debriefing at the hotel and the prep for the next phase of the mission. He had to ask her about Gemma Firth's relationship twice before she heard him and responded. She even meekly accepted his suggestion that she change, so they could hide the wire in the wide lapel of a more sturdy jacket.

"Con, what's our ETA?" he asked.

His point man had taken over driving the limo, and now checked his watch. "Fifteen, twenty minutes, boss."

"Thanks." He closed the glass partition between them, then turned to Raven. "What's your problem?"

She turned from the window, her expression blank. "Huh?"

"You're acting like an anxious rookie." He noted the blink of surprise, then the slight guilty shift of her eyes. "What's got you spooked?"

"Nothing." She moved her shoulders. "It's jet lag, I guess."

He wasn't buying it. "This morning you were ready to wrestle a tiger with one hand and paint your toenails with the other. Now you don't hear half the things I say." He gave her a minute to respond, then demanded, "Are you hedging on me?"

"No."

"Raven."

"All right." She looked down at her hands, then back at him. "There was something, at the funeral. You still have those photos from the crime scene?"

"Yeah." He took the envelope out of his briefcase, and handed it to her. "Here."

She sorted through the photos, and removed a floor shot. "This is the one. Do you know if that mink coat belonged to Portia?"

"Probably. Her blood was all over it. I'll have to confirm that with the D.C. cops." He saw her knuckles whiten. "Why is the coat important?"

"Not the coat, the flower on it. Someone left two lotuses identical to it on her coffin."

To most men, flowers were flowers. But Kalen took the photo and studied it. "You think it's a calling card?"

"Maybe." She pointed to the unusual pink-tipped petals. "Lotuses are white or pink. This one is a hybrid."

"Why didn't you want to tell me about this?"

"I wasn't sure if there's a connection." She went back to staring out the window. "I'm still not convinced."

He still couldn't tell if she was telling him the entire truth, but at least she'd opened up a little. Kalen called the funeral home from the limo and instructed the director to collect all the flowers from the graveside. Then he contacted his forensics unit and told them to retrieve the flowers and compare them to what was recovered from the crime scene.

Raven remained silent and tense, but he didn't

press the issue. He sensed that she was holding something inside, and that pushing her would only result in driving her further away.

That was when he realized how hard it was going to be, when the time came to let her go. "Let's talk about how you're going to work this party."

"Let's not and say we did."

"You need to get him to focus, which shouldn't be hard." All she had to do was walk into a room and every man present would break his neck to watch her move. "You want to get him talking about the brother, the last time he saw him, what he thought of him, how close they were, et cetera."

"I know what to do, Kalen."

He had to shake her out of this trance. "Practice on me anyway."

She skimmed her fingertips through the ends of her hair. "You want the dialogue, or the whole act?"

"Give me the works."

She immediately turned from the window with a glowing smile and shifted closer to him. The transformation was so sudden and complete that he almost recoiled.

My God, who taught her to do this?

"You have a beautiful home, Mr. Dai." One of her hands shyly grazed his arm as she made a sweeping gesture. "Look at all these genuine instruments of torture. I can still see blood on the iron maiden."

Her sarcasm helped clear his head. "Keep it straight, Raven."

She nodded and moved an inch closer. "I'm going to miss Portia so much, she was such a great friend. And I'm so sorry about your loss." Her smile shifted from warm to sympathetic. "I can tell, you were close to your brother, weren't you?"

"Close enough to kill him. Good. So you draw him out as much as you can about the brother." Kalen rolled his hand. "Then what?"

"Were you in Washington when that awful thing happened?" She moved again, now so close she was practically cuddling him, and used her hands to continue gesturing and touching him. "Portia really loved Gangi. In a way, I know she was glad to be with him when he . . ." She slid her hand down his arm and let her fingertips whisper over his.

"You're touching me—him—too much," Kalen snapped.

"No, I'm not. Asian men expect women to flirt with their voices and their bodies." She dropped her hand on his thigh and squeezed. "*This* is touching too much."

He took her hand away before she could feel his muscles knotting. "If you move too fast, you'll blow it. Remember, you just met this morning."

She leveled a direct look at him. "I remember—I nearly stepped on his tongue."

"Go on. Give me a summary—without the groping."

She sighed. "I establish his whereabouts at the time of the murder, if I can, and then I get him to give me a tour of the house. So we can look at his etchings and he can pant all over me. While he's drooling, I get what I can on the tong, his father, and any street war–related intel." She tilted her head back. "Want to give me a few test hickies?"

"You're not funny."

"Neither are you." She threw up her hands. "What do you really think I'm going to do, Kal? Seduce him on the punch bowl table in front of his guests, his dad, and God? Then abscond with him and the tong's treasury?"

He wouldn't put it past her. "This is the one shot you've got to get in with him. Don't blow it."

"I won't, damn it. Get off my back."

They were nose to nose, and all he wanted to do was haul her onto his lap and kiss her until she stopped snarling at him. But her temper brought benefits; her eyes glittered, her cheeks were pink, and she didn't look like a ghost anymore.

All he had to do now was watch her work her magic. Which had all the appeal of taking a knife in the ribs.

"Boss?" Conor tapped the partition. "We're here."

Dai Ruiban instructed his houseman Ran to prepare tea, then frowned as his son ordered that a bottle of scotch be brought as well. "It is too early in the day for alcohol."

Ran Peng, who had served both men long enough to know when to wait, studied the mother-of-pearl inlay of the hardwood floor.

"Bring it," Zhihan told him. When Ruiban didn't contradict that order, Ran departed. "Don't treat me like a child. Not in front of the servants, or my men."

"Then do not behave like one." Ruiban watched his son strip off his jacket and prowl the length of the room until the drinks were served and they were left alone once more. "What of the two government agents?"

"The hydraulic lines bled slowly enough. The incendiary device in the fuel tank finished the job." Zhihan drank his scotch and refilled the glass. "They're dead, and the car was destroyed."

"I told you to make it appear accidental."

"The fire destroyed any evidence that it was not."

"Their superiors will suspect us, nonetheless. Your impulsive act has assured that they will send other agents." The Dai met his son's furious gaze. "We cannot conduct our business under such scrutiny, Zhihan."

"Let them send more agents." Zhihan slammed down his glass. "Let them burn. As my brother burned."

"The American government did not kill your brother." The Dai sipped his tea. "Our enemies are responsible for that. We will have our revenge when we take control of Shandian and the other tongs. That is where you must focus your efforts."

"He died in the Japanese Eembassy," Zhihan snarled. "What better way for the government to send a message to us?"

"The message came from those who covet what we have, not the fools who can only guess at what we do." Ruiban set aside his cup. "Gangi's mistake was in using his mistress as a courier between him and Sayura."

His son clenched his fists. "He used the Brazilian?"

The Dai nodded. "She traveled extensively over the last several weeks, but not to display her body for these fashion magazines. Your brother purchased all of her airline tickets in advance." He made a casual gesture. "Such women are accustomed to selling themselves to the highest bidder."

An ugly color spread from his neck over his face. "The bitch is lucky to be dead."

"She was the only person outside our family involved. We must now discover who paid her to betray Gangi, and who presently possesses the White

Tiger." He allowed a small smile to curl on his lips. "You were wise in inviting the woman's friends here. They knew much about her."

"The dark-haired one with tears in her eyes." Zhihan eyed the bottle, then stalked to the door. "She will tell me everything I need to know."

As Zhihan strode down the hallway, he didn't see the uniformed waiter who emerged from another doorway, nor did he know that the man had been standing outside the door, listening to every word he and his father had said.

Sean Delaney watched the angry young man leave, and wondered how the hell he was going to warn Raven about this without tipping Kalen Grady off to his presence.

And if the Dai don't have the swords, and the son who did is dead, then where in hell are they?

She'd given Kalen everything he needed to know about the flowers, Raven told herself as he helped her out of the car. Bringing up the slaughter in China would only complicate things.

And still she felt terrible.

He looked out at the Dai's mansion, then inspected her face. "If you want a few more minutes to prepare, we can take a walk."

The compassion in his voice startled her. "No. If he sees us strolling around outside, he'll get suspicious." Raven glanced at the house, which was large and imposing enough to look at home in Beverly Hills—or Marseilles. She took the silver mesh and draped it around her neck. "I'm on."

A gorgeous professional hostess met them at the door and showed them to a small, elegant room where the reception was under way. Many of those gathered were male members of the tong, Raven realized as she recognized faces. A number of Portia's friends were also present, mainly women. Almost all were models.

"Hardly any guys," she said under her breath to Kalen. "You'll have to play crutch. Hold on to me like I'm ready to collapse."

"Raven." Zhihan appeared like a cruising shark, circling around her from behind. "I am very happy to see you."

He wasn't happy to see Kalen's arm around her waist, she could tell that. "Thank you for inviting me to your home." She patted Kalen's arm. "This is my assistant, Spike O'Shay. He deals with everything so I don't have to."

"Indeed."

"The media have been after Miss Raven since she arrived in New York," Kalen added, falling instantly into character as the devoted employee. "I keep them from annoying her too much."

"There are no reporters here." Zhihan took Raven's other arm and gestured toward the buffet tables. "Go and have something to eat, O'Shay. You are not needed now."

Kalen held on to her almost a fraction of a second too long, then nodded and moved away. Raven would have sighed with relief, but Gemma and Alake arrived and descended upon her and Zhihan at once.

"You don't mind if I get good and sloshed, do you, Zhihan?" Gemma snatched a glass of wine from a passing waiter and downed it in one swallow. "Funerals are so bloody damn depressing."

"You throw up in everyone else's bathroom, darling." Alake's laugh held a malicious tinge. "Why not his?"

Gemma shrugged. "Can't helping having a stomach virus, luv."

Zhihan frowned as one of the tong members gestured to him, then excused himself.

"What kind of virus? The one where you stick your fingers down your throat three times a day?" Raven eyed her friend. "I thought you'd gone in for treatment last summer."

"I did. I *did*," Gemma insisted. "Spent four horrid weeks at that place Oprah recommended, ate their wretched food and put on ten pounds."

"Where?" Raven looked around her. "In your cosmetic case?"

"Worked it off in the gym. Girl's got to keep her figure tight." The British model slapped her slightly sunken abdomen. "Stop looking at me like that, I've been a good girl, I have."

Raven grabbed her arm before she could exchange her empty wineglass for a full one. "I find out you're purging again, I'll make four weeks at that eating disorder clinic look like a pleasure cruise to St. Croix."

"I told you, I'm fine." Gemma tugged her arm away. "So what's with you and Zhihan being so chummy now? You usually treat men like puppies— pat them on the head, then send them on their way."

She felt rather than saw Kalen approach, and knew he'd heard. *So much for maintaining the illusion that I use and discard men like nose tissue.* "I feel sorry for him, losing his brother that way."

"Sympathy is a good thing"—Alake gave her a sly, appreciative look—"particularly if it puts him in a generous mood."

"Raven does not need my assets, from what I am told." The Dai's heir appeared again, seemingly out of nowhere. "You do not understand true compassion, Alake. It is given for free."

Alake looked amused rather than embarrassed. "Nothing in this world is free, my friend."

As he took her hand in his, Raven felt her stomach roll. His hand was dry and cold, like a corpse's. "Anything worth having is free."

"Oh, God, I need another drink." Gemma wandered off after a waiter.

"I'd better go baby-sit her." The Nigerian girl's gaze fell to their linked hands. "Enjoy sharing your . . . sympathies."

"Are you enjoying yourself?" the Dai's son asked her.

"Not really," Raven said, being completely honest. "I feel a little claustrophobic for some reason."

"Come."

Raven looked for Kalen as Zhihan led her away from the other guests into an adjoining room. Here the furniture and decor reflected a more traditional, Oriental style. But it wasn't the black and silver somberness of the room that bothered Raven.

What made her blood run cold was the collection of antique swords displayed on the walls.

"What a fascinating collection," she made herself say. "Are they real?"

"Quite." He indicated she should sit, then went to the bar.

She wondered how much he'd had to drink. Alcohol usually helped loosen a target's tongue, but the other effects made it hard to maintain control. "They must be very old."

"Some are. My father has been acquiring them for

years. This one he obtained from Takeshi Sayura's collection." Zhihan took down one long, highly polished blade to show it to her. "Most of them are Japanese. The people may be mindless idiots, but they make a superior weapon."

"Wow." *What else would a mindless bimbo say in a situation like this?* "They must be very sharp."

He gave the edge of the blade the merest touch, and instantly a line of blood appeared on his fingertip. "They are. See?"

"Oh, my goodness!" She made her eyes go wide. "You're bleeding!"

"It's only a small cut. Here." He held out the finger to her. "Kiss it and make it better."

She saw Kalen step into the room and quickly snagged the handkerchief from Zhihan's jacket pocket. With her other hand, she gave Kalen the signal to back off.

He hesitated, then moved back out of the room.

"I wouldn't want to give you my germs." She wrapped the cloth around his finger and fussed over it for a moment, then glanced at the sword he held in the other hand. He had some training; he was using the correct grip. "Would you mind putting that thing back on the wall? It's scaring me."

"It should be." Zhihan seized her hand and leaned closer. "It's the same kind of blade that killed your friend."

She froze. "Now *you're* scaring me."

"Silly girl." He replaced the sword and led her to a small loveseat by a floor-to-ceiling window. "Come, sit with me." He treated her like an invalid, adjusting a pillow behind her before taking a seat beside her. "I should not have frightened you like that."

She could smell scotch on his breath and saw that a flush had formed over his cheekbones. *What had the other man told him?* "I'm sorry—it's so difficult to lose a friend, and when I think about how Portia was murdered. . . ." She let her hand tremble as she pressed it briefly against her eyes.

His grip tightened. "Tell me about Portia. How did you meet her?"

She endured his touch for nearly an hour as they talked. During the conversation, she found she had to field a number of direct questions about Portia's activities by pretending confusion and blaming herself for being unable to concentrate.

In return, Zhihan revealed little and grew suspicious at the slightest probe she attempted. He also drank a great deal, which didn't make him talkative but seemed to make his attention wander. Gradually Raven realized he was staring at the door.

"What is it?" she asked as his gaze drifted again.

"Does your assistant not trust me with you?" Zhihan turned back, his expression ugly. "He passes by the door every ten seconds."

"Spike?" Raven produced a weak laugh. "Oh, no, he's probably just waiting for me to tell him what to do." As Kalen appeared in the doorway, she waved him over and gave Zhihan a tolerant smile.

"Yes, madam?"

"I'm going to be here for some time, Spike. You can wait for me in the car." She nodded toward the door.

"Yes, Miss Raven." He gave Zhihan a hard look. "Mr. Dai."

As Kalen left, Zhihan shifted closer, putting an arm on the back of the loveseat. "Send him back to your hotel. I will see to whatever you may need while you are here."

She felt his cold, rough hand slide under her hair, caressing the back of her neck, and smiled. "That would be lovely."

A waiter entered the room, carrying two trays, and approached them. As Raven reached for a glass of wine, his tray bumped her arm. A small splash landed on her trousers.

"I'm so sorry, madam," the waiter said, and offered her a linen napkin.

Zhihan snapped something in his native language, but Raven seized the opportunity and got to her feet.

"It's all right. These things happen." She pretended to survey the damage, then eyed the waiter. "Would you show me to the nearest bathroom, please?"

"Of course, madam."

Zhihan started to rise, but the amount of scotch he'd consumed had made him unsteady, and he sat back down.

"I'll be right back," she told him.

He nodded and let his head fall back on the cushions. "Don't make me wait too long."

"Only a few minutes, I promise." She turned and followed the waiter out through the reception room and down a short hall to a large, elegant guest bathroom.

"Allow me to assist you, madam," the waiter said as he followed her in and closed the door. Immediately he locked it as Raven turned both sink taps on full and disconnected her transmitter.

She looked for cameras, then leaned in to give Sean Delaney a quick hug. "Good to see you, Irish," she whispered against his ear. "What have you got for me?"

Conor Perry liked women. All women—tall, short, thin, voluptuous, serious, frivolous—they were all beautiful to him, no matter what color, shape, or variety. He blamed that on growing up with six sisters. Between them and his young, widowed mother, he'd been trained early on to respect and appreciate their gender.

As he leaned against the hood of the limo and listened to Raven's voice over his earpiece, he thought about what it would be like to have a woman like her.

A man would have to be dead from the brain down not to be attracted to the major, yet he found himself drawn more by her easy laugh than her goddess body. He'd noticed the way she watched and listened to everything going on around her, too. Whatever Brooke Oliver wanted to think, Raven was no dummy. A man could easily devote his entire life to finding out what was going on behind those dark, devastating eyes.

Still, the goddess was already taken, even if she and the poor obsessed devil who owned her heart were too stubborn to realize it yet. He would just have to settle for admiring her from a distance.

"Conor."

Speak of the poor obsessed devil. "Boss." He dropped his cigarette and crushed it under his shoe. He tapped his ear. "Sounds like she's got him dazzled."

"We've got to pull her out of there." He pressed his own transmitter. "Raven? I'm sending Conor in.

Raven, acknowledge." He released a frustrated breath. "Damn it, I can't hear her anymore."

Conor took out his earpiece, checked it, then replaced it. "I'm not receiving either. Brooke? Hyatt?"

"She might have jerked her wire loose," Hyatt suggested. "We've gotten nothing but static for the last three minutes."

"As drunk as he is, Zhihan probably jerked it loose," Conor suggested.

Kalen stared back at the mansion, his gaze murderous. "He's had his hands all over her."

"If he's that smashed, he could be workable." Conor saw his reaction to that. "Right. We get her out. How do you want to do it?"

"You're set up as the photographer. Put on your camera, go in and remind her she's got a shoot scheduled this afternoon." Kalen touched the transmitter on his lapel. "Raven, if you can hear me, I'm sending Conor in to get you out. Stay where you are. Hyatt, pack it up. Brooke, get Jian-Shan on the phone for me. If the Japanese are involved with what happened to the swords, he'll know why."

"Why are we shutting down now?" Brooke wanted to know. "She's got him alone and talking."

"Follow your orders, Captain." Kalen released the transmitter switch.

Conor had worked with the general long enough to realize that his boss was on the brink of full-blown rage. "What's wrong?"

"He's got her in a room full of swords, and he's grilling her about Portia. He mentioned Takeshi Sayura, one of the biggest Japanese crime bosses on the West Coast—almost as if he expected her to recognize the name." He dragged a hand through his hair.

"Something's way off. I want to know what it is before we go any further with this."

"Will do." Conor changed his jacket and slung the camera around his neck. "Don't worry, boss, I'll have her out of there in two minutes."

But as he walked up to the big house, Conor had the feeling Kalen was more concerned about Zhihan putting his hands on Raven than anything else.

Chapter 6

Raven spent as much time as she dared in the bathroom with Sean, going over what he'd learned, then told him to leave before Kalen spotted him.

"I'm not leaving until you do—no arguments." The Irishman took out a vial and pressed it into her hand. "If he starts to get out of hand again, drop this in his drink. It can't be traced; it'll knock him unconscious in two minutes and keep him out for twelve hours."

"All right. Thanks." She tucked the vial away in her pocket. "Kalen will have sent Conor in by now. I'd better go."

"Be careful. The little bastard means business."

She reconnected her wire, then slipped back to the reception, hoping her absence had gone unnoticed. Hope died when she saw Zhihan weaving a path toward her from one side of the room and Conor on an intercept course from the other.

"Where have you been?" Zhihan demanded. "I was looking for you."

"So was I." Conor tugged on his earlobe. "It's time we got back to the hotel, Miss Raven. Calvin Klein's people will be there in an hour to start the photo session."

"You cannot leave." The Dai's son latched on to her arm and gestured for Perry to leave them. "You—go tell these Calvin people to wait until tomorrow."

"I don't have to leave this instant." Raven tucked her arm through his and leveled a look at Conor. "A few more minutes won't hurt, would it?"

"Tell her to quit stalling," Kalen snarled over her earpiece.

Conor grimaced. "I'm just following instructions, miss."

"Yes, those instructions came in *loud* and *clear*," Raven said as she tugged on her earlobe. "But I can't run out on my host just yet." She had to get rid of Conor for a few more minutes, and she saw how to do it when she spotted Gemma heading for the hallway. "Gem, come here. I want you to meet someone."

As Zhihan simmered beside her, Raven performed the introductions. "Gemma's worked with some of the best photographers in the business—you did a shoot with Antoine Verglas last week, didn't you, darling?"

"Bloody slave driver, he was——tied me to a brass bed with black stockings," Gemma muttered as she led Conor away. "You wouldn't do that to a girl and expect her to stick her bum in the air for four hours, now, would you?"

"There are too many people here." Zhihan began guiding her back toward the sword room.

"I know you can hear me, Raven," Kalen said over her earpiece. "Don't fool with him any longer. Make your excuses and get out of there."

"I do have to get back to my hotel, Zhihan." She extricated her arm from his and paused by one of the buffet tables. "I just wanted to tell you how much I've enjoyed myself."

He put his rough hands on her shoulders and pressed his thumbs against the sides of her throat. "Stay and show me."

She leaned back against the table to brace herself as he pressed closer. "I can always come and see you at the end of the week."

His thumbnails scraped against her skin. "I do not wish to wait that long."

Summoning every iota of seduction she could muster, Raven bent her head and let her breath whisper against his cheek. "I'm worth waiting for, you know." She invested each word with slow, sultry meaning. "Let me get all this business out of the way, and then . . . we can enjoy each other."

His bloodshot eyes moved, his gaze fixing on her mouth. "I will not be here. Gemma and Alake are going with me to my home in Chicago." He rubbed a finger across her bottom lip. "Go with us. Be with me."

"We're not set up for you to go with him," Kalen said. "Tell him you'll meet him there."

The thought that he had convinced the two models to accompany him alarmed her. From what Sean had told her, he might even harm them. She had to go to Chicago, but not with him. What excuse could she make? "That's a coincidence—I'm appearing in a fashion show there this weekend. After the show I'd love to get together with you and my friends." She trailed a finger down the front of his shirt. "You do give such lovely, elegant parties."

"A party." His lip curled. "Is that all you want?"

She wanted to spray herself with disinfectant. "Oh, no," she murmured, allowing her hair to brush against his face as she looked down, then up at him through her lashes. "But it's a good place to get started."

"Takeshi Sayura and my father were rivals for years," Jian-Shan said over the speakerphone. "He would have considered it a personal coup to steal the White Tiger away from him, as Raven can tell you."

Kalen had not seen Raven since they'd returned from the Dai's house. She'd gone back to her suite to take a shower and change. He had intended to talk to her about the way she'd handled Zhihan, but decided not to do it in front of the team. When he chewed her ass out for being reckless and stupid, he would do it in private, like he did with everyone else.

"Sayura came up on our list," Brooke said. "He was in China when the swords were stolen." She checked a printout. "He died in a traffic accident six weeks before Dai Gangi was murdered."

"Convenient timing. His people operate up and down the West Coast." Hyatt took off his glasses and polished the lenses with a tissue. "We're talking two hundred, maybe three hundred suspects in ten different cities."

"He wouldn't have entrusted the swords to just anyone," Jian-Shan insisted. "This was more than business. This was revenge. He would have given them to a member of his immediate family."

Brooke shook her head. "Not likely. His sons were with him in China the whole time."

"True, but his daughter, Kameko, resides in Los Angeles. Val contacted her earlier to see if she knew anything about her father's swords, but the lady ended the call rather abruptly. We have been unable to contact her since."

"You mean Kameko Sayura, the jeweler who caters to all those Hollywood celebrities?" Brooke sniffed her contempt. "Doesn't sound like the type, Mr. T'ang."

"The bonds of loyalty among my people are very complicated, Captain. And my wife has taught me never to underestimate any woman." Jian-Shan sounded amused. "General, I suggest you send someone to locate and interview Ms. Sayura. It would also be prudent to perform a thorough search of her home and business. Is Raven there? She knows the woman personally."

Of course she did. Was there anyone Raven didn't know personally? Kalen rubbed his temple. "She's temporarily indisposed, Jian. I'll have her call you later."

Someone knocked at the door, and Conor rose to answer it. Kalen saw him speak to one of the maids, who seemed agitated, then he left with her.

Jian-Shan provided a few more leads, mostly from rumors circulating around the community of weapons collectors, then excused himself to take another call. Brooke and Hyatt went to work on pulling the names of criminals known to associate with Takeshi Sayura. Kalen took a few minutes to review a handful of faxes that had come in, then glanced up at the door.

It had been a good ten minutes, and still Conor hadn't come back.

He thought of Raven, and how well she'd hit it off with his point man, then found himself rising from the table and heading for the door.

"General?"

"I'll be right back."

He used the extra key he had to open Raven's door

slowly. The front room was empty, but he could hear Conor laughing in the bedroom.

"—a little insane to do this," Raven said, sounding a bit breathless. "But it makes me feel fantastic."

"You'll have to show me." Conor laughed again. "Hold still, I've almost got it back in."

He shoved open the door to the bedroom, then stopped at the threshold. Raven was suspended, upside down, by one leg. She hung from a black metal frame fitted to the top of the bathroom doorway. Conor stood on a chair beside her, using a screwdriver on the clamp locked around her ankle.

Raven turned her head and groaned. "We're busted, Perry."

At the same time, Conor said, "Got it," and curled an arm around her waist as the ankle clamp released. He glanced back at Kalen as he flipped Raven over onto her feet and steadied her. "Hey, boss. Uh, Raven kind of got stuck while she was—"

He held up a hand. "Save it. Go help the others pack up the gear."

Conor nodded and beat a hasty retreat.

Raven pushed her hair back out of her flushed face and bent down to rub her ankle. "Mind telling me why you have a key to my suite?"

"The army is paying for it." He wouldn't let himself shout at her. No matter how far she pushed him. "What"—he indicated the suspension frame clamped to the doorway—"is that?"

"It's an inversion rack. It decreases the compressive effect of gravity on the spine and internal organs, reduces lactic acid buildup in the muscles, and realigns the skeletal system." She flexed her foot and grinned. "And it's fun."

"Hanging upside down by one leg is your idea of

fun." *Naturally. Raven wouldn't have a hobby like, say,
knitting sweaters.*

"One of my ankle clamps got stuck in the suspension track, and I couldn't pull it free. Lucky for me,
the maid came in, and I sent her to get help. Oh,
lighten up, Kalen," she tacked on as she rose and
went to the closet.

"It doesn't seem wise, under the circumstances."

"Nothing fun is." She took out a robe and
shrugged into it. "Look, it's a quick way to relax,
and after having Zhihan all over me, I needed it."

The mention of Zhihan reminded him of the ass-
chewing he still had to give her. "What happened to
your transmitter after I left you with him?"

She stuck her head in the closet again and began
sorting through her clothes. "It came loose."

So that was how she was going to play it.

"I fitted you with that wire myself." He walked
toward her. "The plug was tight. So were the connec-
tors. It didn't come loose. Not without help."

"You know, you sound a little tense, Kalen. You
ought to try inversion therapy yourself." She tossed
a pair of wickedly high-heeled magenta pumps out
behind her. "It's like being in traction—your body
weight actually decompresses your spine—and hanging upside down helps stretch out your calves, shins,
quads—"

The last threads of his patience began to snap, one
by one. He used a handful of her robe to pull her
out of the closet and around to face him. "Don't hide
things from me."

She trailed her fingers over his shoulder. "Tense
and paranoid. Sure you don't want to borrow my
ankle clamps?"

He hauled her close. He wouldn't turn this into a

wrestling match—he would simply make a point. "How can I trust you when everything that comes out of your mouth is a joke—or a lie?"

"I told you, Kalen, I've never lied to you." She glanced down at his hands on her arms. "Do you mind? I still bruise rather easily."

He thought of what he could do to wipe that smirk off her face. Anything to keep her from laughing at him. It was the realm of possibilities within the word "anything" that made him take a deep, steadying breath. They'd done this, back in New Orleans— months ago, and it had left him feeling brutal and ugly.

He wouldn't do that again. Not to either one of them.

Slowly, he let her go. "What about the Chicago fashion show?"

"Not a problem." She took an armful of clothes from the closet and dumped them on the bed. Spotting Gemma's satin sack, she picked it up and looked inside. "Good Lord, handcuffs." She chuckled and thrust the sack into the pocket of her robe. "And they say Brits are so conservative. What about the show?"

"Let me rephrase: there *is* no Chicago fashion show."

"Not yet. Wait a minute." She went to the phone, picked it up, and dialed a long series of numbers. After a short interval of silence, she said, "*Bonjour*, Madam Etienne, *s'il vous plaît. C'est* Raven."

"I haven't got all day," he told her. "Talk to your friends when you get back."

"Keep your shirt on, General." She smiled into the phone. "*Bonjour*, Ray, *j'ai besoin d'une*—" She winced and held the phone away from her ear for a few moments as a continuous stream of shrieked French poured out of it.

Kalen knew just how Honore felt. "Do you have this effect on everyone?"

"Only the people who think they have to baby-sit me," she told him, then went back to the phone. "*Je comprends, cherie. Oui.* Yes, you can kick my ass all over Paris as soon as I get back. Twice, if you want. Now listen to me, *c'est une urgence.*" She quickly rattled off several more sentences in rapid French, then added, "*Oui, ici, cette semaine. Est-ce que vous m'enverrez ça par fax? J'apprécie votre aide. Merci.*" She hung up the phone, rubbed her ear, and sighed. "Done."

"What?"

"We now have a fashion show for me in Chicago. Honore will fax all the information to us shortly."

"You got the top fashion designer in France to throw a fashion show just for you. Just like that."

"Just like that." She chuckled at his expression. "Why are you surprised? You're the one who requisitioned a Concorde and an entire hotel."

"I'm a general."

"Yeah, well, in the fashion industry, so am I." She came around the bed and started sorting through the clothes she'd taken from the closet. "I've also got enough money, friends, and fame to do basically whatever I want. Or did you forget?"

"I know what you are." He moved up behind her, and saw her shoulders tense. "It doesn't make you happy."

She snorted. "In comparison to what? Being unknown, alone, and poor?"

He rested his hands on her shoulders, then slipped the robe off and tossed it aside. Her skin had always felt like warm satin under his fingers, and he wanted to rip off her leotard to get at it. "Being with me."

Raven went still. "That was a long time ago—and you said you wouldn't do this."

He turned her to face him. "Do what?"

"This." As he reached down, she took in a quick, shuddering breath. "Kalen—"

"Don't say it." Her hands felt cold as he pressed each one under his, against his chest. "I tell myself the same thing, every time I see you move." He bent his head to breathe in the scent of her hair. She'd washed off the perfume, and now she smelled like sunshine. Like *Sarah*. "Look, but don't touch."

"It's not working," she whispered, lifting her face, pressing her hot cheek against his.

"I know." He left her hands on his chest, and cradled her face between his palms. That strange sense of time evaporating settled over him as he watched her eyes change and darken. The same way they had in that miserable barn in Siberia, where they'd ended up hiding from the militia. He'd pulled her shivering body against his, trying to keep her warm, and they'd ended up all over each other. "It never did."

No other woman had ever felt this good in his arms. If he closed his eyes, he could have been in another time and place. A time when she had been open and generous and completely his, body and soul. As he lowered her onto the bed, he thought of how it had felt to have her wrapped around him in the morning, the slow, lazy smile she gave him when she woke to his touch, the way she would always whisper something loving and sweet before laughing and trying to tackle him.

That woman doesn't exist anymore, his brain told him. *This isn't Sarah. This is Raven.*

He propped himself over her, looking down at the eyes of the woman he had loved, and the gorgeous face of a stranger. He couldn't resurrect the past, and he *had* promised her he wouldn't try. "Old memories. I'm sorry."

She moved under him, twining her long, strong legs around his. "I'm not."

Her lips met his halfway, and the last of his good intentions went straight to hell.

Seeing Kalen appear like some vengeful lover prepared to surprise her in the act had tickled Raven. So had the way he'd ordered Conor out of her suite. She hadn't thought he could ever be jealous, especially where she was concerned.

Now she couldn't think at all.

Kalen's weight held her pinned to the bed, and he kissed her with intense, no-nonsense hunger that enveloped her senses and shut down everything except her own passion, which was so starved that it simply took over.

She'd forgotten how good he was, how clever his mouth could be, how erotic he got with his tongue and his teeth. It was like walking the edge between desire and spontaneous combustion; every nerve ending in her body sizzled with heat.

If it had been just a kiss, she might have been able to resist, turn her head, say something coherent to stop them both from acting like complete idiots. But he used his hands, stroking her throat with his long fingers, cupping her breast through the spandex to brush his thumb over the nipple, and that only added to the burn.

"Wait." She had to feel his hands on her skin. That was all there was to it. Grabbing the front of her leotard, she pulled it down and out of the way, then arched her back. "Now touch me."

"Raven." He looked down at her exposed breasts, his mouth damp from hers, his eyes heavy and dangerous. "Tell me to go. Now."

"Why?" She didn't wait for an answer, but hooked a leg around his thighs and flipped him over onto his back. The fact that he let her—she could never have rolled him unless he'd wanted her to—made her smile. So did straddling his hips, and lowering herself in delicate degrees, until the bulge of his erection brushed against the heat between her thighs. "You don't want to go anywhere right now, do you?"

"I can think of one place." He reached up and tugged her leotard down farther, until it bunched around her waist, then covered her breasts with his hands. "And this is what you want."

"Works for me." She let her head fall back and closed her eyes as he massaged her soft flesh and traced each aureole with the edge of his nails. Her voice dropped to a low murmur. "Oh, God, that feels so good."

She rocked her hips, sliding up and down against his confined penis, moving in rhythm to the touch of his hands. Everything she needed lay beneath a few layers of fabric, but she liked the slow torture of teasing him and herself this way.

"Kiss me," he said, drawing her down.

"I dreamed about your mouth, you know." She pressed her lips against his, but before he could take over she pulled back. "And this spot, right here." She nuzzled his throat, using her tongue to taste him before sliding down a little farther. "And your chest."

One of his hands came up and sifted through her hair, but he didn't pull her away as she unbuttoned his shirt and trailed more openmouthed kisses down the center line of his smooth abdomen. Slowly she worked her way down to the button of his jeans, then she glanced up at him. Her fingers traced the solid, heavy ridge beneath the denim as she watched his expression. "And here, Kalen. I dreamed of how it felt to kiss you . . . right . . . here. . . ."

"Did you?" His hand tightened against her scalp, and his voice dropped to a deep, ragged rasp. "I've dreamed about it, too. About feeling your mouth on me. About watching you do it."

That was when a fist hammered on the suite door, and she heard Hyatt call out, "General? Major?"

Kalen went still, then gently lifted her and set her to one side. As he stood and began buttoning his shirt, she fell back against the bed and flung an arm over her eyes. "Damn it."

He disappeared, only to return a moment later, his expression flinty. "Hyatt's forwarding a call from the tap line. It's Zhihan."

As if cued, the phone began to ring.

Raven rolled over and sat up, hugging her knees with one arm as she picked up the receiver. "Hello?"

The Dai's son didn't waste time with pleasantries. "Are you finished? I want to see you."

Goose bumps rose on her skin, and she tugged her leotard up over her breasts even as she produced a husky laugh. "Zhihan, how nice to hear from you." She wanted to smash the phone into a million pieces and chuck them out the hotel window. She eyed Kalen as her frustration built. "No, I'm sorry, we were just getting started here."

As she chatted about the nonexistent photo shoot, Hyatt edged into the room, followed by Conor. The computer whiz handed Kalen a file and motioned for Raven to put the call on speaker.

If Brooke walks in here, Raven thought as she punched the speaker button, *I'm going to scream.*

"I don't want to wait until then." He sounded angry, and sober. "Whatever they are paying you, I will double it."

"Oh, Zhihan." She made her voice go soft. "There's no reason for you to do that."

"I have money, and you have what I want," he told her. "Come back to my home tonight. We will discuss terms."

She glanced at Kalen, who shook his head. "I'm sorry—I'm very flattered, but there are all these people waiting for me and I'm so confused—please, can we talk about this in Chicago?"

"I want more than talk," Zhihan said, and proceeded to tell her in graphic terms exactly what he wanted.

He doesn't want me, he wants a mannequin drilled with holes and filled with lubricant. Just the thought of letting him do those things to her made Raven want to throw up.

Kalen met her gaze.

That gave her the steadiness to finish the play. "That sounds so hot, Zhihan—you're really turning me on. But imagine how wild it will be when we get together in Chicago." She tangled her fingers in the phone cord, but she never looked away from Kalen. "Waiting makes it so much . . . better."

There was a long silence, then Zhihan said, "When will you be there?"

*   *   *

The team met in the Eisenhower Suite to coordinate moving the operation to Chicago, and a fax from Honore confirmed details for a show at one of the city's convention centers. Raven made a few more calls and had her contacts begin arranging adequate press coverage and local advertising.

Kalen kept his distance, and barely said three words to her.

"The timing isn't great, but Honore just debuted her spring collection." From which Kalen had kidnapped her and, if she'd had any brains, at which she would be in Paris showing this very second. "She's dedicating the line to Portia's memory, and the proceeds from the show to her family in Brazil."

Brooke made a rude sound. "I bet the reporters will love that."

"I imagine they will." Raven rose from the table and stretched, then eyed the general. "I'm calling it a night. Tomorrow I'll need a few more hours to finish getting the word out."

Kalen simply nodded. "Good night."

As she walked out, she wondered if she had hallucinated the entire scene in her bedroom. Did he want to pretend that nothing had happened? That wouldn't work—not for her, anyway.

It was idiotic to get involved with him again, supremely so, considering that they were working together. Yet she wasn't concerned with doing the smart thing, the right thing, the appropriate thing. She wanted him, just as much as she ever had. More, now, because she'd gone without him for so long.

I can have sex with him and get it out of my system, once and for all. Isn't that what any other woman would do?

She let herself into the suite and debated whether

to take a cold shower or hang from her suspension frame for a half hour. She should have arranged for a punching bag. She could use something to beat on—

A hand covered her mouth, and something hard, cold, and loaded with bullets nudged her back.

"Now, if I were a tong killer," a harsh voice grated against her ear, "you'd be lying on the floor this very minute, bleeding out your last, you silly twit."

As he released her, Raven whirled around and smacked Sean Delaney on the head. "You scared the *shit* out of me," she mouthed.

He tucked his weapon into a shoulder holster, and made a circling gesture with one finger. Raven immediately got her scrambler and turned it on.

Only then did she get in his face. "Cute, Irish. Real cute. This your idea of room service?"

"I tried on one of the maids' skirts"—he gestured to the hotel waiter's uniform he wore—"but the hairy legs were a dead giveaway."

She glared. "I still ought to kick your ass."

"Not when you hear what I have for you." He pushed the service trolley he'd brought with him to one side, went to the windows and pulled the blinds. "I've got a line on Gangi's killer—the one who likes to play with flowers. They call him the Lotus. Do you know him, darlin'?"

"Yeah." She quickly locked the door to the suite. "What did you find out?"

"Not so fast." He went to the bar and poured himself a neat whiskey. "This time I want to do a little trading."

Delaney never asked for anything unless he had good reason. "If I can."

"You tell me about this Kameko Sayura the good

general's been investigating, and I'll give you what I know about the Lotus."

Had he not been retired, she reasoned, he would have been able to access the case files involved. And yet something made her hesitate. "Why do you want to know about the Sayura woman?"

He leaned back against the bar and sipped his drink. "Why do you want to know about the Bloody Lotus?"

"He killed my last team, in China."

The drink wobbled in Sean's hand for a moment. "Christ Jesus, girl—he's the one who did your face?"

"Yeah, that too." She rolled her hand. "Your turn."

"Takeshi Sayura's boys stole the White Tiger Swords from that museum in New Orleans and transported them to San Francisco, but they never left the country. Now Sayura's dead, and the swords are still out there, somewhere, up for grabs." He finished the rest of the whiskey and wiped his mouth with the back of his hand. "This was my case, from the very beginning. I'm going to be the one who brings them in."

"All right, here's what I know." She relayed what information she had on Kameko, and added, "I've done a couple of shows where her work was featured, and I've met her twice. The business isn't a cover; she's the real thing. Quiet, shy, but a genius with gold and silver."

"Good, it's easier to deal with a civilian." He nodded and pulled a disk from his jacket. "I got this from a former client, who tried to hire the Bloody Lotus. Couldn't afford the fee schedule."

"Have you scanned it?" When he nodded, she took the disk from him and put it into her laptop drive.

The images that appeared on the screen were accompanied by an aria from an Italian opera. As the soprano sang, photographs of brutally murdered bodies flashed, one after the other. Somewhere in each photo frame a blushing lotus was visible.

As the ghastly images continued to scroll, Raven swallowed hard. "This is a résumé of some kind?"

"The best there is."

She stopped the program and read the disk directory, then touched a key that copied it to her drive without displaying the function on the screen. "There are more than three hundred files here, Sean."

"He does good work, doesn't he?" He came over and held out his hand. "I know you've already copied it, darlin', so you won't mind giving me back the original."

"One wolf recognizes another." Despite her nausea, her mouth hitched. "Do you want to keep a line on Kameko Sayura? I can access the files and keep you updated—"

"Don't trouble yourself. I'm going to see the lady personally." He patted her shoulder. "You'll need new backup from here, darlin'. Have you got someone you can trust, or should I give a few referrals?"

"I can take care of it." She frowned. "Why are you going to see Kameko?"

"Jian-Shan's first wife was murdered because of those swords. So was T'ang Kuei-fei." His expression changed, became almost brutal. "No more women are going to die because of General By-the-Book Grady."

His savage tone troubled her. "Sean, my friend Portia died because of those blades, too. Believe me, I'm just as committed to finding them as you are. But Kalen isn't responsible for the killings."

"Grady doesn't care about your friend—or you."

He flung out a hand. "Think about it—what's the one thing he does care about? The army. That's it—that's all."

"Kalen would have done anything to keep those women alive. You know that." She got up and folded her arms around her churning abdomen. "Sean, you do know that, don't you?"

"He'll answer for what's he done, Raven—if not to a military board of inquiry, then to God himself." He rubbed a fond hand over her head, rumpling her hair like an affectionate uncle. "Now I'm going to get those swords. You keep your back to the wall and your eyes open."

She watched Sean leave with the empty trolley, and wondered if she'd been right in giving him the information about Kameko. Her instincts told her that the Irishman would never hurt an innocent woman, but something had changed him—twisted him up inside. And what he'd said about Kalen only troubled her more.

She didn't want to see Kalen's career in ruins. Not even if, as Sean seemed to believe, he deserved it. Everyone made mistakes, and the army was really all Kalen had. So she would do whatever had to be done to protect him—

Raven sat down and buried her face in her hands. *God, if I want to protect him now, how am I going to be able to leave him when the mission is over?*

"Excuse me, sir."

Kalen looked up from the file he was reading. "What is it, Brooke?"

"I just spotted an unauthorized person leaving the Kennedy Suite on the hall monitors." She kept her expression carefully blank. "It was Colonel Delaney."

Kalen got up so fast his chair nearly fell over. "I'll deal with this."

"Yes, sir." She felt like dancing as she watched the general stalk out, but decided to allow herself a small, triumphant smile instead. Until she caught Conor Perry watching her with his eyebrows raised. "What?"

"Nice work, Captain." He shook his head. "Can't you give that girl a break?"

"What are you talking about? Delaney is AWOL, just like her." Brooke flung a hand in the direction of Raven's suite. "The only difference between them is she bought herself a new face and he didn't."

Hyatt interrupted them with, "Conor, can you give me a hand?"

Brooke followed him to the main terminal, where Hyatt had been working on hacking into Raven's database.

"I've almost punched through her security," he muttered, and tapped the screen, where three rows of jewel-toned circles appeared. "But I can't figure out this last code key. Ever seen anything like it?"

Conor leaned in to study the symbols. "Eight blue, four green, and one red." He thought for a moment, then chuckled. "Clever girl. Type in this word: *brandubh*." He spelled it for him.

" 'Bran-doo'?" Brooke repeated. "What's that?"

"An old Celtic form of chess. It has thirteen pieces—eight sapphire barons, four emerald lords, and one ruby king."

"How do you know that?"

"I'm Irish, it's the law. You ought to learn how to play it, Captain." He met her gaze. "Seeing as it's the general's favorite game."

"That's it!" Hyatt crowed with delight as the final security screen vanished and Raven's main directory appeared. "Look at this. It's like an intelligence treasure chest—operative profiles, contact lists, high-tech and weapons suppliers . . . Hmmm, what's this?" He scrolled down, highlighted a huge data file, and double-clicked on it. A pair of Chinese symbols appeared above the photograph of an ancient stone building. "Brooke? Can you read this?"

"It says 'Shalal Xiudaoyuan,' " she told him, and reached over to tap a key. "That's the name of an old monastery in China. T'ang used it like a warehouse." She hesitated as a list of five names appeared, then pressed another key. "What the hell . . . ?"

The file that opened had been copied from a medical chart. Most of it was in French, but there were a number of photos of a woman with a horrific facial wound. She was so completely disfigured that it was hard to recognize her as even being human.

"Jesus, she must have taken a shot to the face at point-blank range."

"There's more." Hyatt paged down through more clinical notes until he stopped at another set of photos of the same woman on an operating table, with lines drawn on what was left of her face. "The reconstructive work, looks like."

Each subsequent photo showed the woman's face being rebuilt from the original raw horror into a Frankenstein's bride look-alike.

"They had to wait to grow skin grafts, and find a tissue donor for some of the dermal work. She had to have hair transplants, too." Brooke read from the French notes. "Must have taken months."

"Don't you recognize her?" Conor sighed as Hyatt and Brooke turned to stare at him. "Scroll down to the bottom."

Hyatt pressed the keys, which ran rapidly through the woman's transformation. At the end was a photograph of a stunningly beautiful brunette with haunted brown eyes.

They all fell silent for a moment.

"So now we know where she bought her face," Conor said softly. "And why."

For once, Brooke had nothing to say.

"What does the flower mean?" Hyatt pointed to the bloodstained lotus that appeared when he closed the medical file.

Conor studied it, feeling an itch of recognition. "I don't know, but I've seen it somewhere before."

Before Hyatt could open another file, the flower dissolved, and the computer went dead. "Shit." Hyatt quickly rebooted the machine, which came up with a number of system errors. "I don't believe it. She embedded a Judas code in that file."

"Which means?"

"It's a fail-safe device, last resort—if someone hacks into your computer and doesn't know it, a few minutes later the Judas kicks in." Hyatt sat back. "It's programmed to wipe out all the original files from memory. They're gone."

Chapter 7

"*Cher*, you'd better have a look at this."

Val led Lily into the library. The small blond toddler dragged her feet and knuckled her eyes with one hand. She wouldn't look at her father.

Jian-Shan put aside the auction catalog he was inspecting and came around the desk to kneel beside his daughter. "What is wrong, Lily?"

The little girl lifted her face, which was still wet with tears, and sniffed. "I did bad fing."

"She discovered that papers come out of a certain machine in your office," Val said, her voice wry. "Go on, *bebe*, tell Daddy the rest of it."

"Pree pay paz." His daughter stared hard at her patent leather shoes. "I wike cuddor on dem."

"Pretty papers are not always for you to color on, Lily," Val said.

Jian-Shan glanced up at his wife, and suppressed a smile. "How many papers did you take, Lily?"

She shrugged. "Cubbow."

"More than couple, little one," Shikoro said as she brought the crumpled faxes into the library. The housekeeper bowed politely to Jian-Shan before setting the stack on his desk. "Forgive me, I not find these before, *senpai*. Lily good at hiding things now."

Val went over to examine the papers. "She drew some very nice pictures on them, too."

"I did." Lily beamed. "Wid wots uh cuddors." Then she saw her father's stern expression and dropped her chin against her chest. "Sowwy, Daddy. Doan be mad."

"I'm not mad at you, baby." He pulled the little girl into his arms and lifted her quivering chin with a gentle hand. "But if you want some paper, ask Mama or Shikoro first."

The child threw her small arms around Jian-Shan's neck and squeezed him tightly, and he stroked her curly blond head with his hand. To think he had once avoided touching his child because he was afraid to love her—before Val had come into his life. He looked at his wife, who watched them with a gentle smile and suspiciously bright eyes.

She saved both of us.

He picked Lily up and carried her to his desk, where he found a pack of blank paper in one drawer. "Here is some new paper for you to draw on. Will you make a pretty picture of Mama for me?"

Lily clutched the pack with eager hands. "Wide now?"

"Right now." He grinned as the little girl skipped out of the library, followed by Shikoro. "And *next* year we will have the terrible twos?"

"Wait until she decides to decorate the walls. Val took a handful of the faxes Lily had appropriated and began sorting through them. "This is sort of my fault, too. My editor called to find out what I thought of the new cover copy, or I wouldn't have noticed all the faxes were gone." She stopped and examined what appeared to be a blue and purple crayon tornado. "This one looks like it's from Hong Kong, Jian."

He took the fax and studied the Mandarin symbols beneath his daughter's determined artwork. "It is from Li Chin, an old friend of mine. The authorities have determined the cause of Takeshi Sayura's accident—it appears that an incendiary device was used to detonate the fuel tank of his car."

"So he *was* murdered." Val shuddered. "Poor Kameko."

"That's not all that happened." He put down the fax and took the others from her, quickly sorting through them until he found the second page. Lily had only scribbled a rainbow of color across the top of this one, so it was easier to read. "Sayura had recently been in contact with the Chinese Meteorological Administration. He offered to recover something that had been stolen from them in 1994. Something Li Chin refers to as the Xing Huangdi."

Val frowned. "The Star King?"

"I remember something else happening with the CMA's space program at that time." He sat down at his computer and performed an Internet search. "Yes, here it is. In April 1994 there was an accident during the final check on the first Feng Yun Two satellite. Just before the launch, there was an explosion. The fire destroyed the launch vehicle, killed one worker, and injured twenty others. They never disclosed the cause of the accident, and the CMA didn't launch another satellite until three years later."

"What do weather satellites have to do with stolen technology?"

"The People's Republic of China is not as interested in the weather as it is in an earth observation and orbital defense system." He paused, thinking for a moment. "The satellites were funded entirely by the military. They could have contained some type of weapon."

"The symbols on the swords." Val paled. "A treasure of power and death over . . . the earth?"

"I'm not certain." Jian-Shan sat back in his chair. "My father had dealings with the CMA. I recall several meetings he had with some of their top officials at our home." He rubbed his temples. "He never allowed anyone to attend him during those meetings."

"Could your father have staged the accident in order to steal the weapon?" When he nodded, Val reached for the phone. "We have to tell Kameko about this. However she's mixed up in it, her life is in real danger."

"Agreed." Jian-Shan took out his cell phone. "I'll call the general."

Kalen was not available, so he relayed the information to Conor Perry and left a message for the general to call him back. As he ended the call, he saw his wife access their E-mail account as she spoke to Kameko Sayura.

"Yes, it came through. Let me download the image." Val tapped a few keys, then watched as a blurry scan appeared on the screen. It was an old black-and-white photo of a sword. "Yes, I think it's a Nagatoki. I can just make it out—that's a star *kamon* on the hilt. Did you ever see it yourself? Good. Now think carefully—were there newer etch marks on the back of the blade?" Val tensed. "Hello? Kameko? Hello?" She hung up the phone quickly, then hit redial and listened again. Slowly she put down the receiver. "Damn it."

"What did she say?"

"She received a letter from her father this week, mailed shortly before his death. He sent her this photo"—she gestured toward the screen—"and a note she doesn't understand. I think it's the third of the three key swords—the star blade."

"Does she have the sword? Did he tell her where it is?"

"I don't know. Before I could ask her, she hung up. Now it's just busy." She stared at her husband. "Jian, what if they've already gotten to her?"

He picked up the phone. "I think our friend the general must take it from here."

"Wake up."

She opened her eyes to see Kalen standing over her bed, and groaned. "I stopped falling out for reveille ten years ago, General. Go drill someone else around the parade grounds." She pulled a pillow over her head.

He grabbed the pillow and threw it across the room. "You got out of bed for Sean Delaney."

"Okay." Slowly Raven sat up and waved him away. "Give me a minute, then you can flog me or whatever."

He hauled her out of the bed and dragged her to the front room, then pointed to the sofa. "Sit. Down."

She sat, folded her hands, and placed them on her knee. "Yes, drill sergeant."

He eyed her, and for the first time saw what she was wearing. Or not wearing.

"That's why I needed the minute," she added helpfully. "You forgot, I sleep naked."

More swearing. Louder this time, as he marched back into the bedroom. A moment later he came out and flung a robe at her. "Put it on."

"I think you need to cut back on your caffeine intake, General." She stood up and followed orders, yawning. "So what's your problem with Sean now?"

"He's AWOL."

"You're kidding." She saw he wasn't, and sat back down. "Damn, that's kind of funny, when you think about it. Who's going to bail on you next? Captain Holier Than Thou?"

"If you're trying to provoke me," he said, "it's working."

"No, actually, I'm just really tired. And it's a good idea to let me sleep, too. If I don't get at least eight hours, I start to look and sound like Marilyn Manson." She smothered the next yawn with her hand. "Let's skip the usual accusations of treason, betrayal, and sabotage and get right to the point."

He paced a short, tight circle in front of her. "Why was Delaney here?"

"To make mad, passionate love to me." That got his attention. "Kidding. To talk to me."

"About what?"

She sighed. "None of your business."

"Everything you do is my business."

"Not since I quit working for you. But, yes, Sean Delaney came to see me tonight. No, I'm not working for him. No, he's no longer working for me. That's it. That's all." She rubbed the back of her neck. "I'm not going to tell you anything else. You know it and I know it. Now, have I covered everything? Can I go back to sleep?"

"Delaney has gone rogue."

"And?" She lifted her shoulders. "It's not contagious; he didn't get it from me."

"He walked out on the Army in New Orleans— you remember New Orleans, don't you?—and hasn't been back since. He's been spotted with a number of known tong crime figures since he went AWOL."

Raven frowned. "What are you implying?"

"He could even be working for the Chinese now."

She laughed until her sides ached, then wiped her eyes with the sleeve of her robe. "Sorry, but that's just too good. I've got to tell him that one."

He stopped pacing and stared at her. "Who paid for your new face, Raven?"

Slowly her smile faded. "You don't want to go there, Kal. Trust me."

"You had about fifteen hundred dollars in your checking account when you left on that China op eight years ago. Ten grand in savings. I checked; it's still sitting in the bank. So who funded your surgery?"

"You really want to know?" She went to the phone and dialed a number, then put it on speaker. "Jay?"

"Hello, Sarah." Jian-Shan's voice was low and deep, as if he'd been sleeping, too. "Does no one make phone calls during daylight hours in this country?"

"Sorry to bother you, but General Grady would like to know who paid for my reconstructive surgery." She pulled her robe a little tighter as she stared at Kalen. "Want to tell him? I don't think he's going to believe anything I say."

"I covered the cost of your medical care." Jian-Shan's tone became more alert. "Sarah, what is this about?"

"Stay with me, Jay, just for another minute. How did I repay you for helping me with the surgery? Exactly?"

"With money you earned modeling. General—"

"Thanks, Jay. He's going to have to call you back.

Love to Val." She punched the speaker button. "Satisfied?"

"The son of Chinese tong leader pays for you to get a new face, and you think that establishes trust?"

"What is it with you?" She threw out her arms. "My God, Kalen, I was half dead when he pulled me out of that goddamn temple. He could have dumped me in a ditch and I'd have bled to death. Instead, he got me to safety, then out of the country. He sent me to the finest plastic surgeon in the world. And you know what else? He never asked me for a goddamn thing in return—he didn't even want me to pay him back!"

"All right, I'll accept that for whatever reason, Jian-Shan did the decent thing." He swept his hand to one side. "Since day one, you've done everything you could to turn this operation into a circus. First you throw parties, then you stage fashion shows. Now Delaney shows up. I don't care about what happened between you and Jian-Shan in the past. But I want to know what you're doing with Delaney."

She knew she was tired, and she should have told him to get out and talk to her in the morning. But his suspicion grated; it was too quick, too automatic—and, she suspected that it always would be that way. Heat seeped slowly into her veins as the fury built inside her.

He wants everything but gives me nothing in return. She thrust her hands in her robe pockets, then felt Gemma's satin sack. *Maybe it's time the general had a refresher course in Trust 101.*

"Sit down, Kalen." When he didn't twitch a muscle, she tilted her head. "If you do, I'll tell you everything Sean told me. Not there," she added when he went to the couch opposite her. She pointed to a straight-backed chair to her right. "There."

He dropped into the chair, and she rose, taking the cuffs out of the sack inside her pocket as she approached.

His entire body turned to stone. "I don't have time for games—"

"You want to know what Sean said, right?" Smoothly she straddled him and ran one hand down his arm. "Lean back and relax. I won't hurt you." To keep him focused on her face instead of her hands, she nipped his chin, then skimmed his bearded jaw with her lips. Her other hand closed over his wrist, pushing it back into place. "Much." With that, she cuffed his wrist to the chair and slid off his lap.

"What the . . . ?" He jerked, found his arm immobilized, and glowered at her. "This is going too far, even for you."

She took out the transmitter jammer and switched it on.

"I haven't gone anywhere yet. But I will. Eventually. Thirsty?"

She went to the bar and poured a glass of scotch. From the silence she could tell he wasn't struggling to get free, which disappointed her a little. She'd wanted to see him squirm.

The way she had in New Orleans.

"This is a bad idea, Raven."

"You know what's funny about revenge, Kal?" she said as she wandered back over to the chair. "You never know when the opportunity to get some will arrive, but when it does, it's positively irresistible." She held the glass up. "Want a drink? I believe that's how you got started the last time we did this."

"Don't, Sarah," he said in such a low, quiet voice that she nearly took out the keys. Then he ruined it by adding, "You're already in enough trouble."

"I'm not afraid of you, Kalen. And don't call me Sarah." She sipped the scotch, grimaced, and then forced herself to drain the glass. "Ack. This stuff still tastes like used paint remover." She removed the belt of her robe, and used it to tie his other arm to the chair. Then she knelt in front of him. "Next time, I'll order champagne from room service. And whipped cream. And maybe a little Hershey's syrup."

He stared at a point over her head. "There isn't going to be a next time."

"I can see where you'd want to think that. You couldn't get out of here fast enough this afternoon." She rested her hands on his thighs, in exactly the same way he'd begun her interrogation in New Orleans. "Now, where was I before Hyatt interrupted us? I think I was about ready to put my mouth on your—"

"Don't." The big muscles under her hands tightened to steel cords. "New Orleans was different. You'd threatened to expose my European operatives. I had no choice."

"You knew I was bluffing." She lifted her hand and traced his bottom lip with her fingertip. "Otherwise, you would have dumped me in the nearest stockade and left me there to rot, and we both know it."

"What I did . . . was wrong." A muscle twitched along his jaw. "This won't make it right."

"No, but I suspect it's going to make me feel better." She rested her chin on his right knee, fully aware that she hadn't tied his legs. He could easily

jerk his knee up and crack her jaw. But he wouldn't.
"A whole lot better."

"You think that now," he said quietly. "Wait until
you wake up in the morning."

"Shhh. You're making me forget my lines. What
did you say next? Oh, yeah. You reminded me that
I could never say no to you." She let her hands glide
up and whisper over the front of his trousers, and
watched the skin over his cheekbones darken. "But
you never turned it down, either."

As she turned her face and used her teeth to gently
bite the inside of his thigh, he made a low, dangerous
sound. "Stop it, Sarah."

She straightened and shrugged off the robe. "I'm
not doing anything to you that you haven't already
done to me." She sat on his lap and began unbuttoning his shirt, then spread the lapels open and
pressed her breasts against his flat, smooth chest. The
shock of skin-on-skin contact made her draw in a
ragged breath. "That feels good, doesn't it?"

Wood groaned. "You know how it feels," he said
through clenched teeth.

"Fabulous." She let her hair brush against his face
as she nuzzled his neck, and felt his chest heave. "I
can't remember the rest. Does the army have any
new regs against love bites?"

He turned his head, and his mouth touched her hair,
where it hid the scar on her scalp. "Take off the cuffs."

That was her cue to do what he'd done, in New
Orleans—let him go, walk away. That would have
been fair. As she lifted her face, she saw how close
he was to losing control, and thought of all the long,
lonely nights she'd spent, dreaming of loving him
again, hating him for abandoning her.

If he really loved me, he would have come after me. He would have wanted to make sure I was dead, and then he would have found me in that goddamn hospital in Geneva, and he would have stayed with me through all the operations.

But Kalen had written her off. Even when she'd sent him photos of her old face, and her new one, he'd stayed away—and thought her a traitor. What was worse was knowing that in spite of that, in spite of everything, she still wanted him. Her stomach clenched at the thought, but it wouldn't go away.

If I can't have him, then I'm going to have this.

"No." Her voice dropped to a whisper as she let go all the emotions she'd held leashed for years. "I'm not letting you go."

"Fine." Wood cracked, then snapped, and his now-free arm clamped around her. A moment later, he tugged the other wrist free from the shattered wood, shook off the torn robe belt, and stood up. "Hold on to me."

He carried her into the bedroom, but the memory of New Orleans doubled back on her, and Raven swallowed hard against a surge of nausea. As he put her down on her bare feet, she placed one shaking hand against his chest.

"Kalen." She took in a deep breath. "Get out of the way."

"What?"

"I'm going to—" Unable to finish the sentence, she shoved past him and ran for the bathroom. She barely made it to the sink before the scotch in her stomach came up.

"Sarah?" His arm encircled her waist again, and he pulled her hair back from her face. "Go on, get it out."

Raven had no problem obliging him. She threw up until nothing else would come out, then endured the racking misery of dry heaves. Kalen held on to her, keeping her steady through all of it. Finally she was able to breathe, and backed away from the sink, groping for a towel.

"Stand still." He kept one hand on her arm and turned on the water in the sink. Then he wiped her face with a cool, damp towel, and she sagged against him. "Are you done?"

She nodded, and he picked her up and carried her out to the bed. With one jerk he pulled the tumbled covers out of the way, then lowered her onto the mattress.

She looked up, her eyes blurry. "That didn't quite go the way I thought it would. Would you mind waiting to court-martial me till tomorrow? I'm bushed."

His mouth curled into a bitter smile. "You still can't drink worth a damn." He pushed her hair back from her brow. "Are we even now?"

No! her heart shrieked. "I guess."

"We'll talk more tomorrow. Get some sleep." And with that he left.

What Kalen didn't know was that in the years they'd been apart, she'd learned to tolerate alcohol. After all, one didn't live in France without drinking something at every social function. As vile as his scotch was, it hadn't been responsible for her nausea. Nor had the prospect of repeating the past.

What had made her sick was realizing that she was still as much in love with him as she'd ever been.

"I want you to try it again."

Hyatt looked up as Kalen handed him Raven's laptop. "Sure, boss, but she's really got great security on this thing. Could be if I mess with it too much, the hard drive will go into auto lockdown."

"You're the best computer tech in the army," Kalen reminded him. "Find a way."

While Hyatt worked on hacking into Raven's database for the second time, Kalen took a cold shower. He was tempted to pound his head into the tile wall a few times, because the shower did nothing to get rid of the lingering ache of unfulfilled desire.

I could have had her tonight. I could be inside her, right now.

Raven's little reenactment of the night they'd shared in New Orleans had turned him on, so fast and so strong that he had wondered if his self-control would survive it. He'd come close to raping her the last time, and the primal urge to take and possess and mark still pounded in his head.

But this time was different. She's different.

He couldn't pinpoint what had changed, he only knew something significant had happened since he'd seen her last. Maybe she really was getting tired of living abroad and was ready to come home. For a moment he allowed himself to imagine starting over with her—having Sarah back was something he'd dreamed of for years.

But she wasn't Sarah anymore.

When he finished dressing, he went out to find Hyatt still hard at work on decrypting Raven's security. The programmer swore under his breath as the laptop screen went black, then he attacked the keys. A cursor popped up, and Hyatt plugged a Zip drive into one of the computer's ports.

"All right, you bitch, let me in." His glasses slid down his nose as he looked up at Kalen, finally aware that he had an audience. "Sorry, General. I meant the computer, not her." He rebooted the laptop. "Here we go. If this worm program I wrote works right, then it should eat that Judas code and . . ." He trailed off as he peered at a new, small box that appeared on the screen. "It's a riddle of some kind."

Kalen saw the words inside the box—*we think the same way*—and nodded. "Try this: one-two-three-zero."

"That sounds like a code you'd use for your luggage." Hyatt dutifully typed in the numbers, then gaped as the main menu appeared. "Holy cow, it worked." He glanced up at Kalen. "What is that?"

"Our birthday. Raven and I were born on the same day."

Which is why we think the same way, Sarah's ghost whispered inside his head, completing the little singsong rhyme she'd made up.

"That's kind of bizarre, but it worked." Hyatt gestured toward the laptop. "I can download anything and everything she's got on here."

"Let me look through these files you told me about." Kalen checked the time. He wasn't going to sleep anyway; he might as well find out what Raven had been up to. "You can finish up in the morning."

Hyatt nodded and got up. Before he went to his room, he hesitated. "Boss, I should warn you, the pictures are pretty graphic. Hard to believe anyone could survive an injury like that."

Kalen was thinking the same thing a few minutes later when he watched the medical case file images scroll up the screen.

Sarah had been a tough agent; trained to withstand discomfort, hunger, and even a certain amount of torture as part of her job. He'd seen her trudge five miles in waist-deep snow, wrestle a man twice her size to the ground, and perform acrobatic stunts that could have won her a spot on any Olympic gymnastics squad.

But what she'd suffered after the ambush in China was beyond his comprehension.

He knew a little about reconstructive surgery; how time-consuming and painful it was. It wasn't enough that Sarah had endured the horror of the original injury; she'd willingly gone under the knife again and again. For the first time he understood why she had transformed herself into such a beauty. Not only to survive her mutilation, but to completely conquer it.

As the final photo of Sarah, healed and made over into the Raven, showed up, he traced a fingertip over her features. "I understand now, sweetheart. I just didn't know."

He understood even more when the image of the pink-tipped lotus appeared on the screen.

Meko realized she should have told Valence St. Charles everything she knew, but that one line from her father's letter made her panic and hang up on her again.

Until a representative delivers everything, don't betray your dear relatives.

That meant there was more to come, and that other members of her family were involved in the theft. And she felt sure now that her father had been murdered. If they had killed him for stealing these swords, what would they do to her brothers?

"Meko?" Tara stood in the doorway of her office, looking hopeful. "It's after six."

She tucked the letter and photo into her purse, then remembered her promise to take the girl to dinner and a movie. "I wasn't watching the time."

"I put all the display pieces in the safe, so all we have to do is turn on the alarm and go." Tara studied her for a moment. "Maybe this isn't such a good night, huh?" She looked down at the floor and rolled her shoulders. "It's okay. We can hang out together another time."

She sounded so disappointed that Meko banished the thoughts of swords and thieves from her mind. "Pass up a chance to eat the best seafood in town and see Mel Gibson?" she said as she switched off her computer and grabbed her purse. "No way."

"Great." Tara's smile reappeared, then wavered as Meko took a small oblong box from her desk and handed it to her. "What's this?"

"Looks like a birthday present to me."

Tara removed the narrow gold ribbon, then took out the black velvet jewel case. "Oh, my God." She opened it and stared at the bracelet, which Meko had fashioned out of white gold and highly polished blue abalone to resemble seven dolphins chasing each other in and out of stylized waves. Each dolphin had a tiny diamond eye. "It's so totally amazing."

"Try it on."

With reverent fingers, the teenager lifted the bracelet out of the case and held it up. "I can't believe you made this . . . for me?"

"The dolphins are like your spirit." Meko took the bracelet and fastened it around Tara's thin wrist. "Kind and graceful and free."

Tara flung her arms around her and nearly knocked her over. "It's the best present I've ever gotten in my life. Thank you so much."

This is the child I should have had. The one Nick always promised me. Meko hugged her back, then set her at arm's length. "No crying, now. We've got reservations at Louie's."

"Okay." Tara blinked rapidly. "But you can't steal any of my snow crab legs this time."

She laughed as she led the girl from her office. "Then you'd better eat fast, because I'm starving."

Nick Hosyu watched his ex-wife drive away from her jewelry shop, and wondered what a teenage girl was doing with her. "Okay, she's gone. Let's go."

The two men helped him pry open the back service door to the shop, then waited as Nick punched in the code for the silent alarm.

"How do you know she didn't change it?" one of them asked him.

"Because she uses the same one for everything." After he entered the numbers of the date when she had left him, the alarm indicator lights went from red to green. Bitterness made his voice tight as he nodded toward the shop. "It's all yours."

The two men went through the display cases and office and returned within fifteen minutes.

"Nothing. Can you open the wall safe?"

He went into Kameko's office and tried the same numbers on the combination lock. This time they didn't work. "Shit. She finally used something different."

The two men exchanged glances. "We can blow the safe."

"No." That came out harsher than he intended, and Nick laughed. "I mean, you can't. She'll know we were here."

"The boss doesn't care if she knows." The larger

of the two men took a menacing step toward him. "As for you, Nick, until you pay back the ten grand you borrowed, you'll do what you're told, or you'll pay another way."

Sweat beaded above Nick's upper lip as he thought of the alternate methods of payment. "Let me try one more thing." He turned back to the safe and spun the combination again. This time, he entered another date, and the latch clicked open. *God, Meko, won't you ever let it go?* He pulled open the door and stepped out of the way. "Got it."

The men removed the long, flat boxes of jewelry, opened them one by one, and dumped the contents out onto the desk.

"There's nothing here." The larger man went to the safe and examined the interior. "She must have it at the house."

The other man took a handful of necklaces and moved to put them in his pocket. Nick caught his arm. "Put them back."

"What are you talking about? We can fence these easy."

"The deal was, I get you the old man's letter, nothing more." Nick knocked the jewelry out of the man's hand. "It's not here. You're not taking this stuff. It's all she's got."

The larger man laughed. "Still in love with her, huh, Nick? All right, leave it. We don't want anything traced back to the boss anyway."

"I have to put everything back the way it was," Nick said. "Go on, I'll meet you outside."

After the two men left, he carefully replaced every item in the cases, then stacked them back in the wall safe. Before he put the last case back, he paused and admired the designs. He'd always been proud of her almost magical way with precious metals and stones. He'd set up her first business for her, hadn't he? True, it had only been a little kiosk at a local mall, but she'd gone from there to working in Beverly Hills.

After she'd left him.

Nick lifted a jeweled diamond tennis bracelet and watched the stones glitter against his skin.

Then he stuffed it into his pocket and took two more before closing the case and shoving it into the wall safe.

"Just a loan," he murmured. "Just until I get back on my feet, Blossom."

Nick knew she wouldn't mind.

Chapter 8

The operation moved from New York City to Chicago without a hitch. Kalen, Conor, and Raven flew over on a commercial jet, while Brooke and Hyatt transported the van. Instead of staying at a hotel, the team set up their command center in an old army recruiter's office on Michigan Avenue. Raven kept her cover intact by checking in to a five-star hotel one block away.

"We've got about ten thousand square feet to cover on the main floor. Stage entrance is on the right side," Conor said as he laid out the floor plans for the Park West Theater. "That's where the girls will come in. They'll file out in front of the main projection screen and walk down the east and west stage extensions. Raven will have the center extension all to herself." He moved his finger down a diagonal line. "Zhihan and his party will be sitting here, at the guest-of-honor table. The Park West staff is giving us their full cooperation, so the five tables we set up around him will be wired, along with his. Raven will be wearing a remote."

"Which, considering what I've got to model tonight, will be a challenge." Raven brought the latest issue of *Vogue* to the table and pointed out the show-stopping mistral dress. "Same dress I wore in Paris."

"You can't wear that," Kalen said, without looking at the photo. "It's backless, and transparent."

"Almost, but not quite. I've got a flesh-colored chemise I can cut to fit the lines of the bodice, but we'll have to rig the wire differently." She nudged Conor with her elbow. "Feel like taping me up before the show?"

With the waves of cold anger rolling off his boss, Conor felt more like applying for a transfer to someplace safer—like Pakistan. Yet when he saw Raven glance at Kalen and her smile waver, he nodded. "No problem."

"What about video?" Kalen snapped.

"I've set up three cameras—here, here, and here." Hyatt marked the spots with a highlighter. "Concealed on the catwalks around the lighting grids. They'll be forty-five feet off the first floor, but with the zoom lenses that's not a problem. I'm also using the control room upstairs to run everything. This theater has state-of-the-art tech; I'm just going to hook into it and run the show from there."

"Brooke, entrances and exits?"

"One main entrance, four emergency exits, three on Orleans Street and one off the alley. A service ramp entrance, also in the alley. Figure two men to cover the main, one on each of the others." Brooke pointed to the backstage hallway. "If Zhihan decides to go backstage, we'll need another two to cover the front hall and dressing rooms."

"This is overkill." Raven leaned over the table to examine the plans, and Conor saw his boss's eyes zero in on her face. "There's no way he's going to confess to the murders in the middle of the show."

"Your objective is to get him to talk about Portia, and the swords." Kalen turned to Hyatt. "I want a full setup in that utility room we're using for her dressing room. Audio, video, thermal sensors, the works."

The phone rang, and Hyatt turned to answer it. He looked at Raven. "Um, there's a very upset Frenchwoman in the hotel lobby demanding to see you, Major."

"That would be Honore." She straightened and checked her watch. "I need about twenty minutes."

"We're rolling in thirty," Conor reminded her.

"If I'm late, it's because she's beaten me to a pulp." Raven sauntered out of the office.

Kalen waited until the door closed before he turned to Brooke. "Follow her."

With a nod, the captain left, and Hyatt went to move the last of the equipment out to the van behind the office. Conor waited until he and Kalen were alone before he went to the table and cleared his throat.

Kalen glanced up. "What is it?"

Other men would have backed off, but Conor could still see the desperation in Raven's eyes. He snapped to attention. "Permission to speak freely, sir."

"Don't push your luck, Perry." Kalen scrubbed a hand over his beard, then rubbed his eyes. "Look, I haven't had much sleep this week, and my temper's punchy. Whatever's on your mind, just say it."

He thrust his hands in his pockets. "I don't know what kind of history you've got going with the major, and it's none of my business."

The frayed temper immediately appeared. "You got that right."

"But whatever it is, you're pushing her too hard. She's already scared enough with this guy, and yesterday—" He shook his head at Kalen's blank expression. "Don't you see how pale she is? She looks like a good gust of wind would knock her on her backside."

"She got sick the other night."

Conor folded his arms. "Was that before or after you busted the chair in her room?"

Realization dawned on his boss's face. "Jesus Christ, Con, I didn't hit her."

"You didn't have to." He planted his hands on the table. "I saw the photos of what they did to her face. Before she got the doctors to fix it. She's been through enough shit, boss. Back off before she crumbles."

"Or?"

"Or you'll have a couple of real fine reasons to court-martial my ass."

"You don't want to threaten me, Lieutenant."

"I don't make threats, General." He matched his boss's tone and expression to the exact same chilly degree. "That's why you keep me on point. I deliver."

For a moment the two men stared at each other, neither of them backing down. Then, slowly, Kalen shook his head.

"You want to tell me what's got you acting like a Doberman in the manger?" Conor suggested.

"She wasn't beautiful before all this happened to her, but she was mine. In the ways a man can only dream of. I took it for granted—no, I took her for granted. I never thought I'd lose her the way I did." He looked blindly at the plans on the table.

"Now she's Raven, every man's goddamn wet dream."

"Did you love her, or her face?" Conor asked. He nodded when Kalen gave him a filthy look. "That's what I thought. So it's simple, then."

"What is?"

"You tell her, General. You tell her, and you get her back."

By the time Raven reached the lobby, Honore Etienne had the hotel manager, the assistant manager, the restaurant manager, and half the lobby staff hovering around her. One of the maids was translating some of what Honore was shouting, but prudently left out the more colorful phrases.

"Trying to start a riot, Ray?" Raven asked.

"*Cherie!*"

"Miss Raven." The hotel manager practically tripped over his own feet hurrying to her. "I'm so glad you're here. This lady—"

"—needs to take her medication," she whispered to the agitated man.

"Ah." He nodded. "Would you be so kind as to . . . ?" He stepped out of the way as the Frenchwoman flung herself at Raven.

She hugged her friend and nodded over her shoulder. "No problem."

"*Depuis combine de temps êtes-vous ici? Où est le poste de police?*" The older woman flung her head around. "And where is *le generale*? I have many words to say to him, the vile kidnapping beast that he is."

"I just got here last night, and you are not going to the police station." Raven tucked her arm through Honore's and began guiding her toward the restaurant. "Come and have a cup of tea with me." She caught the eye of the restaurant manager. "I'm sure they can find us a nice quiet table where we can talk."

The manager escorted them to a cozy corner table, well away from the rest of the guests, some of whom had witnessed the tantrum in the lobby and were still whispering. A waiter appeared with a pot of tea and a beautiful tray of petite pastries only a few seconds after they sat down.

"At least the service in this wretched place is acceptable. You should see what they do to you at the airport." Honore sniffed as she dropped a lump of sugar into her cup.

"I'm sorry I dragged you into this."

"No, you are not." Then, with the kind of regal indignation that only a true Frenchwoman could summon, she lifted her chin and gave Raven a grand gesture. "Very well, *cherie*, I am waiting. Tell me everything."

Raven laughed out loud. "God, I've missed you."

She brought her friend up to date on everything that had happened since she left Paris, leaving out the details on the mission and her personal clashes with Kalen. Yet as much as she tried to make it sound like a routine job, Honore wasn't fooled.

"So. This is why you abandoned me, then forced me to fly half my staff across the world. For *le generale* and this army scheming." Honore finished the puff pastry she was daintily picking at and patted her lips with her napkin, then automatically applied fresh lipstick. "You still love him."

"I do not."

"You are like the mule about this." The designer

shook her head sadly. "I should beat you with a stick, but I will not risk hurting my godchild."

Raven rolled her eyes. "Since when did I become your godchild, Ray?"

"Not you. The baby."

All the noises around them seemed to vanish as Raven stared at her friend. "What did you say?"

Honore put away her lipstick and regarded her with a decidedly hostile glare. "You did not know? With all this sickness and no appetite and fragility? What did you think it was, *cherie*? The pox of chicken?"

"Chicken pox," she muttered absently. Everything inside her seemed to disintegrate, like a carefully-stacked house of cards hit by a tornado. "No. It's not possible. I'm not. I can't be."

"What are you, sixteen and stupid? Of course you are pregnant." Honore leaned across the table. "You have known it, in your heart, all along. You would not admit it, but you knew. How many cycles have you missed?"

Raven blinked. "A couple, but—"

"You see?" She made an elegant gesture.

"Hold on a minute. I've had an irregular cycle for a long time," Raven told her, feeling desperate. "Ever since I came back from China. The doctors told me it was from the stress. They said it could stay that way for years—"

"*Mon Dieu*, must I go to the store of drugs and buy the pee-pee test?" The Frenchwoman sounded furious. "You risk the life of your child for him, this man who abandoned you."

"For my country."

"France is your country. This America, it aban-

doned you as much as he did." Honore rose from
the table. "I am going to the nose-powdering room
and say many more bad words about you. You stay
here until I feel better and come back."

Stunned, Raven stared at her empty teacup until
a passing waiter offered to refill it for her. She nodded and gratefully sipped more of the now-
lukewarm tea.

*That's why I've been so sick, why I can't stand the
smell of perfume or cigarette smoke—or cornflakes, for that
matter. I'm going to have a baby.* She touched the flat
span of her stomach. *My baby.*

Kalen's baby.

He'd gotten her pregnant in New Orleans, of
course. She frowned as she thought of that night, and
how much it had preyed on her conscience since
then. They had been like two animals, ripping at each
other, and somehow, in the middle of that terrifying,
primal merging, they'd created a new life.

What am I going to tell him?

It was tempting to think of keeping the baby a
secret—it was hers, and could be hers alone. After
the mission was over she could leave the country
and never return. With a little effort, she could make
sure Kalen would never find her again. She'd grown
up without a father, and her baby could, too.

Then she thought of the picture her mother had
kept by her bed, the one of her father in his uniform,
just before he shipped out on a peacekeeping mission
to the Middle East. She barely remembered him herself, but she remembered how her mother had kissed
the photo every night and had reminded Sarah to
include her father in her prayers. And how her
mother had wept when they sent his body home,
and had quietly faded out of life every day until

she finally succumbed to a bout with pneumonia and joined him when Sarah was seventeen.

"I can't run and hide from this." She caressed her stomach, and a tear ran down her face. "Can I, baby? We'll have to tell the general he's going to be a daddy."

"That is the first intelligent thing you have said all afternoon," Honore sniffed behind her.

"Well, I was dumb enough to get pregnant. This is going to seriously screw up my schedule for the next year." She felt dazed. "Have you ever considered doing a maternity line?"

She bent down and enveloped Raven with her arms. "It will work out, *cherie*. I will do whatever I can."

Neither woman noticed the blonde watching them, or how she performed a neat about-face and strode from the restaurant to the lobby desk.

"I need to make a long-distance call," she told the desk clerk. "Is there a pay phone nearby?"

The clerk directed her to the private phones located at the back of the lobby. Brooke dialed a long series of numbers and waited until a voice answered.

"This is Captain Oliver with the CID." She rattled off her identification number. "Connect me with the inspector general's office, please."

"You know this place pretty well?" Kalen asked Raven, who had gone back to staring out the window and giving him the silent treatment.

"The Park West? Sure." She studied the condition of her manicure. "It used to be an old vaudeville house back in the twenties. Now they've renovated it, and performers like the Rolling Stones and Whitney Houston use it for private concerts."

"I suppose you and Jagger are friends."

"Not since he dumped Jerry Hall. But Michael Jackson borrows my hair stylist whenever he's in Paris." She eyed him. "Want his autograph?"

Conor lowered the glass partition. "We're here."

As she climbed out of the limo and strolled past the Park West's lighted logo sign—showing the arched body of a shapely woman dancing inside a spiral of light—Kalen watched it illuminate her face. She looked better than she had on the flight over from New York. Stronger, more determined. At the same time, he had the feeling that more had changed than just her outward appearance. She wasn't ignoring him to provoke another fight. She was genuinely preoccupied by something—and it wasn't him.

He intended to find out what as soon as they were alone.

The exterior of the Park West didn't do the inside justice. The elegant theater contained five tiered levels, two large balconies, and bars around the room. A small army of staff were already working with Hyatt on rigging the main floor for the fashion show. Startling forty-foot columns of blue silk spilled from the darkness overhead down to the floor and rippled gently at the slightest touch.

"Honore will be setting up backstage with our people," Raven said as she walked up the front hall toward the utility room Hyatt had prepared for her. "I'll need twenty minutes for my hair and face, minimum." She looked around Kalen. "Where's Conor? I've got to dress, now."

He shook his head as the team cryptographer appeared beside them, carrying Raven's prep case. "Brooke will rig your remote and do the rest."

"Captain, would you excuse us for a minute?"

Raven pulled him into the utility room and slammed the door. "In case you haven't noticed, General, the Nordic goddess out there hates my guts. I assure you, the very *last* thing I'm going to do is let her touch my hair or my face."

"She still rigs the remote."

"Conor was going to do that." Her expression changed. "Oh, so you don't want me tempting your point man. What do you imagine I'll do, General? Knock him to the floor and molest him the first time he cops a feel?"

"Conor is busy. Brooke will rig your remote. I don't give a damn who sprays your hair or paints your face." He yanked open the door. "Captain, get started."

As Brooke came in and opened the case, Raven stripped off her sweatshirt and reached for the zipper of her jeans, then hesitated. "You're going to watch?"

He smiled at her. "Maybe I'll take pictures. How much did *Playboy* offer?"

Brooke's gaze bounced from Raven's face to his, then back again before she faked a cough. "Should I step back outside, sir?"

"No." He leaned against the wall. "Get her rigged. Now."

In order to be wired, Raven had to strip down to her panties, which she did quickly and silently. As Brooke taped the wire to follow the line of her sternum down to her navel, she stared at her reflection in the mirror. "Where do we secure the transmitter? In the crotch of my G-string?"

"I have a thigh strap." Brooke produced the Velcro band, clipped the remote on and secured it around Raven's upper leg. "When you put on your stockings, fasten one of your garter belt clips to the band."

She stood up and looked as if someone had fed her a whole lemon. "If you'll sit down, Major, I'll do your hair and makeup now."

"That's okay." Raven put on the robe she'd brought and waved her hand. "The general wants to watch me do that, too. Run along now."

Brooke flushed. "Sir?"

Kalen opened the door. "Walk the perimeter backstage now, Brooke. We'll catch up to you in a few minutes." When she stalked out, he shut the door and locked it. "Don't bait my cryptographer."

"Tell her to stop looking at me like I'm a great big walking worm." Raven grabbed the case and sat down at the well-lit vanity. "This part is really boring. Sure you don't want to go test some spy equipment or something?"

He knew how easy it would be to get into another verbal fencing match with her. Instead, he moved up behind her and watched her apply her cosmetics. "Are you feeling better?"

"As in, do I feel like throwing up? No." She whisked a fan-shaped brush over her skin, then closed one eye and darkened it with a gold-tinted green shadow. She started to do the other, then put down the applicator. "But then, Zhihan has yet to make an appearance."

"You know how to play him." He pulled her hair back and held it away from her face. It was so thick he had to use both hands. "Keep up the babble; he expects that. See if you can get him to tell you more about his father's swords. Don't let him corner you like he did in New York."

She nodded and finished the other eye, then touched up her lashes with mascara. "If this doesn't work, I need some computer time tomorrow."

He watched her paint her mouth with a soft, ripe rose color. "For what?"

"I have an idea I want to play with." She etched a line of silver highlight gloss across her bottom lip. "I need to run some logistics."

"Hyatt can do that."

"So can I." She tugged her hair free of his grasp and bent over to shake it as she sprayed it with styling mist. "Would you hand me my curling iron, please?"

He handed it to her, and she began curling her hair with her head still upside down. "All this for two minutes of walking around a stage."

"You should stop by when we do the fall collection premiere. Armand takes three hours to do my hair for that one." She finished curling and sat up with a sigh of relief. "Although I'll probably miss the next one."

Kalen watched as she plunged both hands into her hair and scattered the loose curls. "Why?"

She stared at his reflection for a moment, as if deciding something. "I'll tell you after the show."

There was a knock at the door, and one of the agents assigned to the back entrance stuck his head in. "Excuse me, General, but we've got a delivery van outside. The driver says he isn't moving until he talks to the man in charge. Something Ms. Etienne ordered."

"Better go take care of it," she told him. "I'll finish up here."

Kalen nodded. As he left, he didn't see Brooke come around the corner, or the look on her face when she glanced at Raven's dressing room.

The Lotus had followed Raven from New York, but the constant presence of her entourage made it impossible to get her alone. The best opportunity had come when she rendezvoused with the French fashion designer in the hotel restaurant, but shooting her from that distance had seemed too impersonal. It would also ruin the chance of seeing her eyes just before her face was destroyed for a second time.

And this time, you will not crawl away to make yourself over again, the Lotus vowed.

Then the information regarding the secret operation Raven was involved in had been delivered, and the hunt had to be sacrificed. She was far too close to the truth, and there was more at stake than the Lotus's personal pleasure. Because the military was involved, her death would also have to appear to be accidental—and well documented.

Which meant killing her at the theater.

There were a number of interesting possibilities, but the killer had decided to attack from above. Preparation had taken very little time or effort. Now all that was left to be done was to wait for the show to begin and for Raven to take the stage.

For the last time.

Brooke slipped silently inside the dressing room. The major was still sitting at the vanity, putting on makeup and fussing with her hair. For a moment the image of the ghastly, ruined face from the computer files popped into her mind, then she banished it.

Whatever Raven had suffered, she'd obviously gotten over it. And now she was going to ruin Kalen Grady's life by sticking him with a baby he didn't want.

That couldn't happen. Not when Brooke was supposed to have his children.

"Get bored walking the perimeter?" Raven asked.

"I wanted to talk to you." She locked the door behind her. "Alone."

"Woman to woman?" Raven put down her eyebrow pencil and turned around. "Did you need some tips on how to do your hair? Pulling it back like that is murder on your scalp, you know. Plus it makes the ends split."

Reminded that she was only dealing with a bimbo model, Brooke felt confident enough to stroll around the room. "So this is what you gave up the army to do. Dress up." She pointed to the heavy makeup case. "Trowel all that glop on yourself and strut around half naked in front of a bunch of cameras."

"Dress up to strut around half naked." Raven arched a brow. "Were your parents, like, really strict with you or something?"

"You know what I mean." Brooke picked up a silk stocking, then let it fall from her hand as if it was a used Kleenex. "You had a solid career, you contributed something significant to the world. How could you abandon your duty? Your country?"

"Easy." Raven stood and belted her robe. "I mean, compare the jobs—now all I have to do is stand still and look good. No more blowing up armories, chasing down informants, or taking out terrorist cells in countries where I can't read the road signs. And modeling pays better, too."

"That's right, I forgot. You're rolling in it."

Raven shrugged. "I have a few pennies saved for my retirement."

"Plus the villa in Provence and the apartment in Paris." Brooke picked up a hand towel and draped it over the microphone Hyatt had installed in the room. "I have a one-room efficiency that I see the inside of maybe twice a week."

Raven went to get the mistral dress from the garment bag hanging on the clothes rack. "I hear there are some nice places in Maryland, if you don't mind the commute. You ought to relocate. Maybe you could get a cat or something."

Brooke moved fast and caught her arm. "You think you're better than me, don't you? I graduated top of every class I ever took. I've got a whole closet full of black belts. I could take you out in ten seconds flat."

"You could try." Raven leaned in and gave her a slow smile. "But I wouldn't recommend it."

"Come on." She gave her a shove, hoping that would get her to take a swing. "Karate, judo, kickboxing? You call it."

Raven only chuckled and shook her head as she took the dress out and went hung it on the back of the door. "Much as I am tempted, honey, I've got a show to do. Run along now."

"Coward." Brooke came up behind her. "That's why you bailed on him, isn't it? You were afraid he wouldn't love you anymore." She prodded her in the shoulder. "He doesn't. He thinks you're nothing but a high-maintenance whore."

By then Raven's smile had disappeared. "One day, Captain, you're going to get a very hard, very painful lesson about life." She went back to applying her cosmetics.

Brooke snorted. "Yeah, I'm just shaking in my shoes here, thinking about big bad Raven coming to take me down. What are you going to do? Blast me with your blow-dryer?"

"Oh, it won't be me." She pointed to Brooke's reflection in the vanity mirror. "It'll be that bitch in there. And when she's done ripping you and your dreams and your hopes to small pieces, you'll have to go on with whatever's left." A note of sympathy entered her voice. "I sure hope you can deal with that better than I did."

Brooke launched herself at Raven, then found herself slammed facedown on the floor. A hard knee pressed against the center of her spine as the woman who had thrown her there bent down by her face.

"I should have mentioned, my black belts got so dusty I had to throw them away," she said, as if they were girls trading beauty secrets. "You're going to get up and leave now, and we'll just forget all about this. Or you can come at me again and I can break your nose this time. You pick."

As soon as Raven released her, Brooke shoved herself up and wiped the blood from her face. Her nose wasn't broken, but it had been a close thing.

"You're going to be sorry you ever came back here," Brooke promised her as she went to the door.

Before she slammed it behind her, she thought she heard the major say, "Babe, I already am."

Raven barely noticed the usual backstage chaos as she went to find Honore. The brief tussle with Brooke Oliver hadn't affected her much—she'd been expecting that. Yet she felt oddly disconnected from everything, ever since Honore had made her face the fact that she was pregnant. All she could think of was how much her life was going to change, and how to tell Kalen. She'd nearly done that in the dressing room, until she remembered Hyatt was listening in. No wonder Brooke had thrown the towel over the mike.

The models wearing Honore's new Mistrals line were dashing around, vying for a place in front of the wall mirrors, some looking in vain for shoes or accessories to match their dresses. In comparison, Raven moved almost in slow motion, so lost in her thoughts that she almost screamed when Gemma Firth grabbed her and gave her a noisy air kiss next to her cheek.

"My, aren't we jumpy? I'd offer you a Valium, darling, but you're already looking half dead." The British girl gave her another squeeze and added in a stage whisper, "Chin up now. The harridan from hell is right behind you."

"Gemma, have Pierre fix your hair. You look like fried poodle. You." Honore latched on to Raven's arm. "You look like limp poodle. Come here." The fashion designer guided her to a chair and pushed her down. "How many times do I tell you, let the stylists do their job?"

"It looks fine."

"It looks fine for grocery shopping. Not for my show." Honore picked up a comb and started spot-teasing Raven's heavy mane. "Your friends have everything ready for this, *oui*?"

"Yes." She winced as the older woman tugged on her roots. "Take it easy, Ray, *Vanity Fair* won't touch up pictures of my bald spots."

"You should have used foundation; you are too white. The photographers will think I starve you. I will have to tell them the big secret." She paused. "You didn't tell *le generale*?"

"Later." As the music cued for the opening of the show, she stood up. "Stop fussing, I look fine."

Honore pinched her cheeks with both hands. "Lick your upper lip. Smile. Just so. Now you look *trés elegante*."

She felt *trés moche*. "Showtime."

*   *   *

Kalen had one of the best seats in the house, next to Conor, who was poised to snap photographs of the models as they emerged.

"Get that delivery van squared away?" his point man asked him.

"Yeah." Kalen had argued with Honore's assistant for fifteen minutes before letting them unload the special delivery. "You're not going to believe what they've got planned."

Conor grinned. "Knowing Stretch, she'll probably ride out on top of a Bengal tiger."

A lovely young woman walked to the podium on-stage and inclined her head as the media erupted with applause. "Welcome to the Park West Theater, ladies and gentlemen," she said. "This evening we have something very, very special for you. As you know the House of Etienne has been a leader in haute couture for nearly three decades. Yet not once in thirty years has Madam Etienne brought her debut collection across the Atlantic."

The reporter sitting at the table beside Kalen's leaned over. "I heard the old lady hates America even more than she hates the grunge look."

Kalen thought of Honore. "I wouldn't say that to her face, friend. Not if you like your teeth where they are." When the reporter turned away laughing, he touched the transmitter on his lapel. "Stations."

"Control room green," Hyatt said over his earpiece.

"Backstage green," Brooke added.

The other agents posted at the various exits reported in one by one, until music began thumping from the speakers around the stage.

A group of teenage boys ran out onto the stage,

shouting phrases in French, Spanish, and English. They were dressed in ragged baggy pants and T-shirts, and wore heavy silver chains around their necks. At first they looked like a gang getting ready to fight, then they split up and formed three ranks. Bright white lights began flashing over the stage.

"Boys' choir?" Conor looked dubious.

"Worse." Kalen's mouth curled. "Street dancers."

The boys began dancing, using moves from the inner city in a raw display of energy and style. Each youth seemed to barely avoid colliding into the others, and it finally became apparent that they were following a distinct if chaotic choreography. Over and over the three lines of bodies merged, then split apart.

"How do they do that?" Conor wanted to know, pointing to one dancer who had flipped into a handstand and was dancing upside down. "Without passing out, I mean?"

Kalen shook his head as another boy dropped into a painful-looking split. "I have no idea."

The house lights dimmed as the announcer appeared in the center of the dancers, who hoisted her up on their shoulders. "And now, ladies and gentlemen, the House of Etienne presents . . . Le Mistrals!"

Pastel-colored spotlights replaced the glaring white beams focusing on the dancers and began to sweep in slow, intricate patterns over the stage. Half the audience got to their feet as the models began appearing, each stalking up to one of the boys and tapping him on the shoulder. The dancer responded by doing tight somersaults, then landing on his feet before the model, who threw up her hands and walked away. The teenager followed, performing more acrobatic stunts in the model's wake as she sauntered out onto the narrow stage platforms that extended into the audience.

"Mother of God, they look naked," Conor muttered as he rose and began snapping off shots of the models walking past.

Kalen watched each girl complete her walk, pause, and pose for the cameras as the dancer behind her assumed a tough-guy stance. Then with a smile, the model turned, took the boy's arm and let him escort her back to the main stage. As they had in Paris, the models gradually formed a gauntlet in front of the center stage extension, this time interspersed with the street dancers.

The house lights dimmed even more, making the slow-moving spots appear solid. Then the music changed and rumbled down to a seductive beat. The boys began to clap and stomp the stage slowly in time.

Conor nodded toward center stage. "Here she comes."

As Raven appeared, he noticed two things—she was still distracted, and her skin looked almost as fragile as the snowy lace that barely covered her breasts. The reason he noticed was that one of the brighter spotlights was moving in an odd way—jittering over the stage instead of sweeping slowly, like the others.

Zhihan left his table and walked toward the end of the stage, a strange expression of anticipation on his face. The sight of him made Raven hesitate, then she looked up, frowning. Gemma stepped out of the line of models and walked up beside her, taking her arm and leaning close to whisper something.

Following his instincts, Kalen got up and followed the man, pushing past photographers and cameramen to get to the front. Then, as the audience clamored for the star of the show, he heard the sound of cables snapping. The spotlight spun crazily on the stage directly in front of Raven.

He wasn't going to make it to her in time. "Sarah! Incoming!"

Raven spotted him, then shoved Gemma back, causing the model to knock over two dancers before sprawling on her hands and knees. The move cost her precious seconds, however, and as she pivoted to jump off the stage, a large black blur dropped out from the darkness above them.

Kalen dove on top of the stage, knocking her off her feet. He caught her in his arms as she fell and rolled with her off the other side of the stage only a split second before the heavy spotlight smashed through the stage, precisely where she had been standing. The tremendous crash echoed through the screams of the audience.

He managed to land on his back, still holding Raven on top of him. She stared down at him, her white face curtained by her dark hair.

"That was nice," she whispered. "Thank you."

"Yeah." Hands reached to help them, but he shook them off as he got to his feet and helped her up. "Are you okay?"

"As okay as I get with scrambled brains." She flexed her arms and legs, and rolled her head from side to side. "How did you know that light was going to fall?"

"It was moving wrong." He put an arm around her and addressed the gathering crowd. "The lady is fine. Please, let us through."

He escorted her backstage, where Conor and two other agents were waiting, and ordered them to clear the area. Honore fluttered around them, so upset that she couldn't speak English at all for five minutes straight. Raven took the first seat she saw and gratefully accepted a cup of coffee from one of the stagehands.

The designer went out with the show manager to inspect the stage, and Kalen's expression kept everyone else at a discreet distance.

"You okay?" he asked her again.

"A little shaky." Raven stared out through a gap in the curtains at the audience. "You saved my life, you know."

"Yeah." He wanted to carry her out of the theater and to his house and lock her up for the rest of her life. But all he could do was the job at hand. "Now I want the one who tried to take it."

Chapter 9

"Dai's out front, demanding to see her," Raven heard Brooke say outside her dressing room door. "I don't think he's in the mood to wait around much longer."

Kalen's voice went deep and quiet. "Nobody's getting access to the theater until Hyatt finishes checking the rest of the lighting and the catwalks. Have you finished your sweep?"

"Yes, sir."

"Then do it again." A pause. "Your nose is bleeding, Captain."

"I bumped it, sir." Footsteps hurried away.

Raven quickly finished changing out of the Mistral dress and inspected the damage. This time her hasty exit from the stage had caused the skirt to rip in three places. She hung it up carefully, then reached for the replacement dress Honore had brought her. Something tucked in her case fell to the floor, and she stooped to pick it up. Her hand froze as she saw what it was.

A single white lotus with pink tips. Something had been impaled on the stem. An old, stained strip of camoflage tape, with a name embroidered on it in dark blue letters.

Ravenowitz.

The falling stage light hadn't been an accident.

He had been in here. The one who had killed the rest of her team. The one who had stood over her and shot her in the face. The Lotus. He could still be in the theater. Right now.

"Kalen." She could barely get his name out at first. Then, clutching the name tag until her fingernails cut into her palms, she shouted, "Kalen!"

He jerked open the door and was holding her a heartbeat later. "What's wrong? What is it?"

She couldn't pry her fingers apart, couldn't release it. All she could do was hold it up for him to see. "He—he was in here." As Kalen carefully worked her fingers loose and took the flower, she ripped the name tag from the stem.

"Do you see this?" She smoothed it out, then crumpled it in her fist. "It still has stains from my blood." She looked wildly around the room. "He knows my real name. He knows who I was."

"Calm down."

She flinched away from his hand. "He knows *who I am*." She shook her head as she inched toward the door. "I can't go through that again. Not again. I can't, I'm sorry, I'm so sorry. . . ."

"Raven. *Raven*." He caught her and made her look at him. "I'll take you back to the hotel. We'll talk about it."

"I can't go back there." Why didn't he understand her? "He'll *find* me. He'll find me and he'll shoot me, he'll shoot me like he did before, and then I'll have to go back to Switzerland, and—"

"Stop." He gave her a small shake. "I'm not going to let any of that happen to you. I'll keep you safe."

Her heart pounded wildly as she clutched his arms. "It's not just me. I have to tell you about—"

"We'll talk more about it in the car." He urged her through the door, past Brooke and Conor. Without looking back, he said, "Tell Zhihan she's not coming."

Horror had her so numb she wasn't aware of how fast Kalen got her out of the theater and through the back service entrance, where her limo was waiting. He put her in the front seat and strapped her in with the seat belt.

She glanced to the left as something penetrated her daze. "There's no driver."

"I can still drive." He went around the front of the car and got in behind the wheel. "Okay?"

She wouldn't feel better until she was on another continent. Or planet. Maybe NASA's Mars program was hiring. "No. Kalen, this is bad."

"I know." He started the engine. "Sit back and relax."

He drove away from the theater and through Old Town, taking back roads for a time. Raven didn't realize he was driving out of the city until she saw Lake Michigan disappearing behind them.

"Where are you going?"

"Are you in a hurry to go back to the hotel?" When she shook her head, he gestured to the road. "So we take a little ride, and we talk."

She closed her eyes, steadying herself. "I'm supposed to be at the Dai's party, right now, aren't I?"

"Why didn't you tell me you recognized that lotus when I showed you the photos in Paris?"

"I wasn't sure it was connected."

"You knew when you saw it that this lunatic was the same one who hurt you." When she opened her mouth to deny it, he covered her hand with his.

"Raven. I know he left a lotus in your hand after he shot you and left you for dead in the temple."

There were only two people who knew about the lotus—the killer and Jian-Shan. Raven knew her friend would never tell Kalen what had happened. That left only one other possibility. "You had Hyatt hack into my laptop and read my personal files."

"Twice." He didn't sound the least bit guilty. "If our positions were reversed, you'd have done the exact same thing. I read the entire case file you put together. Why didn't you tell me?"

"You saw the photos of what he did to my face." When he nodded, she ducked her head. "If I had shown you those, you wouldn't have let me come here."

"Probably not." He glanced at her and squeezed her hand. "It's time you told me everything that's not in that file of yours. Start from the beginning."

"We went in through the jungle, exactly as planned. All the intel was right on the money; we found the boards hidden in some old prayer scrolls. Then we set up and waited for the smugglers to show. They did, and we moved in." She cleared her throat. "My memory gets a little patchy here. The doctors said it's from the trauma."

"Tell me as much as you can remember," he urged in a gentle voice.

"Dunhill and Myers were behind me, and Haverson was in front. Something didn't feel right, I think I heard something, and I turned around." Raven curled her fingers tightly around his. "I saw six of them. They were all rigged out in army-issue gear, jungle camouflage, just like us. Except they were wearing cold-weather masks. I couldn't see their faces."

"They were the second team."

"That was what I thought, until the smugglers opened fire. The second team disappeared. Haverson was shouting something. 'Take cover,' I think. Then there was more shooting, from a different direction— behind us. I remember the second team advancing on us. Shooting, at us." She swallowed hard. "Something hit me—Dunhill falling back, I think. I went down under him. I saw . . . he . . . his face was . . . the blood went everywhere, all over me." She ground the heels of her palms against her eyes, but the tears came anyway.

"I don't want to put you through this again, but I need to hear all of it, Raven."

"I know." She wiped her face with her sleeve. "I rolled Danny over, but he was gone. Then someone kicked me, and I was on my back, looking up into a barrel. I don't remember anything until I opened my eyes again, and saw Jian-Shan standing over me. He carried me out of there and into the jungle. The pain was so bad I kept passing out.

"When I finally woke up, I was in a farmer's cottage in some mountain village. Jian-Shan was sitting next to me, holding my hand. He told me that I was the only survivor. Then he told me what the Lotus had done to my face. He was using exploding rounds, but something went wrong. The bullet was defective; it exploded before impact. It's the only reason I survived, but it . . . it chewed up my face pretty bad."

"Did Jian-Shan know who sent in the second team?"

"No. He was sent there with his men to take out the smugglers—he said they'd double-crossed T'ang on some deal—and he thought at first we only got caught in the middle. Then he confirmed everything I remembered about the second team."

"From there, he smuggled you out of China and got you to Geneva." He watched her nod. "Did he ever tell you why?"

"Later, he did. He told me about a wall in his father's home. It was decorated with the dismembered faces of men that T'ang had murdered. He said saving me was the first time he'd ever turned his back on his father's evil. But you know, honestly? I think seeing me survive my injuries horrified him. I was like a walking, faceless corpse."

"The files you have on the operation are huge. I have about ten more subdirectories to plow through yet. All these years you've spent away, you've been looking for this lotus killer, haven't you?"

"I've tried, from a distance. He's one of the best and most exclusive assassins in the world. Sean brought me a disk—some sort of bizarre résumé he sends to prospective clients. I copied it to my hard drive, if you want to have a look. There are kill photos on it, Kalen." She looked out the window as they approached the city again. "Hundreds of them."

"Was the Lotus part of the second team?"

"I don't remember. Jay said he saw someone walking away from me, after the shooting was over—but he wasn't dressed in fatigues. He wore a red robe, like a Buddhist priest, with a cowl covering his head."

"I did some checking of my own, after I came back from New Orleans. The only way the smugglers or anyone could have known you were coming was from someone inside the department." He didn't try to hold on to her hand when she pulled away. "Even then, the mission was highly classified. Eyes-only for a handful of people."

She heard the way his voice changed. "And?"

"And one of them was Sean Delaney."

Kameko hadn't moved her very successful jewelry designing business to Los Angeles to end up hiding under her bed while two burglars ransacked her home.

But here I am. She looked sidewise as something else crashed in the kitchen. *And there goes the good crystal.*

Like any American city, L.A. had a steady, significant amount of crime. Some of her friends and colleagues had obtained gun permits, claiming the weapons were necessary to protect their homes and businesses. Even Nick had repeatedly urged her to carry a .22 in her purse, although she suspected he wanted her to use it more to protect him from the leg-breakers from whom he kept borrowing gambling money than to protect herself. But, thanks to her father, Meko had seen enough violence in her lifetime, and she wouldn't hear of it.

Now, as footsteps thudded down the hallway outside her bedroom, she wondered if her decision had been totally naive.

Someone kicked in the door of the spare bedroom next to her own, and she clenched her fists. As terrified as she was, a chilly certainty settled over her. *I can't stay here like this. They'll find me. They'll want to know where the swords are.*

The thought of what they would do to her to find them made her crawl out from under the bed. Because she had had her home built on the side of a hill, jumping out of the bedroom windows was impossible—it was a fifty-foot drop to the ground. And she didn't have time to fashion a rope out of her bedsheets.

She'd always been good at hiding when she was a little girl, and now she quickly scanned the room. The armoire and the closet were too obvious; they would be the first places to be searched. The adjoining bathroom offered no sanctuary either. She lifted her gaze to the delicately embossed drop-ceiling panels overhead.

Will the frame hold my weight?

She climbed on top of her bed, and reached up to lift and remove one panel. As she did so, she heard the workout machine in the spare bedroom crash into the wall, shaking the house. She muttered a prayer under her breath and jumped up, grabbing the ceiling frame with her hands. The metal supports groaned as she pulled herself up, but they held.

Awkwardly she maneuvered herself until she was lying flat against the ceiling frame, then dragged the panel back over to cover the gap. Because the panels were opaque, she saw only the shadows of the two men as they burst in.

She held her breath and went still.

One of them cursed in Japanese, then demanded, "You are sure that is her car outside?"

"I told you, I saw her walk into the house," the other man said. "She's here, somewhere."

"You know what the boss said. We don't leave until we have the swords."

Meko cringed as one of the intruders knocked over her armoire, which landed on the floor with a tremendous crash. If only she had neighbors to hear the noise—but the main reason she'd had her house built on a hill was to get away from the otherwise crowded confines of the city.

I wanted to be left alone, and now I get my wish.

"Now, boys," a new voice said. "Is that any way to treat a lady's things?"

Kameko watched the two dark shadows rush across the room as a third entered. There was a hissing sound, and both men cried out, then she heard two thumps on the floor.

"It can't be very comfortable up there," the third man said. "Do you need helping climbing down, darlin', or can you manage by yourself?"

She slid the panel aside to see a silver-haired Caucasian man standing on her bed, directly beneath her. The two intruders lay unconscious on the floor. "Thank God you're here."

He lifted his big hands as she swung her legs over the edge, and caught her by the waist as she dropped out of the ceiling onto the bed.

"They cut the phone lines before they came in," she told him as she stepped down on the floor. "I didn't know what else to do but hide." She stared at the men as an even more horrifying thought occurred to her. "They're not—you didn't kill them, did you?"

"No, they'll just be taking a wee bit of a nap now." The man guided her out of the bedroom. "You're Miss Kameko Sayura?"

"Yes." Now that the danger was over, she felt as if she would keel over in a dead faint. Talking gave her something to concentrate on. "Who are you?"

"My name's Sean Delaney." He led her into the living room, to one of the overstuffed sofas there. "Sit down, darlin', and catch your breath."

"I'm fine, I'm just . . . a little shaky. Not every day I have burglars break into my home." She sat down and clasped her hands together. "Mr. Delaney, I'm so grateful for what you did, but I have to ask—why are *you* here?"

"I stopped in to have a word with you, and I heard the noise from outside." Delaney had a weathered, handsome face that only grew more charming as he smiled. "From the sound of things, I thought I should come in to see what was making all the racket."

She uttered a single laugh. "It's a very good thing that you did. I'm all alone here, and when I think of what those men could have done to me. . . ."

"There now, darlin', don't dwell on it." He patted her arm like an affectionate uncle. "Can I get you something to drink? A glass of water, maybe?"

"Please." She frowned. "No, I mean no, thank you. I have to find a way to call the police."

"I already did that, too, from my car phone. They're sending out a patrol unit, but it may take a few minutes. Something about a big pileup on the freeway." He walked over to the mantle above her fireplace and picked up one of the framed photos. "This is you, isn't it? The pretty little girl in the kimono."

She focused on the picture. "Yes."

"You were a tiny thing. Still are." He admired the photo and went to the next one. "And this fine gentleman?"

"My father." Meko felt an odd prickling along the back of her neck, and rubbed it. "He died a few weeks ago."

"I'm sorry to hear that." Delaney put down the frame and walked around the perimeter of the room. "Were you close to him?"

Why was he questioning her like a cop? Her unease increased as she realized he was carefully inspecting everything in the room. "No, we weren't. I haven't spoken to my father for years. Mr. Delaney—"

The charming smile flashed at her again. "Call me Sean."

"Sean. Why did you come here? Why did you want to speak with me?"

"I work for the Central Intelligence Division of the U.S. Army, Miss Sayura. And I know how scary that sounds, but it's really more of a desk job than anything." The Irishman came and sat down beside her, close enough for her to smell his scent. Sean Delaney smelled of leather and smoke and faint male sweat—and for some reason, she found that very appealing.

She looked at his cable knit sweater and faded jeans. "But you're not wearing an army uniform."

The grooves in his cheeks deepened. "I'm off duty now."

"Oh."

"Miss Sayura, your father sent something to you before he died." He wasn't asking a question. "I need to see it."

"He wrote a letter to me, but I threw it away." She didn't know why she was lying to him, but he must have sensed it, for his smile faded. "It was just a letter."

"And in this letter, did he tell you where he hid the collection of swords his men stole from the museum in New Orleans?"

Don't betray your dear relatives.

She wouldn't cover for her father, but the thought of her brothers made her heart pound. Especially Ichiro—he didn't deserve to suffer again for their father's crimes.

"No." The fact that she was telling the truth now

didn't make her sound any more convincing. "He didn't mention anything about that."

"That's a shame. Your father kept a house in San Francisco, didn't he?"

No one knew about Takeshi Sayura's waterfront home, which made her panic even more. Sean hadn't shown her any identification, and she was as vulnerable with him as she'd been with the two burglars. "Mr. Delaney, I'd like you to go now."

"I'm sorry to say that I can't, darlin'." He stood up and pulled something out of his jacket pocket. It was a very efficient-looking gun. "Not without you."

Kalen escorted her up to her hotel room, and found Gemma and Alake waiting for her.

"You're a sight, luv." Gemma threw a thin arm around around her shoulders and gave her a real kiss on the cheek. "That's for saving my ass tonight, even if you did give the audience a good look at my knickers in the process."

"Did you and Spike have plans?" the Nigerian model asked, sending a smoldering look at Kalen. "I still need a date for Zhihan's party, if he's not busy with you."

"I have some calls to make for Miss Raven," Kalen said. "Will you be going to the party, then, madam?"

Raven understood what he wasn't saying—she didn't have to go unless she wanted to. At that moment, all she wanted was a weapon, a Kevlar vest, and a detachment of marines to stand guard around her.

If Zhihan is the Lotus, I'm the only one who can get to him.

"Yes, I think I will, Spike." She smiled blindly at the other models. "Why don't I meet you girls downstairs in ten minutes?"

They agreed to wait for her, and left. Inside her suite, Kalen bolted the door and watched her drop onto the nearest chair. "You're in no shape to keep playing the game."

"That never stopped me before. Remember how bad it got, in Siberia?" She gave him a wistful smile and went to get a new dress. "Fourteen inches of snow and no transport out for twenty hours. I thought for sure they'd find us frozen inside two great big ice cubes."

"We nearly were, when they pulled us out of there." Once she'd stripped off her street clothes, he checked her remote. "We should leave it where it is. Don't let him put his hands on your leg."

"In this dress?" She pulled the burgundy sheath over her head and tugged it down into place. The bodice molded to her breasts and pushed them up like an erotic offering. "He won't even realize I have legs."

"You don't have to do this." He rested his hands on her bare shoulders. "You've done enough. We're calling it quits here. I'll clear your records, and you can go home."

"We haven't bagged the bad guy yet, and this is home." She tilted her head and rubbed her cheek against the back of his hand for a moment, then moved past him. "Have you seen my makeup case?"

He didn't argue with her, which was a rather novel experience. Instead, he went over the plan. "Once you're inside, see if you can slip away and get up to the second floor, east wing. Hyatt's sweep indicated a high concentration of computer equipment in that area of the house. Plug the relay modem in, hide it, and get out. I'll send Conor in to retrieve it once we've downloaded his database."

"Hang on." She copied some files from her laptop and handed the disk to him. "This is the intel I got from Sean. I know, you think it's possible he's the Lotus, but I don't believe that. Hyatt can run a comparison between the dates on the kill photos and Zhihan's financial records. If there's a match, then that should be all the evidence we need. If I can't get to the second floor, send Conor in to do a handoff with me." She concealed the relay modem in a small empty tampon box and put it in her purse.

He raised his brows. "Tampons?"

"Men have an aversion to feminine sanitary products," she told him as she refreshed her makeup. "You would not believe what I've smuggled through customs using that little box."

"Don't tell me." He went to the hotel phone to call Conor, Brooke, and Hyatt back from the theater and told them to wait outside the rear lobby of the hotel. "I'll walk you down to the bar."

"I'll be fine." No, she wouldn't, not with him looking at her like that. She took her favorite silk cloak from the closet and draped it over her shoulders. "Kalen, please. I know I lost it before, but that was shock. I wasn't prepared. Now I am. Trust me."

He plucked at a fold of the long cape. "No leaping off any more tall buildings, Superwoman."

The tenderness in his voice almost made her cave in, right there. "I can still dodge trains and bullets, though, right?"

Kalen bent down and pressed his lips to her brow. "Behave." He gave her arm a squeeze and left the suite.

Raven took a moment to collect herself, then went down to meet the other two models at the bar. Gemma had already ordered a taxi to take them to Zhihan's lakefront Chicago home, and on the trip over both models grilled her about the accident and the dashing way Kalen had saved her life.

"I thought my eyes would pop out of my head when I saw that bloody damn light smashing down on us." Gemma sighed. "Then watching that bloke of yours dive into you and right over the stage. Lord!" She sighed. "If he had black hair, he'd be a dead ringer for Pierce Brosnan."

"You are very lucky to have hired such an excellent bodyguard," Alake commented. "I should like a man like him the next time I visit Uganda. Do you hire him out temporarily?"

"He's not a bodyguard, and he doesn't do temp work." As the taxi stopped in front of a large, well-lit mansion, she leaned over to pay the driver. "Spike is just very observant, and very loyal."

Gemma huffed. "He's more than that, luv. Give the man a nice fat raise. He deserves it."

A maid ushered them in and took their cloaks, then directed them to the ballroom. Inside, the post-show party was already in full swing, and when the three models were announced a huge round of applause broke out.

Playing to the crowd, Gemma grabbed Raven's hand and lifted it up. "You can't keep a good woman down, ladies and gents. Not even if you use a bloody wrecking ball."

Everyone laughed, and Raven submitted to a number of half hugs and air kisses as they made their way into the ballroom.

"Raven." People parted on both sides as Zhihan

walked forward and gave her a shallow bow. "I feared you would be unable to attend."

Why, because you tried to crush my skull? "I wouldn't have missed it for the world," she said, and returned the bow.

Chapter 10

Ran Peng watched Zhihan move around the room with the dark-haired woman, and silently applauded the young man's hard-won self-control. Only a week ago he had been prepared to drag the model to the nearest unoccupied room and beat her until she gave him the information he wanted. Now, at last, the Dai's heir was beginning to show himself worthy of the cunning and intelligence long associated with his ancient family name.

None too soon, either, for Zhihan's undisciplined behavior since the death of his elder brother had become unacceptable to the Dai.

You must watch him for me, Ran, his master had commanded before leaving for San Francisco. *Watch him and guide him until I send for him.*

Ran had done that, to the best of his ability, and he believed he had succeeded. Yet his pleasure soon evaporated as he saw Zhihan rapidly consume several drinks as he steered the model through the clusters of guests. He used every excuse to put his hands on the young woman, and while the temptation was understandable and even forgivable, the danger he created by such scandalous conduct was not.

And if Zhihan embarrassed his father again, Ran

Peng suspected that the Dai's wrath would fall heavily upon him.

At last Ran received a sealed note from one of the guards, giving him the excuse he needed. He gestured for one of the housemen passing by him with a tray, and the servant instantly attended him.

"Go to young master Dai." He gestured across the room. "Tell him I have an urgent message that has just arrived, and must speak with him at once—alone."

The houseman bowed, set down his tray and hurried off. He reappeared with Zhihan a few moments later.

"You heard from my father, old man?" Alcohol had blurred Zhihan's speech to a barely intelligible slur. "What does he want now?"

"Come, master." Ran led the boy out of the room, holding him up as he stumbled. When they were out of earshot of the guests, he halted. "Master Zhihan, forgive me, but you are drinking too much again."

A guest passed them, and Zhihan slouched against the nearest wall. "What did my father tell you?"

The servant glanced both ways, then said in a low, urgent tone, "He asked me to look after you. To remind you that, in his absence, you are the Dai."

"You are quick to judge, old man, but slow to see." Zhihan lost his leer, straightened, and folded his arms. In a cool, crisp voice he added, "What do you see now?"

Ran bowed low. "That I am a fool, master."

"You are not the only one." Zhihan laughed, an unpleasant sound. "You've seen the American woman—she's a beautiful *gai*, isn't she? And she hangs on my every word. The more I drink, the more questions she asks me. Is that not interesting, Ran?"

"Yes, master." The old man remembered the note and took it out of his jacket. "This came for you. It is not marked."

"I know who it is from." Zhihan opened the envelope and removed the single folded page inside. He read the letter, then smiled. "I must call my father at once."

"And the woman?"

"She will be staying tonight."

That troubled the old servant. "But if she is indeed a prostitute, hired by your father's enemies—"

"Oh, not to bed her," Zhihan said with a dismissive gesture. "But she will tell me everything I want to know."

Ran knew about the heir's perversions, mainly from the housewomen he'd beaten in the past. Part of his duties had always been to clean up whatever mess Zhihan left behind. Although he was loyal to the Dai, now Ran genuinely wondered if the wrong son had died. "Zhihan, you cannot kill her. She is too famous, your father says."

"You have not indulged yourself enough here in America, have you? You should try one of them. These women enjoy being abused." The Dai's son leaned back and closed his eyes, as if reminiscing. "Some of them beg for it."

As he had been trained to do since birth, Ran accepted what he could not change. "And if she does not tell you what you wish to know?"

"She will tell me anything I desire." The Dai's son gave him a chilling smile. "And when I am done with her, her face will become famous for different reasons."

"Mr. Delaney—"

"Sean, darlin'." He shifted toward her, still holding the gun between them. "Call me Sean."

He'd forced her to leave her home and drive him to San Francisco. He'd even made her take her own car. *She had plenty of things to call him.* Meko gripped the steering wheel tighter. "Mr. Delaney, you know this is kidnapping."

He took something out of his pocket. "I know. You'll want to turn right up here, and take U.S. 101 North."

Meko kept silent until they were on the highway, then the words seemed to burst from her. "Let me get off at the next exit. You can go on from there." That made him chuckle, and the sudden, intense desire to hit him made her blink. She had never felt this annoyed with anyone, not even Nick. "I mean it—take the car. I promise, I won't tell anyone about this—"

"You'll call the police from the first phone you can get to and scream bloody blue murder. I would." With his free hand, he lit a cigarette. "Be a good girl and keep your eyes on the road."

"What are you doing?" She coughed and waved her hand in front of her face. "Put that out!"

With a chuckle, he opened the car window and pitched it. "I take it you don't smoke. Smart girl."

She cracked her own window to clear the remnants of smoke from the Mercedes. "I don't abduct innocent people at gunpoint, either. And I'm not a girl."

"Oh, sure, you're—what? All of twenty-five? Twenty-six?"

"I celebrated my fortieth birthday in December, Mr. Delaney." She couldn't help a small smirk when she saw his expression. "One of the benefits of an Asian heritage—the look of youth far past the blooming years."

"You could have fooled me."

Meko fell silent as she tried to think of a way to get herself out of this mess. Traffic was thinning dramatically, and soon theirs would be one of the few cars left on the highway.

Finally she decided to try reasoning with him again. "My father *is* dead, you know. His house has been closed for months, ever since he went overseas."

"That makes it a good hiding place."

She gnawed at her lower lip. "Don't you think those men who broke into my home have already ransacked my father's house?"

"They wouldn't know where it is, darlin'. Your father was good at keeping secrets." He watched her intently. "What did he tell you about the swords?"

"I told you, my father and I have been estranged for years. He wouldn't tell me anything. He disowned me." When he didn't respond, she hit the steering wheel with one hand. "Why won't you believe me?"

"I know all about the code of silence you people maintain, even when you hate each other." The glow from the dashboard lights turned his handsome face into a bleak mask. "As soon as you tell me where the swords are, I'll let you go."

"I don't know what swords you're talking about!"

"Pull over." He pointed to an emergency stopping area just ahead of them. "Right there."

Meko slowed down and eased off the road, then put her Mercedes in Park. He wasn't going to dump her off in the middle of the highway, was he? "Mr. Delaney, surely we can work this out. There's no reason to become violent."

"Me, violent?" He grabbed her then and hauled

her across the seat. "Do you know how many men and women and children your father injured or killed since he started operating here in America?"

She swallowed and shook her head.

"Hundreds. Maybe thousands. That's how organized crime works. It profits off the fear of a lot of people. When the fear doesn't work, then they make some families into examples, to keep the others afraid."

She thought of some of the things she had seen as a child. Visitors to her father's house, bringing envelopes and clearly terrified. "I am a law-abiding citizen. An *American* citizen. I'm not involved in any of my father's criminal activities. I never have been."

"No, I imagine you've kept your head buried in the sand for years. That's what women like you do, isn't it?" He bent his head close to hers, until his breath warmed her mouth. "There's a war going on, right now, between the Chinese tongs, and maybe your father's people. People are dying, and not just the criminals."

A tong war—over some swords? "I didn't know about this."

"You can watch the six o'clock news and see it happen, every night. Little kids playing in their yards get caught in crossfire. People's homes are set on fire. Women like you are murdered for no reason but to send a message to their sons or husbands or fathers. More and more innocents will die until those swords are found, and I'm going to find them." He got very close, his grip hurting her now. "Do you understand me?"

She nodded, too afraid to move.

"Good. Slide over. I'm driving now." He opened the passenger door and got out, then came around to get behind the wheel. "Don't think about jumping out. You'll either break your neck, or I'll have to chase you down." He put the car into Drive and pulled out onto the highway. "And with the mood I'm in, darlin', you don't want me catching you."

Meko wondered what he intended to do to her when they arrived at her father's house and found no swords. He wouldn't kill her, not after the way he'd talked about the victims of her father's crimes. Sean Delaney might be crazy enough to kidnap her, but he wasn't a monster.

She hoped.

"Talk to me, Raven," Conor said over her earpiece.

She scanned the hall before responding. "I'm on the second floor. Zhihan left with one of the servants. Is Hyatt tracking me?"

"Yes—the equipment should be about thirty feet away, northeast."

"Where's Kalen?" she asked as she moved toward one of the closed doors at the end of the hall.

"Installing the phone tap." The connection crackled. "We're getting interference over the line."

She reached under her skirt to check the remote connection. "I'm still plugged in."

"He may have a signal-scatter unit, Hyatt says." Conor's voice faded in and out. "Better make it fast, Raven."

"What are you doing, skulking around up here?"

She turned to see Gemma emerge from one of the rooms. "Hey, Gem. Great party, huh? That the bathroom?" She started toward it.

"Uh, I wouldn't go in there." The British girl caught her arm. "The loo's backed up."

"Is it." Raven got close enough to catch the scent

of her breath. "Peppermint. Nice. Doesn't quite cover up the smell of the puke, though."

"Stomach virus, remember?"

"Don't bullshit me."

"Then don't patronize me, Rave." Gemma's voice turned vicious. "Unlike you, I compete with sixteen-year-olds, and they all weigh about seventy pounds dripping wet. Save your lectures for someone who wants to hear them."

"I'm not going to lecture you." Raven shoved her up against a wall. "I'm going to kick your scrawny English ass. Last time you started binge purging, you tore up your stomach so bad they had to operate on you."

"Did me a bit of good, that. Got rid of most of the hunger pangs."

"Goddamn it." Raven hit the wall next to Gemma's head. "Don't do this to yourself again."

"I've got to fight for every contract I get, you stupid gint—but you wouldn't know about that, what with your perfect face and perfect body." She shoved Raven's hands away. "Piss off."

"Gemma!" She swore under her breath as the other model stalked off and Conor's voice crackled over her earpiece, wanting to know her status. "Okay, sorry, I'm moving now."

The door he'd indicated wasn't locked, and she walked in quickly, prepared to act surprised that it wasn't a bathroom for the benefit of anyone inside. It was another beautiful room, richly decorated in scarlet, gold, and black, with authentic antique Oriental furnishings.

"Hello?" She waited a moment, then touched her transmitter. "Okay, I'm in."

She took the tampon box from her purse, removed

the relay modem, then found the sophisticated computer array concealed inside a large black-lacquered Oriental cabinet. She had to pull the drive tower out to plug in the unit, then hook it to the phone jack.

"Here we go." She sat down and booted up the system, which thankfully had only industry-standard security. It took her all of thirty seconds to hack past that and open the database. She switched on the modem. "Ready for transmit, Conor."

His reply broke up, but she made out the word "standby."

She closed the doors and moved away from the cabinet, then began searching the room. She doubted Zhihan would be stupid enough to leave any evidence lying around, but she'd expected better security on his PC, too. According to Hyatt, the download would take at least twenty minutes, so she might have to slip back out and return later to retrieve the relay unit.

Someone opened the door, and she had enough presence of mind to drop onto the bed and stretch out, pillowing her head on one arm.

"Raven." Zhihan stepped inside as soon as he saw her, then closed the door behind him. He was carrying an open bottle of wine in the kind of grip used to club someone over the head. "What are you doing in here?"

"Relaxing a little." She produced a sleepy smile and jammed her thumb down on her transmitter. "Did the maid give you my message?"

"Message?" he echoed in a soft voice as he approached the bed. He didn't sound drunk, however. He sounded . . . pleased.

"To meet me up here, silly." She forced herself to

giggle. "I was getting tired of all those people. I thought you and I could spend some time together . . . alone."

"Did you?" He sat down on the bed beside her and put one of his rough hands on her abdomen. "I did not get any message. Which maid did you tell?"

"You're here now. That's all that matters." The look in his eyes was starting to spook her. "We can talk without being interrupted."

"You do not go to a man's bed to talk." His fingers slid down to her hip and squeezed. "You liked what I told you on the phone, eh?"

As his fingers inched farther down, she thought of the thigh strap and her blood turned to ice. "Wait— I have a little surprise for you." She rolled over and off the opposite side of the bed, then circled around, running her hands from her hips to her breasts. "Let me do a little private show for you."

Zhihan pulled the pillows up against the headboard, then settled back against them and took a drink from the bottle. "Go ahead."

She knelt in front of the bed, smiling up at him. "You're going to love this." Quickly she reached up under her dress to jerk off the thigh strap and the wire, then shoved the unit under the bed as she stood to shed her shoes. As she shimmied her hips, slowly lifting her skirt to reveal the tops of her stockings, she decided to use protection as a reason to leave the room.

"Oh, dear." She let her skirt fall and giggled again. "I forgot, I have to visit the little girls' room. You know, to get ready before we . . . do anything." She reached for her purse, which sat on the end of the bed, only to find Zhihan's fingers around her wrist.

"You can primp later." With one jerk he pulled her down beside him and clamped a hand around her throat. "I want you now."

She could smell tea on his breath. He wasn't inebriated; it had all been an act. *Why is he trying to make me think he's drunk?*

He massaged her throat. "You look frightened. Are you afraid of me, Raven?"

She edged away and tried to sit up. "I'm more afraid of doing it without protection," she said, then went still as he cut off her air.

"I tell you what. If you give me a disease," he muttered against her ear, "I will kill you, very slowly."

She summoned another laugh, pretending to take the threat as a joke. "And if you get me pregnant, I'll kill you too."

"Stop your babbling." He let go of her neck and seized her by the hair, dragging her head back. "I want to see you naked now. Take off that dress." He shoved her off the bed.

Carefully she got to her feet, and reached for the side zipper, checking her watch as she did. Somehow she had to keep this up for another fifteen minutes. Maybe if she got him to talk, it would slow him down. And if that didn't work, the Ming vase on the mantel would leave a nice dent in his head. "I feel a little funny, enjoying myself so much." She fumbled with the zipper, maintaining the illusion that she was eager to have sex with him. "With Portia dead and all, it doesn't seem right."

He took another drink, maintaining the illusion that he was drunk. "You still miss your *gai* friend?"

Gai meant whore in Chinese, and Raven suppressed a surge of fury. "Yes, but she and I were close. Almost like sisters." She inched the zipper down another notch, and felt the air touch her bare skin. "You must feel the same way about your brother."

"He was good, my brother. Strong—stronger even than our father." His mouth thinned as he stared at her, then he climbed off the bed. "He should not have died that way."

"It was a terrible thing." She backed up a step, then forced herself to stand still as he came at her. "I'm almost done, it's just that this zipper is—" She broke off as he slapped her, hard.

"I am tired of this game. Your friend betrayed my brother." He grabbed the front of her dress and ripped it away from her breasts. "You know what she did, who paid her." He seized her throat again, pushing her back toward the bed. "Tell me."

Raven let herself fall back, then curled over and tried to get up on her knees. But Zhihan descended, hitting her again, this time with a knotted fist to the jaw.

She wanted to hit him back so much it took every ounce of strength she had to cower and beg. "Zhihan, please!"

He got her pinned, his knees digging into her thighs, his fingers gouging into her breasts. "Who gave her the money to turn on my brother?"

"I don't know!"

"You'll tell me." Before she could get her hands up, he punched her a third time, then flipped her over and shoved up her skirt. She felt him fumbling with his trousers. "You'll scream for me when I'm done with you."

Raven's vision grayed as he shoved her facedown into the mattress, then abruptly he let go and got off her. She turned her head to see Kalen standing in the doorway, his shirt untucked, his hair in disarray.

"Hey." He staggered in and waved one hand. "Miss Raven doesn't allow that sort of thing."

"Get out," Zhihan roared, launching himself at Kalen, who smoothly pivoted, caught the back of the man's jacket and flung him into the wall. Zhihan fell to the floor with a thump and didn't move.

She crawled off the bed, coughing and rubbing her throat. "Good . . . timing." When he stared at her, she looked down at the ruins of her dress, then pulled it up to cover the scratches and bruises on her breasts. "It looks bad, but he didn't—"

"He did enough, the son of a bitch." Kalen reached down and hauled the unconscious man up against the wall, then drove his fist into his belly.

"Boss." Conor appeared and grabbed Kalen's arm before he threw another punch. "Easy now, you'll kill him."

"Not right away." Kalen shook off Conor and hit Zhihan again. "I'm going to enjoy myself first."

"Kalen, I'm okay. Stop." Raven hurried over and latched on to his arm. "Please."

"Con." He didn't let go of the sagging body. "Take her out of here."

Confused by the blind hatred on his face, she shook her head. "Listen, nothing happened. He just got a little rough with me. I would have disabled him if it had gone too far."

"Before he choked you, or after?" He dropped Zhihan and swung toward her. "Did he rape you?"

"No." She flinched as he dragged her up against him. "Kalen, you're hurting me."

"Why didn't you get him out of here, take him back down to the party?" He shook her. "I told you not to let him corner you! Have you forgotten everything I taught you?"

"He was acting drunk. I thought I was safe!" she yelled back. "And I haven't forgotten a goddamn thing!"

"I hate to break this up, but the servants around here aren't deaf," Conor said as he checked Zhihan. "He's not drunk, but he's going to be out for a while. Major, what about the download?"

She stalked over to the cabinet and opened the doors. The lights on the modem were dark. "It's done."

Conor pulled out a handheld radio. "Hyatt, have you got the database?"

"Yeah, but there's not much here," Hyatt's voice replied. "Some Asian porn sites and records on their legit business. That's it."

Raven eyed the equipment. "You two had better go, before someone else wanders in here. Give me a minute to pull the equipment and get my dress back together."

"Make it fast." Kalen walked out, followed by Conor.

As soon as they were gone, she took her cell from her purse and called Jian-Shan. "Jay, it's Raven. I need your help."

Gemma Firth had envied Raven from the moment she'd set eyes on her. No woman looked like that without help, and other girls whispered that she'd gotten her face from the world's finest plastic surgeon. He'd done his work well; Raven didn't even have scars. Her rise to fame had been so quick it shocked even the most jaded in the industry, but Gemma knew it was deserved. Raven had a great body, a fantastic voice, and endless charm. More reasons to hate her—and to befriend her.

"Bloody perfect bitch, she is." Gemma stalked downstairs and looked around. No one was smoking, of course, no one did anymore—at least not in public. Her own nicotine urge hit her hard, as it did after any time she purged. "Time to have me a smoke."

She spotted a pack of European cigarettes sticking out of a purse left on a chair, and casually picked it up as she strolled by. It wasn't the first time she'd nicked something that didn't belong to her, and as always she got a little thrill out of the theft.

The temperature outside was dropping, so she stopped by the coatroom to pick up her wrap. Then she saw the fabulous black silk cloak Raven had worn to the party, recognized it as one of the other woman's favorites, and smirked.

Why not go two for two?

"May I help you, ma'am?" the pretty little maid attending the room asked.

"Yes, luv." She might not be able to compete with Raven, but she could bloody well burn a few holes in her precious cloak. "I need my cape—it's the black one, right there."

The maid handed it over, and Gemma felt so pleased she tipped the girl. Then she shrugged into the cloak and slipped out of the house.

"Looks like a million quid, feels like tissue paper," she muttered as she followed the little stone path around to the side of the mansion. Wearing Raven's cloak had made her feel better, but the damp, chilly breeze coming in from the lake made her wish for her own much warmer wool cape. She took out a cigarette and lit it, sighing with pleasure as she inhaled. "You'd think she'd have a bloody Russian sable or something."

The path took her into a garden, but not like any she'd ever seen. There were no flowers and only a few straggly plants around a lot of big, ugly boulders stuck in some black dirt with swirly lines raked through it.

"Must be some kind of Kung-fu garden plan," she muttered under her breath. A sound made her glance back over her shoulder. Through the windows of the ballroom, she saw a couple of the guests looking out and pointing at her.

They think I'm Raven.

"Go on, have a good look, why don't . . ." She trailed off as she noticed the large statue of Buddha in the center of a huge patch of raked sand. "Oh, that's too wicked. I couldn't. I shouldn't." She clamped a hand over her mouth to stifle her giggles. "Serve her right, though, it would."

Something shuffled behind her, and she turned to see a shadow moving toward her. A camera flashed. *Ooooh, a photographer. How perfect.*

She skipped up to the statue and climbed up onto the raised platform at its base. "Hello, mate. Want to help me get Raven on the front page of every entertainment section in the country tomorrow?"

Keeping her face and dress well hidden, she started dancing in front of the statue, caressing it with her hands. She made sure she appeared as lewd and suggestive as possible.

The shadow moved closer, now only a few feet away.

Suppressing more giggles, she hooked a leg over the Buddha's, and ground her hips against the prominent belly.

"Give it to me, big boy," she whispered, doing her best imitation of Raven. "I need your love tonight. . . ."

There was another sound—a click—and a voice murmured something. Gemma frowned; it almost sounded like praying. She forgot her ruse and turned toward the shadow as it pointed a gleaming object at her.

That's not a camera, it's a—

Before Gemma could complete the thought, the photographer shot her in the chest.

Chapter 11

The gunshot threw all of the party guests into an immediate panic.

Kalen sent Conor outside, then notified the team. "Hyatt, Brooke, we've got live fire up at the house." He turned back to climb the stairs, but Raven was already rushing down them.

"Where?" she asked as she looked around.

"Single shot, side of the house. Zhihan?"

"Still down for the count." She eyed the milling crowd, who were clustering in groups around the most hysterical individuals. Zhihan and his men were noticeably absent. "A tong hit?"

"Unlikely. They'd use more ammo." He moved into the room, looking for anyone who was armed. "Conor, what've you got?"

"No sign of intruders, but there's—" His point man broke off into vicious swearing.

"What?" Kalen demanded.

"I've got a victim with a gunshot wound to the chest out here," Conor's voice sounded ragged. "Raven. Can you hear me? It's your friend. The Brit girl."

Raven's eyes flew wide. "Gemma?"

"We copy, Con." Before she could move, Kalen took her arm. "You're going back to the van."

"The hell I am." She tugged free and ran, yelling to one of the servants, "Call 911!"

He caught up with her outside. "The shooter could still be out here."

She didn't stop. "Then I suggest you use that gun in your hand, General, and protect me." They found Conor in the garden, where he was kneeling beside Gemma's still form and pressing his hand against her chest. He barely spared them a glance.

"Gemma." Raven dropped down on the other side of her. "Oh, my God."

Kalen noted the blood splatters on the Buddha statue, then intercepted one of the housemen entering the garden. "Did anyone see anything?"

"I see lady out here before." The Chinese man looked at Gemma and cringed. "She dance around Buddha. Then there was big bang, and she fall down."

"Did you see who shot her?" Kalen hissed in an impatient breath as the man shook his head. "Con, how bad?"

"Bad. Punctured her lung, close to her heart." Conor lifted his hand to inspect the wound and Gemma made a gurgling noise. He rolled her on her side, and blood trickled from her mouth. "She's hemorrhaging. We need to evac her right now, boss."

The servant wrung his hands. "I call 911. They say they be here, five minutes. She not die?"

"No." Raven was nearly shouting. "She's not going to die."

Kalen left Raven with Conor and scouted the immediate area, meeting up with Hyatt and Brooke. Both reported finding no one during their sweep. By the time they returned to the garden, medics had arrived and were taking over for Conor and Raven.

"One—two—three, lift." The EMT and his partner shifted Gemma's limp form onto a stretcher and strapped her down. "We're taking her to Northeast Regional."

Raven picked up a crumpled silk cloak and clenched it in her fist. "I'm going with her."

Kalen closed his eyes briefly. "You can't—"

"This is *mine*. Her blood is all over it. He thought she was me." Raven shoved the ruined silk into his hands. "I'm going."

"Con." Kalen handed the cape off, then lowered his voice. "Perform another sweep, see what you can find before the local PD gets here. I'll go with the unit."

Raven sat beside him in the back of the rescue unit as the technician worked on Gemma, but she didn't say anything. She alternated between staring blindly at the British model's colorless face and looking at her own hands.

"What's her condition?" Kalen asked the tech when he finally sat back to watch the monitors.

"One of her lungs collapsed, but there may be more internal damage. She's critical." He tapped the monitor. "The bullet may have nicked her heart; she's losing a lot of blood." He reached for Gemma's wrist, then frowned as he bent closer. "She's got something in her hand."

Raven went still beside him as the technician removed a flower from Gemma's fist. "May I see that, please?"

"Sure." The tech handed it to her. "Guess she grabbed it in that garden, huh?"

"Yeah." Kalen watched as Raven crushed the bloody lotus in her hands. "Looks that way."

When they arrived, Raven jumped out of the unit and accompanied the gurney as far as they would let her. A charge nurse stopped them just outside assessment and indicated they'd have to go to the critical-care waiting room.

"Your friend will be going up to surgery as soon as we stabilize her." The nurse touched Raven's arm. "We'll keep you posted on her condition."

"Come on." Kalen took her hand. "Let's find a coffee machine. It's going to be a long night."

Brooke Oliver didn't like losing. Especially to someone who had no concept of duty, honor, or country. So she had stopped in the lobby of the theater and made one final phone call. She'd done her duty, maintained her honor, and served her country—all by reporting Major Ravenowitz to the inspector general. She'd been obliged to tailor the truth here and there, to protect General Grady, but that was part of her duty as well. As she entered the critical-care waiting room to report to him, she felt serene and satisfied with herself.

All I have to do is arrange the time and place to have the MPs pick her up, then good-bye, Raven.

The major was standing by a small window, staring out into the empty street. The general stood beside her, his arm around her waist. Her head rested lightly on his shoulder. Brooke had never seen them touching each other before. Not like this.

What if he really does love her?

She cleared her throat, and Kalen glanced over his shoulder at her. She remembered to display the right amount of impersonal interest by asking, "Is Miss Firth all right?"

"She's still in surgery." Kalen leaned in and murmured something to Raven, then left her and gestured for Brooke to accompany him out into the hall. "What's the status on the Dai?"

"The son left O'Hare ten minutes ago on a private chartered jet to San Francisco. Hyatt picked up the call he made from the house tap just before he left; Zhihan is going to deliver the swords to the Dai."

"Shit. Do we know where the swords are?"

"No, he wasn't specific. From the conversation, Hyatt believes he's going to attend some kind of meeting with his father and the other tong leaders."

"Delivering the swords as part of a unification agreement, no doubt," Kalen said, and rubbed the back of his neck. "With the Dai triad taking over as head of all the tongs in the U.S."

Brooke smiled a little as she thought of the day when she could rub away his aches for him. While Raven made license plates in some jail factory. "It's possible."

"Excuse me, sir?" A nurse appeared, carrying a plastic bag. "Are you here for Miss Firth?" When he nodded, she handed him the bag. "These are her personal belongings, but she won't be able to keep them with her until after she's out of the intensive care unit."

"I'll take them." Raven stepped out into the corridor. "She's out of surgery?"

"Yes. She's still in critical condition, and will be for at least another twenty-four hours." The nurse excused herself and left.

Raven looked inside the bag. "No handcuffs this time."

"Pardon me?" Brooke raised her brows.

Raven's mouth hitched. "A private joke, Captain." She took out a purse and opened it. "The nurse said they needed her ID and insurance card. I hope she's got them . . . on her. . . ." She removed a pair of plane tickets and read the front of one. "These are for San Francisco. A charter flight on a jet—it leaves in an hour."

"Did Gemma tell you she intended to go to San Francisco?" Kalen asked, and Raven shook her head. "On the same night Zhihan goes."

"Whoever shot her thought she was me." Raven clutched the ticket. "So maybe I should take Gemma's place."

They left Conor to guard Gemma, while Kalen requisitioned a commercial flight to take Brooke and Hyatt out to the coast. Arrangements were also made with the local FBI to set up an exchange point, to which Raven would lure Zhihan once she arrived in San Francisco with Kalen.

Knowing her friend had taken a bullet meant for her haunted Raven, to the point that everyone had to repeat things three and four times before she heard them. Even the prospect of getting on the private chartered jet and facing Zhihan in San Francisco didn't faze her.

This time, we finish it.

Kalen remained equally silent, until they got on the plane. "Raven, we need to talk about this."

"There's nothing to discuss. He wants me, I want him in jail. I call him from the airport and tell him I know who murdered his brother, and to bring the swords to our prearranged location. If he's the Lotus, he'll come just so he can kill me."

"He was unconscious when Gemma was shot," Kalen reminded her. "We know he's not the Lotus."

"He could have had an accomplice do her. If he's not the Lotus, he'll come anyway, to find out who killed Gangi. You take him into custody, make a plea bargain with him for the swords, acquire them, throw his ass in jail for a few decades." She waved a hand. "End of story."

"It won't be that easy." He took her cold hand in his. "A million things can and probably will go wrong."

"That's why you're here, General Genius. To fix them." She pulled her hand from his, then saw the dry, dark red smears on her fingers. *Must have gotten it on my hands when I picked up the cloak.* "I have to wash up."

She got up from her seat and walked to the back of the plane. There were no attendants, thanks to some maneuvering by Kalen at the airport, and the only other person on the plane was the charter line pilot who was busy flying it.

She liked flying, so the small size of the jet didn't bother her. The interior, on the other hand, did. Everything was glass, onyx leather, and chrome fittings.

Like a flying hearse.

Raven's stomach rolled as she walked through the curtained partition and found a private executive suite, complete with bed and bathroom. Someone had left a flower in a black marble bud vase by the bed. If it had been a lotus, Raven would have screamed, but it was only a rose. A dark, red rose, the color of old blood, Gemma's blood—

She carefully made her way into the bathroom and tried to throw up as quietly as possible. Only somehow Kalen heard her, because he was behind her a minute later, supporting her with one arm, holding her hair back as she retched.

"It's okay, baby, let it out." His voice was as gentle as his hands. "Get it all out."

When she was finished, he helped steady her until she could get to her feet, then told her wash her face and left. He came back a moment later with her carry-on case so she could get what she needed to brush her teeth.

"If the army thing doesn't work out, you'd make an excellent valet," she tried to joke as she went to work at the sink. "And God, I'm airsick."

"Good to know I have an alternate job placement to fall back on." He didn't leave, but stood in the doorway and watched her clean up. "Are you hiring?"

She nearly choked on her toothpaste before spitting it out and rinsing her mouth. "Uh, no. I can dress myself."

"Pity."

As he continued to play voyeur, she wondered why he was being so nice—and provocative. The old Kalen never teased or flirted; he considered it a waste of time. She glanced at him, and saw the intent way he was following every move she made. He had a way of looking at her that made her wonder if he was counting her heartbeats by observing the faint pulse in her throat.

Better lighten this situation up real quick, before it gets out of hand.

"Now I understand those little monogrammed sacks tucked behind the seats," she said as she dried her hot face on one of the beautifully soft towels provided by the airline. "Designer barf bags."

"You aren't airsick, Raven."

No, she wasn't. She ran a brush through her hair but decided to forgo the makeup. Then she found herself telling him the truth. "That rose by the bed reminded me of Gemma. All that blood on the sand."

"I threw it out." He came up behind her, took the brush out of her hand, and stroked it through the heavy length over the back of her neck. "I missed untangling your morning rat's nest."

Her mouth curled. Although her hair was wonderfully thick, the individual strands were so fine that she constantly battled snarls and knots. "Who always messed it up during the night, playing with it?"

"I couldn't resist." He put the brush down and ran his palm from her crown to the middle of her back. "It's like wrapping my hands in silk ribbons." He stepped back and tugged gently. "Come out of here."

"Do all private jets come equipped with a bed, I wonder?" she murmured as she let him draw her out of the bathroom.

"Only the good ones." Kalen slipped an arm around her waist. They were standing so close now that only a whisper separated their bodies. "Feeling better now?"

She nodded, but didn't meet his gaze. "I should go do something official. Have you got any paperwork I can forge your signature on?"

"It'll keep." He trailed his fingers down her cheek. "You're always trying to run away from me."

"Kind of hard to do that, twenty-two thousand feet above the ground." She couldn't help leaning in to return the caress. "Especially since you wouldn't let me bring my bungie cords."

"You scared the hell out of me, that night in Paris. I saw you go over the side of that roof and thought—" He stopped and shook his head. "You take too many chances."

"And you worry too much." She ran her fingers through his shaggy, bleached mane, then pulled back her hand. "Kalen, what are we doing?"

"Arguing, as usual." He eased her up against him, closing the various gaps between them. "I like doing it this way. Beats dodging flying garbage cans."

The warmth of his body seeped through her clothes, touching her skin. They'd never needed blankets when they'd slept together—they'd always generated plenty of heat. She wanted to curl up with him now and thaw her frozen soul in his arms. "Old memories stir up some old feelings, don't they?"

"And desires," he said, bending down to brush his mouth lightly over hers. "It's been all I could do to keep my hands off you."

"You're not doing too well now," she whispered, sliding her palms down his chest. The heavy thud of his heart sped faster, pounding against her fingers. She looked down at the press of their bodies. "But then, neither am I."

He lifted her chin. "I don't want just sex. I want you, Sarah. Every way I can have you."

She should have shouted at him, told him not to call her that, pushed him away and stalked back to the front of the plane. All she could manage was a wretched whisper. "I'm not Sarah anymore."

"Yes, you are." He brought a handful of her hair to his face. "You smell like her." He turned his head, tracing his tongue along the full lower curve of her mouth. "You taste like her." He cradled her face between his hands and inspected her features. "Your eyes, your voice, the way you put your hands on me—it's all the same, Sarah. Nothing's changed."

"You saw the photos of what the Lotus did to me."

Kalen caught the tear that spilled down her cheek with his thumb. "Yes."

"Then you know." She blinked back the rest of the

tears. "He took my face away from me, Kalen. Even the photos don't show how bad it was. When I saw what he'd done, I wanted to die. There was nothing left of me in the mirror." Her throat felt raw. "He made me look like a monster. Then I turned into one."

"You did what you had to do. You survived." He traced the perfectly arched line of her brow. "And there's not a man on the planet who would call you a monster."

"You don't get it. I had a choice." She released a bitter laugh. "I was carrying a photo of you and me in one of my pockets."

He frowned. "I don't understand."

"The surgeon could have made me look the way I did before. I told him to make me look like this"—she touched her face—"for revenge, on you. For sacrificing me and the others." She slipped out of his arms and sat down on the bed. "The only reason I did this was to get even with you. To make you see me everywhere. Like some kind of designer Marley's ghost."

"It worked." He gave her a wry look. "I haven't been able to buy a paper at the newsstand for the last five years without seeing you on the cover of something."

She dug her hands into the silk coverlet. "How can you joke about it? When I did it just to hurt you?"

"Sarah, you thought I had set you up. You had every right to do what you did." He sat down beside her and took her hand in his. "I'm surprised you didn't come back to the States and shoot me in the head."

Knowing that he understood took a huge weight off her shoulders. "The thought had crossed my mind." She laced her fingers through his. "So, where do we go from here?"

He brought her hand to his mouth and kissed the backs of her fingers. "We do what we should have done six years ago."

"Which is?"

"I tell you how sorry I am." He pulled her onto his lap. "And I am, sweetheart. I wish I could make up for what happened to you. It's no excuse, but when they told me you were all dead, I went a little crazy. And when I discovered you were still alive, and you wouldn't come back to me, I imagined the worst. I should have trusted you. Forgive me."

She nodded, struggling with tears again to get the words out. "I should have come home to you, Kal. I assumed you'd betrayed me even when a part of me knew you would never do such a thing. I wish I could go back. I'd do everything differently." She knuckled her eyes. "I'm so sorry."

"Shhhh." He pressed her against his chest, rocking her. "It's all right now."

Kalen held her for a long time, murmuring soothing words as he rubbed her back. She'd never felt as safe as she did in his arms. Gradually her despair evaporated and she knew it was time to tell him about the baby.

When she lifted her face from his damp shirt, her mouth skimmed the line of his jaw, and she felt him shudder. She'd been so miserable she hadn't realized how tense he was—or why. Now she ran her hand up his arm and felt the hard knots of his muscles bunching under her touch.

He still wants me. And he'd ignored it to comfort her. "Kalen?"

"It's okay." Carefully he set her aside. "But *I'd* better go find some paperwork to do."

It was easy to catch his hand and bring it to her heart. "I'm still hurting." She splayed his tense fingers over her breast. "Make it feel better."

He stared at his hand, and a trickle of sweat ran down the side of his face. "It's been too long, Sarah. I can't give you what you need."

Stubborn man. "You can't touch me, like this?" She laid her hand over his, and moved it slowly over the tight bead of her nipple. "You can't hold me close?" She straddled his lap, inching closer. His free arm came up around her hips. "You can't"—she brushed her lips against his—"kiss me?" As the heat poured off him, she added one more refinement by delicately rubbing herself up and down the length of his erection. "You can't find a place . . . to put this?"

An instant later she was flat on her back, under him, her body pinned to the bed by the weight of his. "Oh, I can do all that, and more. I've had six years to fantasize about what I'd do to you."

"Well, then." She smiled up at him. "What are you waiting for?"

He muttered something under his breath, then pushed a hand under her head and brought her mouth to his.

Raven could have laughed with delight, but she was too busy reeling under the ferocious kiss. Kalen snarled her hair in his fingers as he took her mouth, kissing her the way a starved man would fall on a feast. The deep, erotic thrust of his tongue stroked hers as his hands began tearing at her blouse, ripping the fabric apart. She twisted under him, wanting to help but unable to do more than clutch at him with frantic hands.

"Hold still." He pushed himself up and wrenched the remains of the blouse away, then ran both hands over her breasts, catching the edge of her skimpy bra with his fingers. "Are you attached to this?"

She glanced down at the bra, which was hand-dyed blue silk and cost a small fortune. "I've got more."

"Good." He tore it in half and stripped it away, then slid down to tug off her jeans. "The panties?" he asked as he threw the jeans across the room.

Raven reached down and tore the delicate material apart herself. "What panties?"

Kalen looked down at her, his hands clenched into fists, as if he didn't trust himself to touch her. "I missed this." Then, his eyes intent, he used his fingertips to trace the narrow oval of her navel. Raven groaned as his hand drifted down to the trim dark curls below. "Does it hurt here, sweetheart?"

She arched her hips, trying to push herself against his palm. "There are a couple of places . . . Kalen . . ."

"Let me see you." He moved off the bed, and his big hands eased her legs apart. His voice dropped to a low rumble as his cheek brushed the inside of her thigh. "You tell me how this feels." Then he began to use his mouth and tongue on her.

Raven's hands curled into the coverlet as the sensations blasted through her, huge rolling waves of pleasure and need blended and roaring inside her. She couldn't take her eyes off him, couldn't resist the delicious thrill of seeing his eyes staring back at her as he ran his tongue up and down her, parting her and penetrating her, then retreating back to smooth, slow caresses that were too shallow to be anything more than teasing.

"Kalen, please."

He lifted his mouth from her. "Tell me, Sarah."

"I can't think, the way you're—ah," she gasped as his fingers exposed her clitoris and he gently blew on it. "That's the place."

"This pretty little thing, here?" he asked, and even the words acted like a caress. Then he swept his thumb over it, back and forth. "Does that hurt?"

"No." She pratically moaned the word as he increased the pressure. She'd forgotten how sensually demanding he could get in bed. "Kalen, please."

"Tell me exactly what you want. This?" He changed the caress to a teasing circle. "Do you like this?"

"Yes, but—"

"Not enough, not this time." He bent his head and moved his mouth over the tight, pulsing spot. "Do you want me to kiss you, like this?"

The firm texture of his lips inflicted even more torment, but when she tried to move against him, he held her hips down. "No—yes—Kalen, damn it!"

"I know what you need, sweetheart." He pressed one more, delicate kiss against her. "Are you ready for me?"

Her body hummed as her hands fisted, driving her nails into the coverlet. If she were any more ready, she'd explode. "Yes, yes, please, Kalen, oh, God—"

He settled his open mouth against her, and rubbed his tongue over her with firm, slow strokes. Raven pressed a fist against her mouth, muffling the sounds that erupted as he took her higher and higher, but what pushed her past the final limits of sanity was when he sank two fingers inside her.

Her first orgasm burst over her, sending her hurtling into that dark, secret place only Kalen had ever taken her to. He kept her there, working his mouth on her, demanding more, taking everything she had and pushing her back up to those dizzying waves of pleasure to a second climax, then a third.

"Kalen!" Her hands found his hair, and pulled. She couldn't stand it anymore, not alone. She dragged in enough breath to speak. "I need you, please, I need you inside me."

"Beautiful." He stood up and pulled his shirt up over his head. His gaze moved over her like another caress. "You're so beautiful when you come."

What he said, and the sight of his bare chest made her curl over and sit up. She had to touch him, had to get those clothes off him. Her hands shook as she tore at the button and zipper of his jeans. Then he pushed them and his shorts down, and kicked them away, while she curled her fingers around the rigid, thick shaft of his penis. She opened her mouth, wanting to taste him, to give him what he'd given her, but the first touch of her lips made him groan and push her back on the bed.

"That can wait." He eased between her shaking thighs, pressing the smooth, slick head against her. "This can't."

She lifted her hips, caressing him. "I've dreamed of this. Of you, moving inside me. Filling me up." She closed her eyes. "Then I'd wake up, alone."

"No more dreams. No more empty fantasies. Look at me, Sarah." When she did, he smiled down at her. "I want to see your eyes." He laced his fingers through hers, and shifted closer, pressing in. "Relax, sweetheart." He moved slowly, inching into her by slow degrees. "Let me in, yes, like that. That's it."

"Sorry." Raven shifted, biting her lip as she tried to accommodate him better. "Did you get bigger, or am I shrinking?"

"You're nervous." He went still and brushed her hair back from her face. The fact that he could control himself, even at this point, made her want to weep all over again. "I won't hurt you. I can stop right now if you want me to."

"You do and I *will* shoot you in the head." She lifted shaking hands to clutch at him, moving her hips to try to lodge him deeper. "Come inside me, Kalen. I don't want to be empty anymore. Now, please."

He pushed into her until their bodies met, then stayed buried inside her, his face tight, his hands hard on her hips. "God, you feel so good on me."

Raven was torn between watching his eyes and relishing the uniqueness of being with him in this most basic, satisfying way. In all the lonely years since they'd been together, she'd considered taking lovers. Yet she hadn't, mainly because she sensed that no one would ever be able to erase the memory of Kalen's touch.

And Kalen was the only man she'd ever loved. Would ever love.

He moved, stroking carefully in and out. As he thrust in, she used her inner muscles to return the intimate caress. It increased the heated, sweeping pleasure generated by the slow friction of their bodies, to the point that Kalen began to shake and groan.

"I wanted this to last," he muttered, bending down to kiss her as he pressed in, impossibly deep now.

"It's a short flight," she reminded him, panting against his mouth, rolling her hips under his. "Next time."

That seemed to snap whatever threads of control he had left, and he dragged her back, propping himself over her before he started moving again, thrusting in deep and fast, sending her over the edge again, pushing her higher and harder until there was no more coherent thought, there was only Kalen on her, inside her, all around her.

She linked her hands behind his head, her eyes intent on his, feeling him tense as his body hammered into hers. "Come to me, Kalen. Come to me, now, please—"

"Sarah." With a deep, tortured sound, he buried himself inside her and shuddered through his climax.

"Oh, God." She kissed his chin, his cheek, his mouth, breathless, laughing, crying as he held her close. "I missed you, love. I missed you."

Chapter 12

Six hours of driving in near-total silence had given Meko plenty of time to think. Sean had let her take the wheel an hour ago, but she had no intention of taking him to her father's house; Nine Dragon was the last place on earth she wanted to see.

What had she shouted, that afternoon in the garden? *If you do this, Father, I will never step one foot in this house again.*

Yet she didn't know where else to go. The Irishman had stayed alert, and kept the gun on her throughout the journey. Maintaining the minimum speed limit on the highway had prevented her from jumping out of the car. She was too frightened to try anything else.

I can't crash the car; I might kill us both. It's too early for anyone but drunks and street sweepers to be out. She glanced sideways at him. *He doesn't look like the type who would shoot an innocent bystander, anyway.*

"Have you got it all figured out yet, darlin'?" he asked without looking at her.

Meko focused on the road again. The Bay Bridge loomed ahead of them; her father's house was only a mile away. "If you let me go, I'll give you the address."

He chuckled. "You'll give me the address of a MacDonald's, and call the cops from a pay phone."

The fact that he could practically read her mind didn't improve Meko's mood. "Mr. Delaney, I'm tired. My house has been burglarized. You kidnapped me. I've driven all night to bring you somewhere I never wanted to see again. I've tolerated the gun, the shouting, the threats, and everything else, and I think I've been pretty reasonable about it." She adjusted her grip on the wheel. "However, if you call me darlin' or laugh at me again, I will drive this car into the first tree I spot. Is that understood?"

"Absolutely, ma'am."

"Thank you."

She drove across the bridge and into the heart of the city. It had been ten years since she'd lived here with her family, and she'd left a happy bride. Now she was returning as a kidnapping victim. Though there hadn't actually been a great deal of difference between the situations, this time she knew she was being held hostage to fate, the last time, she hadn't.

"Why did your father disown you?" Sean asked, startling her.

She cleared her throat. "I divorced my husband, moved out on my own, and started a business. My father found those three things completely unacceptable."

Sean made a humming sound. "Was he an old-fashioned man?"

"Does Barbara Bush like pearls?" She glanced in the rearview mirror, but the street behind them was empty. "You see, I was the first woman in the family ever to be educated in the United States. I won a full art scholarship and went to Berkeley."

"How did your father feel about that?"

"Since he didn't have to pay for it, he didn't care. What my father didn't know was that I also studied and applied to become an American citizen. He thought he could send me back to Japan whenever he wished. Like when I told him I was divorcing my husband." Her mouth curled. "When he found out what I'd done, he was very upset."

"Told you never to darken his door again, did he?"

"In his eyes, I was as good as dead." And she had very nearly felt like it, at the time. "Which should illustrate the state of our relationship, and why I couldn't possibly know anything about these swords."

Sean's voice changed, became more grim. "How close are we?"

Meko hadn't realized it, but they were only a few blocks from Nine Dragon now. What choice did she really have? There was no one left there; the Irishman couldn't hurt anyone but her. Besides, she knew the house, and he didn't—there were possibilities for escape there that she didn't have while driving the car. "It's just up ahead."

Takeshi Sayura had commissioned a team of Chinese architects and archaeologists to design and build his miniature palace in the style of one of the homes of Emperor Qianlong, complete with an exact reproduction of the famous Nine Dragon Screen.

"Your father had a fondness for big lizards?" Sean murmured as he took in the sixty-foot glazed-tile wall forming the front boundary of the estate. Yellow, white, blue, and purple dragons playing with pearls danced over two hundred and seventy hand-glazed tiles, protected from vandals behind a taller, wrought-iron security fence.

"My father wanted to be an emperor." Meko

pulled up to the security gate and punched in her old code. She didn't expect it to work, but the gate creaked as it swung open. "He was half Chinese. Maybe it was in the genes."

"There are more than nine dragons."

"There are nine important dragons. Nine, being the highest single-digit number, was a symbol of the emperor's supremacy. Dragons were always used as imperial symbols as well. The five other dragons along the borders represent my father's children." She glanced at the small blue dragon in one corner, curled and huddled away from the others, its body wrapped protectively around a bright white pearl. That had been *her* dragon.

"So you have four brothers? Sisters? Some of each?"

"Two living brothers." She drove the Mercedes up to the front of the house and parked it. "My sisters are both dead."

The damp, cold air of San Francisco made her shiver as she climbed out of the car. She had the spare key to her father's house on her key ring, and wished as she unlocked the front door that she had thrown it away years ago. But keeping it meant keeping one last connection to the family who had scorned her and to the brothers she was not permitted to see. Her father would have been gratified to see her using it to allow a criminal into his home.

You have always been an ungrateful, unnatural daughter to me. You bring no honor to my family, Kameko.

The inside foyer light was on, showing that the electricity to the house was still on. Meko started to wonder if her father had left someone to watch the house—the only person he would trust would be Xun, the gardener. But Xun had been an old, arthritic man ten years ago; he could be crippled or dead by now.

The dead bolt on the door clicked as Sean locked it, making her turn around. "Well?" She held out her hands. "We're here. What now?"

"You're going to show me where your father would have hidden the swords." Before she told him she didn't know, he held up his hand. "You know the house; you know your father. Guess."

She pursed her lips. "This way."

Meko led him to the back of the house, to her father's private room, and pushed open the intricately carved rosewood doors.

"What's this?"

She folded her arms. "My father used to receive visitors in here." When Sean gestured for her to go in before him, she sighed. "I don't want to go into this room."

"The sooner I find the swords, the sooner you can leave." He followed her as she stalked inside, then stopped behind her. "What's wrong?"

She turned in a slow circle on the marble floor, her eyes wide. "I didn't know my father had redecorated."

What had been a simply furnished reception room had been transformed into a completely unrecognizable chunk of seventeenth-century Chinese artistry.

"I don't believe it." She walked up a narrow ramp and climbed the three steps leading to an immense, elaborately worked chair. "This looks like . . ."

"Like what?" Sean prompted.

She trailed her fingers over one massive carved arm and stared down at the incense urns and bronze figures on the inlaid dais. "It's the Dragon Throne."

Sean began searching through one of the large cabinets lining one wall. "It seems like he took the idea of being the king of the castle a bit seriously."

"I didn't know he'd become this . . . obsessed." Meko looked up at the large characters etched over the throne. "It's the same. Purity and righteousness."

Sean abandoned his search and came to her. "What are you muttering about?"

"This isn't possible." She backed away, then bumped into a vertical tablet positioned at the right hand of the throne. When she saw the inscription, she almost screamed.

Sean took her arm. "What is it?"

She pointed to the tablet. "It says, 'The first step in adjusting the universe is to keep constantly in mind the shaping of one's own character.' "

"A fine sentiment."

"Yes. The emperor of China thought so." She shook her head, still dazed. "My father couldn't have pulled this off. They're national treasures." She saw Sean's blank look and sighed. "This—all this"—she gestured to the throne and the contents of the exquisitely decorated room—"looks exactly like Emperor Qianlong's throne room."

"And what did he do in the throne room?"

"The emperor held his levees, his birthday parties, and every other important celebration right here." She walked around the throne. "There would have been a cortege of household courtiers all around him, while those of inferior dignity and rank stood in the court below. When the emperor called on them, they would prostrate themselves, paying obeisance to him. This is the same room where Titsingh and Van Braam were banqueted by Qianlong in 1795. After that, no European ever entered that throne room until 1900."

Sean cocked a white brow at her. "It's an interesting history lesson, darlin', but it isn't helping me find what I came for."

She wanted to hit him. "Don't you get it? What if this is all real—the throne, the tablets, the art, everything?"

"Then I'd suggest that when we're done you call China and ask them if it's missing. You could get a nice reward for giving it back." He guided her away from the throne. "Now, show me where a man could hide three hundred swords in here."

Kalen eased away from Sarah, slipping from her body carefully so as not to wake her. He wanted to stay inside her, keeping her wrapped around him for the rest of the flight, but she was exhausted. He picked up his jeans, and the foil pack of condoms he'd tucked in his pocket fell out. He picked it up and studied it with a faint frown.

"You forgot to use those." She hadn't moved, but her eyes were open and watching him.

He wasn't sure if he wanted to have this conversation right now. Not while he was still warm and slick from making love to her. "Not exactly."

"Either you use them, or you don't. There's no middle of the road." She dragged the sheet around her and sat up. "You don't have to worry, I'm in great shape."

"I noticed."

She made a face. "I mean, I'm healthy. You won't get any weird disease from me."

He shoved the condoms back in his pocket and pulled on his shorts and jeans. "Go back to sleep. I'll wake you before we land."

She didn't lie back down. She dropped the sheet

and climbed off the bed, stepping between him and the closet-size bathroom.

"Whoa." Her hand landed in the center of his bare chest. "What is it? What did I do?"

"Nothing." He dragged in a breath and looked over her head. "I need to get cleaned up."

"You're disappointed." She snatched her hand away. "I know I'm a little tired. I'll be better next time."

He clenched his teeth. "You were fantastic. Making love to you demolished me."

"But you're disappointed—no, you're angry." She squinted up at him. "Why?"

"Because of this." He put his hand on her abdomen and splayed his fingers over it.

"I guess you don't want me to get my navel pierced, huh?"

"When did you plan to tell me, Sarah?" He rubbed his hand over her, over the child he suspected they'd made together. "Were you going to tell me at all?"

She stepped back, her movements careful. "Are you psychic?"

"Jesus." He laughed once. "Sarah, I'm your lover. I know your body better than you do. Your breasts are heavier, the veins on them are prominent, and you've got the beginnings of a pretty little belly going there."

"I am not showing yet," she told him with immense dignity.

"Add in all the vomiting and nausea, and an idiot could have figured it out." He eyed her again. "I'm the father."

She looked at the carpet under her feet. "There hasn't been anyone else."

He nodded, hiding his reaction. Knowing for sure

that it was his baby growing inside her made him want to drag her back to bed and make love to her all over again. But he wasn't in the clear just yet. "Then we get married."

"No."

He went over and took her by the shoulders. "Why not?"

Her eyes flashed. "You're just having a knee-jerk Catholic reaction. Get over it."

"It's our baby, Sarah, not a head cold. We're in this together, for life." He let go of her and went into the bathroom. Splashing cold water on his face didn't help chase off his temper. Neither did hearing her kick things around the room behind him. Yet when he came out, Raven and her clothes were gone.

If you yell at her again, she's going to bolt. Be calm. Be reasonable. And don't argue with her.

He found her out in the main cabin galley, calmly pouring two plastic cups of chilled bottled water. "We're not done talking about this."

"I am." She handed him a cup, then rummaged around in the cabinet under the counter. "Want some really expensive honey-roasted cashews? Or"—she pulled out a plastic-wrapped sandwich—"something pinkish on rye?"

She'd retreated behind her Raven facade again, but given the time frame he decided it was better to move on to the next phase of operations. He left her and went to place a couple of calls. Conor reported that Gemma was holding her own and requested permission to stay with her until she was out of critical condition.

"Have you got full security at the hospital?"

"Yeah, five guards at different points, and a couple of patrolmen running people through a metal detector in the main lobby." Conor sounded tired. "I'd feel better if I could watch her myself, though."

"Stay with her, then." He watched Sarah raid the cabinets and pile a small mountain of junk food on a tray before sitting down with it as far away from him as she could get. "I'm sending Raven back to Paris."

"Now?"

"Yeah. I'll check in with you later." He hung up the phone and saw her digging through her bag. "What do you need?"

"This." She produced a small jar of peanut butter and proceeded to dip a handmade French chocolate bonbon into it. She ate the conglomeration with relish, licking her fingers until she sighed. "It ain't Reese's Peanut Butter Cups, but it's close enough. Want some?"

"No." He wondered when she would progress to pickles and ice cream. "You're going to make yourself sick."

"I get sick every day anyway." She shrugged. "Might as well enjoy it."

He made two more phone calls before the pilot announced they were descending for the landing.

"We'll be in San Francisco in ten minutes, folks," he said over the intercom. "Skies are clear and it's a beautiful seventy-two degrees."

With a good-natured sigh, Raven disposed of her junk feast then sat down beside him and fastened her seat belt. "All right, look: once we bag the bad guys, we'll talk more about what we're going to do with this baby. I can find a place somewhere in the vicinity of the Pentagon."

"You're going back to Paris."

She shook her head. "I don't have to live in Paris full time. I've got some contracts to finish, but in about two months every photographer in the world is going to say 'Euuuuwww' when they look at me."

"What I mean is, you're leaving for Paris today. You're done working for me."

Meko helped Sean search the throne room, but they turned up nothing. Even the modern filing cabinet, concealed inside an antique Chinese version of a clothespress, revealed only dust and the beginnings of a cobweb.

"I'm tired, and I'm thirsty," she said as he slammed the last drawer closed. "May I go get something to drink?"

"I'll go with you."

Of course he would.

The kitchen proved bare of dishes and supplies, except for several forgotten gift bottles of liquor in one of the top cabinets and a chipped crystal vase under the sink. Ever practical, Meko rinsed it out, then filled it with water from the tap.

"Would you like some?" She held it out to Sean first.

"No, thank you." He watched her sip from the vase. "You're a polite little thing, aren't you?"

"This is the very first time I've ever been kidnapped, so I don't know exactly how I'm supposed to act." She leaned back against the counter and drank again before adding, "Would you prefer I swear and throw this vase at you? I think I could do that very well, too."

He laughed, but it was forced. "No, thank you, I'm not up to a fight." He gestured to the kitchen chair.

"Sit down, rest a bit. I'll have another look around."
He paused at the kitchen door. "You don't want to
be running out of here while I do."

"Mr. Delaney, you have the car keys, and I'm too
tired to run." She pillowed her head with an arm on
the table and closed her eyes. She waited until he
left, then silently rose and listened at the doorway.
She could hear his footsteps moving down the hall
toward the family bedrooms. "However, I can walk
just fine."

She tiptoed out of the kitchen, keeping to the sides
of the hardwood floor to avoid the squeak spots. She
made it all the way to the front door and breathed
a sigh of relief.

"You don't seem that tired to me," Sean said behind her. "Get your second wind, darlin'?"

Meko grabbed the doorknob, but he latched an
arm around her waist and dragged her up off her
feet. She struggled against his hold, twisting against
him and kicking his legs. "Put me down!"

Sean turned her around and propped her against
a wall instead. "You're not doing great things for my
confidence in you, Miss Sayura."

She closed her eyes. "I had to try."

"Don't do it again." Sean let her down on her feet,
then took her hand. "Come with me."

He dragged her along with him through the rest
of the house, room by room. Then he walked the
grounds outside, keeping her close with an arm
around her shoulders. They found nothing but a neglected garden and an empty garage.

"You see, they're not here," she said as he led her
back to the house and into the kitchen. "No swords.
Can I go now?"

"What other properties does your father own?" he asked as he opened the cabinet and searched through the bottles of liquor.

"In this country?" She frowned as he took down a large bottle of American whiskey. "I don't know. He had a home in Kyoto, and Tokyo, and a couple of office buildings in Hong Kong. Perhaps more now; as I've said repeatedly, we haven't spoken in years."

"He told you where the swords were." Sean opened the bottle and drank directly from it. "All you have to do is tell me, and you can go back to your life."

"I don't know where they are." She flinched as he sat down beside her, but all he did was offer her the bottle. "No, thank you. I don't drink alcohol."

"It's not alcohol, girl, it's liquid Irish magic." He took another, longer drink. "And drinking a little whiskey might loosen a few of those thousand knots you've tied yourself up in."

She turned toward the window and saw that the sun had just risen above the rooftops to the east. "I'd rather have coffee."

"I thought you Eastern ladies preferred tea."

"Stereotypical thinking, Mr. Delaney." She wagged a finger at him. "Like saying every Irishman is a drunk."

He toasted her with the bottle. "Oh, but every Irishman is."

The level in the bottle had gone down by a quarter already, and she wondered if he intended to get drunk. *I'm sitting in my father's house with a philosophical kidnapper who drinks whiskey at eight o'clock in the morning.* If she wasn't so worried about exactly what her father's letter had gotten her involved in, the situation would be almost ludicrous. She glanced at Sean, and for a moment she saw something terrible in his eyes.

"Maybe I should go look around again."

"Stop being so jumpy." Sean sighed. "We'll figure this out, the two of us."

"We're not in this together," she said, suddenly angry with herself for feeling sorry for him. "You're the criminal, I'm the victim. You're going to jail, I'm going to testify at your trial. People will feel sorry for me, not you. Do you know how difficult it is to get a good job when you've had a felony conviction?"

"There'll be no trial, and no testifying. They catch me, I go directly to jail." He drank again. "As well I should, for the rest of my life."

Now he had her totally confused. "You did this to me because you *want* to go jail?"

"I'm doing this for a beautiful lady who died right in front of me. Her name was T'ang Kuei-fei." He regarded her for a moment. "Did you know her?"

He's already half drunk. Meko shook her head.

"She died protecting the only thing that ever mattered to her. I promised her she'd be safe—that I'd keep her safe. I even stopped her from betraying the general." He laughed at himself and swallowed more whiskey before offering her the bottle again. "Are you sure you don't want a wee sip? You're looking very pale all of a sudden."

"Thank you, no." There was no way to make sense of what he was saying, but it seemed sensible to keep him talking. "This general is . . . someone you work for?"

"General Kalen By-the-Book Grady. He's in charge of domestic and international covert operations for the army. Sounds grand, doesn't he? Don't tell anyone that, by the way. It's all classified."

She tried to imagine the Irishman in the army. And failed. "So you did covert work for this man?"

"He's not a man, he's a machine. As cold-blooded a bastard as you'll ever meet—and yes, I worked for him." He wiped his mouth with the back of his hand. "He used me, used my nieces, all to lure T'ang along, to get him where he wanted him." He stared at the bottle. "Grady's the reason Kuei-fei died. Him and his obsession with T'ang and Shandian."

Meko was starting to make a little sense out of what he was telling her. "If this General Grady was responsible for the lady's death, then why are you working for him?"

"I'm not. I'm going to find the swords myself—the swords are the key to controlling Shandian. He knows it, and I know it." He leaned forward, his eyes filled with malice. "And when I have them, I'm going to throw them in a furnace and melt them down to nothing. Then we'll see how long the Almighty General Grady stays on the short list for the Joint Chiefs."

"Indeed." The random flares of ferocity frightened her, but it explained much as to why he was so driven. "Do you think after you melt them down and destroy the general's career, you'll be able to forgive yourself?"

He jerked back so fast he nearly fell over backward. "You don't know what you're talking about."

"Don't I? Seems very simple to me. You did promise Kuei-fei that you would keep her safe. You didn't keep your promise, Sean." She tilted her head. "That makes you equally responsible. What you're doing is an irrational response to your involvement in these crimes and your own guilt over her death."

He started to say something, then shook his head. "You're a perceptive girl."

"I told you, I'm not a girl." Feeling more sure of herself now that he was properly soused, she took the bottle away from him and went to the sink. Pouring out the rest of the whiskey gave her a great deal of satisfaction. "And you have had enough of this."

"What are you doing?" He staggered toward her, then watched the last of the whiskey disappear down the drain. "Fine, I'll just get me another bottle from your father's stash."

"No, you will not." It took all the nerve she had, but she stepped between him and the liquor cabinet. Then she took his hand. "You and I are going to leave this place. I'll take you wherever you want to go. You need help, Sean."

Like a child leading a blind man, she walked him out of the kitchen and toward the front of the house. He made no attempt to stop her, and even rubbed his thumb across the back of her hand.

An affectionate gesture, one that made her feel uneasy again. "I'd better drive again."

He stopped, but he didn't hand over the keys. "You have a lot of nerve for such a little girl."

"You don't." She glared up at him. "You won't find absolution in a bottle, no matter how many you drink." She thought of her father. "The only place to find it is inside your heart."

It happened so quickly that Meko didn't have time to defend herself. One moment Sean was staring down at their hands, the next he had lifted her up to his eye level.

"You think you know me? You don't know anything about me." He yanked her close. "I could do anything to you. I'm a dangerous man."

Somehow she managed to look amused. "You're drunk, Mr. Delaney. Now put me—"

The rest of the sentence was muffled as Sean covered her mouth with his.

He's kissing me.

Sean tasted of whiskey and anger, and something more desperate than both. Meko should have fought, should have hit him with her fists, kept her mouth clamped shut—something. But all she could think to do was hold on.

"Christ Jesus." He lifted his head. "You've got a sinful mouth."

"Don't—"

He kissed her again, moving with her, lowering her onto something covered with a dusty sheet, until she was under him and his weight was pressing her into the hard surface of the shrouded table. And it wasn't enough to hold on anymore, she was gripping his jacket like a drowning woman, unable to catch her breath, unable to think—

No. Not here. Not in this house.

She shoved him with all her strength, and Sean fell off the table. The thump he made when he hit the floor sent her scrambling to her feet. She had backed away nearly into the entrance hall when she realized he wasn't moving.

"You have the manners of a pig," she said in Japanese, then paused. No response. In English she said, "Did you hear me?"

Sean remained motionless, sprawled on his back where he'd fallen.

"Mr. Delaney?" She took a few steps forward. "Sean?"

He didn't move.

Meko cautiously approached, then saw his closed

eyes and slack, open mouth. "Oh, no." She knelt quickly and put her hand under his head. There was no blood, but a sizable lump was forming.

He muttered something, then his slow, even breathing turned into a faint snore.

Meko sat back on her heels. "The very first time a man kisses me properly in seven years, and I knock him unconscious. Well, he kidnapped me first."

She took the keys from his pocket and went out to the Mercedes. The cell phone she'd been unable to get to was in her glove compartment; she took it out and dialed 911. As the emergency operator answered, she glanced at the house, swore, and hit the End button.

He's not a criminal. She blew out a breath and redialed the number of the woman who had called her about the swords.

"Hello?"

"Hello, Ms. St. Charles? This is Kameko Sayura. You're not going to believe this, but I need your help." Quickly she relayed the details of her bizarre abduction. "Mr. Delaney mentioned the name T'ang; is he somehow connected with you or your husband?"

"Sean Delaney is a retired army colonel, but I think he's a little mixed up." Val sounded confused. "Miss Sayura—"

"Meko, please."

"Meko. My husband suggests, if you are willing, that we contact Colonel Delaney's superiors rather than the police. Given the nature of this operation he's involved in, it may be best to allow them to handle the situation from here." Val sounded sympathetic as she added, "I know you've been through quite an ordeal, but I'm sure the army will be happy to make whatever reparations you desire."

"I don't need anything. Mr. Delaney, on the other hand, needs medical treatment and perhaps some extensive therapy." She agreed to let Val contact the appropriate authorities, but told her she would stay with Sean until they arrived.

He might have a concussion, she told herself as she went back into the house. It was the right thing to do. Or would have been, had the man been lying where she'd left him.

But Sean Delaney wasn't there, or anywhere else in the house. He had completely vanished.

Chapter 13

Raven had already decided to railroad Kalen's plans when they touched down at the San Francisco Airport. She simply had to decide for which reason—kicking her off the operation, or deciding how to handle her pregnancy.

I'm fired, and we have to get married. She snorted. *We'll just see about that.*

"I can hear those little wheels inside your head spinning from over here," he told her. "The flight to Paris is standing by, waiting for you, and I'm putting you on the plane personally."

"You can't make me go."

"You're an AWOL army officer," he reminded her. "I can pretty much do anything to you that I want."

She took a piece of her hair in her fingers and studied the ends. "I'm a celebrity. All I have to do is scream, and reporters will come scurrying out of the woodwork. I see them eating up an exclusive on how the army's covert operations work."

He only smiled a little. "I'll shut down the airport."

"You wouldn't." Her head snapped up. "Damn it, Kalen, don't do this to me. Not now, not when we're this close to nailing him. I've wanted this for years."

"You've done your part. It's over."

She crossed one leg over the other and regarded him steadily. "I'm not marrying you, you know. As in never. Not if you were last breathing male on the planet, et cetera."

He didn't blink an eyelash. "We'll deal with that later."

"I mean it." She hated it when he gave her that poker face. "There is no way in hell I'm tying myself down to a man who thinks he can run my life however he chooses."

"Our baby needs two parents." He leaned forward. "A mother and a father."

"I can buy whatever Junior needs. In the twenty-four-karat gold model." She showed him some teeth. "And daddies aren't all that expensive. Not when Mommy looks like me."

That penetrated his calm for an instant, before he looked back at whatever report he was reading. "You keep right on thinking that way, sweetheart, if it makes you happy."

He figured he had her right under his thumb. The man's gall knew no boundaries. As she started to tell him that, the plane touched down smoothly on the runway, and other priorities took over.

Priority number one: I am not going back to Paris.

Her lack of success in evading Kalen at airports didn't bother her. So she was 2–0 with him on escape attempts. She would pretend to go along with his plan, to the point of getting on the Paris flight. All she had to do was find a way to get back off.

How secure are those baggage compartments, I wonder?

"Welcome to San Francisco, folks," the pilot announced in an oddly strained voice. "Uh, you may want to step to the front of the plane now."

"Trouble." Kalen got up at once, reaching for his briefcase. Before he could remove his service revolver, three very large Asian men entered the cabin. One of them was holding the pilot against him like a body shield. Another had a pistol jammed under the pilot's chin.

"You will come with us," the one with the gun said, in a beautifully polite voice, "or this man's brains will exit through the top of his head."

"I'll do whatever you say," Kalen replied. "Just let the woman and the pilot go."

The polite one smiled a little. "Our master wishes to see both of you. Now, out of the plane."

Raven used the opportunity to palm a small bottle and her stiletto from her carry-on and insert both up her sleeves. She had no chance to pass the knife to Kalen, however, for the third man pulled a gun and got between them as soon as Kalen moved forward.

"Sarah, I'm sorry. This is like Vladivostok all over again," Kalen called back to her.

"Oh sure, you say that now." Vladivostok had been the most successful operation they'd ever worked together, during which they'd used an outrageous diversion to retrieve a downed reconnaissance pilot in mid-transport. She instantly recalled the code phrases they'd used back then. "What's the point, Kalen?"

"For you, about six." He grunted as the man behind him prodded him in the back. "You get outside, you secure your bags and go quietly."

He wanted her to try to disable the man behind him, grab the pilot, and leave him behind. "Kalen—"

"I love you, Sarah."

That wasn't code for anything, but by then they were nearly at the bottom of the stairwell. She let the knife and the bottle drop from her sleeves into her hands, and caught his gaze when he glanced back at her. She gave him a single nod.

Kalen turned and stumbled.

Or appeared to stumble—he fell against the man in front of him, who was holding the gun, and sent him flying over the side of the stairs. The man between them whirled around.

"Hi, there." Raven sprayed him in the eyes with her perfume in one hand, and slashed the backs of his fingers holding the gun with her knife. "No touching the world-famous model, now."

He cried out, instinctively releasing the weapon and clutching at his face. She caught the gun and pushed past him, catching the pilot by the arm as Kalen shoved him toward her.

"Go!" he shouted, then knocked the third man down the stairs.

Raven looked into the pilot's face. "Hold on to me— we're jumping." Then she hauled him over the side of the stairs and fell four feet to the ground, rolling with the impact beneath the solid protection of the ramp.

Shots immediately rang out, but Raven used the cover of the plane to drag the pilot back behind the fuselage. She looked around wildly, then spotted a baggage handler driving a full luggage cart in their direction. The pilot saw it at the same time and took her arm as they ran for it. Bullets ricocheted off the tarmac all around them, but they jumped on the back of the cart, and Raven shouted for the driver to turn around and head for a nearby hangar.

"What are you doing?" the pilot shouted as she jumped off near an empty plane.

Raven shook her head and waved the cart driver off. "Go on, get out of here!"

She had to circle back to the plane again, keeping low and moving from cover to cover to remain undetected. The shooting had stopped, but a long black car had pulled directly onto the runway. As she came around the tail end of the plane, she heard Zhihan's voice.

"—you now, General Grady. Where is she?" When Kalen didn't respond, he barked out something in rapid Chinese, and she heard the sound of a gun striking flesh. She saw Kalen fall, and she nearly darted forward, until she saw the half dozen other men clustered around him and Zhihan. "Put him in the car."

She backed away, and scanned the immediate area. There was an empty utility truck, sitting three hundred yards away. It would have to do.

She moved carefully over to the passenger side of the truck, and climbed in as noiselessly as possible. It took her another minute to hot-wire the ignition and start the engine. By then, Zhihan's car was traveling at high speed toward the nearest exit.

"Oh, no, you don't." She put the truck in gear and jammed her foot down on the accelerator. "Hold on, Kal. Hold on."

"Already hard at work?" Val brought her husband's morning tray into his study, where she suspected it would sit neglected until he finished whatever new computer schematic he was working on. "Is that the file Raven transmitted to you?"

"Yes. I've been checking the Dai's financial records against the data Colonel Delaney provided her." He absently reached for his tea and sat back for a moment. "Still no sign of Sean in San Francisco?"

"No. Kameko called me from her hotel. It's as if

he disappeared into thin air." Val frowned as she studied the screen. "That's an odd entry." She pointed to a cluster of double figures that broke the regularity of the column.

"Yes, it seems the Dai is keeping two sets of books, like any accomplished criminal."

"No, I mean, the figures themselves—don't they seem a bit strange?" Val leaned over and highlighted one double entry, then cut and pasted it into a separate window. "Look at this one—2,500,005, and 5,000,052. They're mirrors of each other." She highlighted another, similar entry and moved it. "And these two: 1,000,005, and 5,000,001." She studied the others. "It can't be coincidental; the first series of numbers all end in five, and the second all begin with five."

"Unusual, but each entry has different businesses listed as accounting references. The dispersal coding is disparate as well, some reference accounts payable, accounts receivable, overhead, housekeeping. . . ." Jian-Shan put his cup aside and stared at the screen. "Sayura Enterprises, 3,000,005 and 5,000,003. Dated the week Takeshi died."

"How much would an assassin want to kill an important man like Sayura?" Val asked softly.

"The going rate for a professional hit would be about three hundred thousand in U.S. dollars." Jian-Shan began separating all the entries. "Quon Food Service, Bao-De Dry Cleaning, Ming Hoa Restaurants. All within the last year."

She made a soft sound of regret. "If the owners or someone else important involved in all those businesses was killed around the same time—"

"—then we have the evidence to prove an assassin was hired. I think I understand the fives, too—five is a symbol in Chinese mythology. It represents the halfway point between earth and heaven."

"If I remember correctly, all respectable assassins ask for half of their fee up front and the other half upon completion of the kill." Val sounded sick. "Jian, why didn't Kalen's people recognize this? We're no experts, and we figured it out."

"I don't know. What concerns me now is this." He brought up one of the last double entries, indicating that more than two million dollars had been paid. Two business names were listed beside the entry, which had been coded as housekeeping. "The Sing Gardens and Leong Factories. They can only be business fronts for the On Leong and Hip Sing tongs."

"Kalen said Zhihan had been called to some kind of summit meeting in San Francisco—to meet with leaders from both of those tongs."

"Not to meet them," Jian said, reaching for the phone as it rang. "To execute them." He lifted the receiver to his ear. "Hello?"

They won't kill him right away. They'll interrogate him first, maybe keep him alive for barter.

Staying three cars back was risky, but she couldn't take the chance of their discovering she was shadowing them. It took all her control not to speed up and ram the back of the black car, too. Only the knowledge that Kalen might still be unconscious and the number of thugs Zhihan had with him kept her from taking the chance. The fact that the only weapon she had on her was a knife didn't help, either.

I'm right behind you, love. Hang on.

She followed the car into the narrow streets of Chinatown, where vendors were already setting up sidewalk tables of colorful goods to sell to passing tourists. She wondered just how deeply the Dai had spread his tentacles over this portion of the city—lookouts could be posted anywhere. Luckily, the truck she'd stolen was unmarked, and no one seemed to be paying attention to her.

"All right, boys," she muttered under her breath. "Where are you taking my kid's father now?"

They left the merchant rows and moved into the older sections, where most of the immigrant population lived. Here there were fewer cars for Raven to hide behind, so she was forced to drop back even further. She hissed as Zhihan's car took an unexpected turn and disappeared.

"Damn it." She sped up. "I'm not losing you."

At first it appeared as if she had. Wind chimes hanging from second-story casements tinkled gently as she inched past each building, looking down the side streets for Zhihan's car. Then she heard the sound of an automatic door creaking and turned her head to see a huge garage door closing, and in the rapidly narrowing gap, the taillights of the black car.

"Gotcha."

She drove past the old warehouse and parked two blocks away, then checked the area. Most of the buildings were old and utilitarian, seemingly warehouses and small factories. There was a noticeable absence of traffic, and no one appeared to be on the streets at all. A search of the interior of the truck turned up a Forty-Niners baseball cap and a dark blue windbreaker.

"Great." She rolled her hair up and tucked it under the cap, then put on the jacket. "All I need now is a gun." Unfortunately, there were no weapons to be had—she would have to rely on her knife, and her wits.

Carefully she moved down the street, sticking close to the buildings while trying to walk as normally as possible. Diagonally across from Zhihan's warehouse stood an abandoned gas station, and on the side of the boarded-up building was a pay phone.

"Please, don't be out of order," she muttered as she went around the back of the station. Again, luck was with her; she picked up the phone and heard a dial tone. "Yes."

The first number she dialed was the secure emergency line Kalen had given her. Hyatt answered at once.

"Hyatt, this is Raven. Where are you?"

"We just got in, we're having breakfast over on the wharf," he said. "Major, what's wrong?"

"We've got problems." Quickly she relayed the details of everything that had happened since they'd left the plane and then gave the address of the warehouse. "I need an extraction team here ASAP."

"I'll get on it immediately. Hold for Captain Oliver."

There was a pause, then Brooke asked, "Are you staying at your present location, Major?"

"Of course I am." Raven could have screamed the words. "I'm not moving an inch until we get him out."

"Good. We'll be there in ten minutes. Don't do anything until we arrive." The captain hung up.

"You're welcome," Raven said and slammed down the phone.

Ten minutes seemed like an eternity. She didn't dare approach the building, not alone and unarmed. Instead, she sat down beside the phone and leaned her head back against the building. "This is going to blow the entire operation, and he's really going to be pissed off at me."

Once the extraction team went in, the only thing they could arrest the Dai and his men for was kidnapping, which could be easily beaten in court. She could hear the expensive lawyer arguing now, claiming that Kalen and Raven had commandeered the Dai's private chartered flight. Finding any evidence to link Zhihan directly to the murders was as unlikely as getting a snow cone in hell. Unless—

She got to her feet and used the phone to call Jian-Shan in New Orleans. "Jay? It's Raven."

"Raven, thank God. Where are you?"

"In San Francisco. In a whole bunch of trouble." Raven looked across the street at the warehouse building. "We were ambushed at the airport. I got away, but the tong heads have Kalen. I need to know before we move in, did you find any evidence on that database?"

"Are you alone?" he asked.

"Yes, why?"

"You need to know something first."

Raven listened as Jian-Shan described the odd bookkeeping entries, and her heart constricted as the implication set in. "Then Zhihan is the Lotus."

"We can't be sure yet, but it appears so." Jian-Shan sounded grim. "Raven, who examined these computer files before me?"

"Hyatt." She closed her eyes for a moment. "Oh, God, and I just told him everything. I've got to warn Brooke. Jay, stick by the phone, all right? I'll talk to you soon. 'Bye." She hung up, and tried to think of what to do.

"Major Sarah Jane Ravenowitz?"

A plainclothes CID agent stood on either side of her, both holding weapons.

Raven heaved a sigh of relief as she saw Brooke appear behind them. "Yes, and boy, am I glad to see you guys." She looked around them. "Where's Hyatt? Where's the rest of the extraction team?"

"Major Ravenowitz," the taller one said as his partner grabbed her arms and cuffed her wrists. "I'm placing you under arrest for violation of punitive articles eighty-five and eighty-six of the Uniform Code of Military Justice, and for conspiracy to kidnap and unlawfully detain a superior officer. You have the right to remain silent and the right to seek counsel."

"Kidnap?" She looked from the agent to Brooke. "What?"

"Hyatt spoke to the general five minutes before you called," the captain told her. "Nice try."

"What are you talking about?" She lunged, but the cuffs were tight, and so were the hands holding her. "Kalen is over there, in that warehouse. Hyatt is the traitor."

"No, that would be you, Major." Brooke turned away. "Get her out of here."

Kalen regained consciousness in the car, but forced himself to remain still and lifeless in order to listen to the orders Zhihan was giving his men.

"This one is a general," he was saying, "so the body cannot be found. Is that clear?"

"We can dispose of him in the bay," one suggested. "But what about the woman?"

Zhihan made a disgusted sound. "I will have her soon enough."

No, you won't, Kalen thought as they dragged him out of the car. Remaining limp took some effort, especially when he was dumped onto a cold concrete floor and kicked in the ribs.

"Give it to me," Zhihan said.

He didn't have time to brace himself for the wave of cold water that hit him in the face, or the brutal hands that jerked him to his knees. As he coughed, someone grabbed him by the hair and yanked his head up.

"Good morning, General Grady." The Dai's son wiped his hands with a silk handkerchief. "I was quite surprised to learn who you are. A man of your rank, working as a field agent? Is there a shortage of army personnel these days?"

Kalen said nothing.

"You are not very friendly, are you? That will change." Zhihan nodded to the men holding him, and they dragged him up onto a hard-backed chair. "The word on the street is you have been quite ruthless in your persecution of my people."

Kalen grunted as one of the men looped a rope around him and pulled it tight to pin his arms at his sides.

"Still nothing to say? How unfortunate." Zhihan turned as another hireling rushed up to him with a cell phone, and relayed some information too quickly for Kalen to follow. "Ah, excellent. We have visitors, across the street. It seems your friend Raven has been arrested."

That made him speak before he thought. "You're full of shit."

"No, boss, I'm afraid he's not." Hyatt walked in, with Brooke at gunpoint. "It's amazing what a jealous woman will believe—Captain Oliver here's been so determined to nail Raven that she's completely lost her edge."

Brooke turned and spit in Hyatt's face. "You weasel."

"That's not very nice." Hyatt backhanded the blonde across the jaw with his gun, sending her to the floor. "Tie her up with him."

Kalen never took his eyes off Hyatt. "You're good, Smith. I never suspected it was you."

"Why would you? Guys like me are invisible." The computer programmer grinned. "Which is why we end up spending our golden years as millionaires in the tropics."

Zhihan's men tied Brooke to another chair and set her back to back with Kalen.

"You couldn't have sent in the second team on the temple raid," Kalen said. "You were just a clerk back then."

"A clerk in resource management." Hyatt chuckled.

"You bought yourself a life sentence in Leavenworth," Brooke said, spitting out blood.

"No, actually, once we're all through here, I'm headed back to D.C. You two will end up as missing-person reports, and no one will ever know I was responsible." He smiled at Kalen. "Well, Raven will probably figure it out, but who's going to believe a deserter?" He lifted his gun, leveling it at Kalen's head. "Anything you want to say to the boss before I blow his brains out, Cap?"

"No," Zhihan said, holding up a hand. "My men will interrogate them first, then they will deal with them."

Kalen grunted. "Why not do the job yourself, like you did with Gangi and Portia?"

Zhihan strode over and slammed his fist into Kalen's face.

"You are not fit to say his name. I loved my

brother, and whoever killed him will suffer a long, long time before they die."

"Didn't you know?" Kalen would have laughed, but his mouth hurt too much. "You hired the same assassin who killed your brother. He left a lotus there, right next to Portia's body."

"You lie."

"Look at the photos of the crime scene yourself," he told him. "They're still in my briefcase."

Zhihan hit him again, shouting something, and Kalen blacked out.

"Major."

Raven held out her hands for the MP to remove her handcuffs. "Is the base commander in there?" She nodded toward the hearing room.

"The CO, and every high-ranking bird in the vicinity." The officer eyed her. "What did you do, try to kidnap Colin Powell?"

"No, that's next week." She straightened the uniform jacket she'd gotten from supply, and tucked her hat under her arm. "How do I look?"

"Like the mini poster inside my locker back at the squad room." The MP opened the door to the room and stood sideways. "Major Ravenowitz, sir."

Raven strode in, stopped ten feet from the long conference table, and stood at attention. "Major Sarah Ravenowitz, reporting as ordered, sir."

"At ease, Major." General Eckard gave her a sour look. "Nice of you to visit us after so long a vacation. Get bored sunning yourself on European beaches?"

Besides the general, there were four colonels and half a dozen lower-ranking officers sitting at the table. None of them looked happy. An enlisted man stood up as a court reporter began typing.

"This special hearing is convened at Oakland Army Base temporary field command unit, Oakland, California, pursuant to Court-Martial Convening Order number oh-nine-seven-three, this headquarters, dated March fifteenth, for the arraignment of Ravenowitz, Sarah J., Major, United States Army, Central Intelligence Division."

Sarah took a deep breath. *Here we go.*

"Major Sarah Jane Ravenowitz, assigned to Third Special Battery, Field Agent CID Division, Washington, D.C., did in the country of China, on or about 8 December 1995, without authority leave her place of duty with intent to remain away therefrom permanently."

It sounds really grim when he says it like that. And a cold chill ran down her spine as she finally realized what she had to do. *It's his life. I can't save it any other way.*

"This emergency session is being held before Military Judge William T. Eckard, General, Seventeenth Battalion, Pacific Coast Division, and a convened committee of adjunct officers assigned to the Inspector General's Office, Pacific Coast Division. By order of General Eckard, this hearing is now convened."

Every gaze in the room was fixed on her, and Raven wouldn't have been surprised to see someone toss a noose up over one of the old ceiling beams.

"I'd really like to know, first of all, what you're doing in this country, Major. Seeing as you've avoided it, and extradition to it, for seven years. But we'll save that for the court-martial."

Keeping her expression blank, she stared past them at the American and Corps flags displayed on the wall. "Permission to speak freely, sir?"

Eckard templed his fingers. "This is a hearing,

Major, not an opportunity for you to protest your highly unlikely innocence. The only reason we convened was the serious nature of your allegations and the incident report you made regarding General Grady. Which I would like you to now repeat for the entire committee."

"Yes, sir. General Grady was abducted by armed Chinese nationals in the employ of Dai Zhihan, the son of Dai Ruiban, a well-known international crime figure and tong leader, at oh-seven-hundred hours from the San Francisco Airport."

"Have we confirmed this?" one of the colonels asked.

"Working on it, sir," a major replied.

Raven waited for a moment, then went on. "General Grady's last known location was the warehouse in Chinatown, which I reported to my arresting officers." She made eye contact with the general. "Sir, I don't know if he's still alive, but if you don't send an extraction team in there right now, he will be killed."

"Excuse me, sir," one of the colonels said, "but this officer has been an AWOL deserter for nearly eight years. She's also been accused of collaborating with these same Chinese nationals. Now she's caught and presents this sudden dramatic plea. I have to question her motives, at the very least."

"My team was killed and I was left for dead in China seven years ago, Colonel. Until recently, I believed that the army was responsible for that. However, I have never worked for the Chinese. In any case, it doesn't matter—*I* don't matter. We have to get General Grady to safety, now."

"We?" Eckard's brows rose. "Young woman, the only place you're going is back to the stockade to await trial."

"That's the other reason I'm here, sir." Raven took a deep breath. "I know the man who abducted the general, and what he plans to do with him. I want to lead the extraction team in to get him."

A few of the officers chuckled, until the general waved a hand. "And why in God's name would I allow you to do that, Major?"

"Because if you do, I will voluntarily sign a statement confessing to all the charges being brought against me. I will also plead no contest at my court-martial." She saw his eyes narrow. "I'm not bluffing, sir. If you have the statement prepared at once, I'll sign it before I go."

"You realize that in doing so, you're sentencing yourself to a minimum of twenty-five years in prison."

She nodded. Her freedom for Kalen's life. A pretty decent trade.

One of the officers picked up a folder. "We have excellent evidence against you, Major. We don't need a confession."

"With all due respect, sir, I may be a deserter, but I'm also an international celebrity, and I command instant attention from the media. I could demonstrate that, but I don't think the army needs the expense or the embarrassment of a highly-publicized trial. Do you?"

"Blackmail pisses me off, Major," the general said. "That's what I think."

"I don't like it either, sir." She scanned the faces behind the table. "But obviously, this is not for my benefit. This is for General Grady."

"Hmmm." Eckard considered that. "Tell me something, Major. Precisely what is the nature of your relationship with the general?"

"General Grady was my supervisor when I worked for the CID. He also risked his own life to save a pilot and myself at the airport." *He's the man I love, the father of my child, and if you don't do this, I will go crazy.* "General Eckard, do you know Kalen Grady?"

He nodded slowly. "I have worked with him on several occasions in the past, Major."

"Then you know what kind of man he is, and why the army can't afford to lose him." She lifted her chin. "Whatever it takes, we have to get him back. If you don't send me, you're wasting your best chance to get him out alive."

"Very well, Major." Eckard gestured to the bailiff. "I will release you into the custody of the senior field agent for the CID. You may lead the extraction effort to retrieve the general."

The knot in her stomach loosened a notch. "Thank you, sir. You won't regret this."

"I already do." The general waved a hand at her. "But let me be clear about one thing, Major. Those agents going in with you will have standing orders from me. If you try to desert again in the middle of this operation, you will be shot on sight."

Chapter 14

"What have you gotten yourself into now, Stretch?"

Raven looked up from the vest she was preparing and grinned. "Conor, you're supposed to be in Chicago!"

"I got a real bad feeling last night and decided to jump on a plane." He picked up an assault rifle and checked the load. "From what I've been told, this has turned into a total fubar."

"Not yet." She pulled on the vest, zipped up the front, then tested the cable clips. "I'm going to get him out."

"Need a demo man?"

"As long as he's you." She picked up another vest and tossed it at him. "Suit up."

While Conor changed and strapped on the gear, Raven checked and rechecked her lines, then coiled them and clipped the bundle to her belt.

"I heard you drove a hard bargain with the CO to get this command," Conor said casually. "What did you promise them?"

"Autographed eight-by-ten glossies." She handed him an extra clip. "Why, do you want one?"

He shook his head. "Whatever it was, Kalen isn't going to like it."

"Let's concentrate on saving Kalen's life, okay?"

The rest of the team were already waiting in the briefing room when she and Conor emerged.

"Lights." She waited for the sergeant at the back to switch them off, then turned to the projector screen. "These are the floor plans for the warehouse. We've got north and south access hatches, and an atrium." She tapped a larger square in the center of the roof. "Bravo team goes in first, takes defense positions along this gallery. Charlie team enters through the back and takes out the electrical room. Once you've doused the lights, Alpha and I will enter through the atrium, we converge and move in."

"What's the retrieval protocol?" one of the men asked.

"First team to find the general pulls out. Getting him to safety is everyone's top priority. Thank you, Sergeant," she said, and the lights came back on. "Any other questions?"

One of the younger men lifted a hand. "Major, do we know how many hostiles are inside?"

"Fifteen confirmed. I'd estimate twenty, thirty more." She moved around the desk and perched on the edge of it. "Remember these men are armed, street-trained, and highly unpredictable. Use whatever force is necessary to protect the general." She nodded as another sergeant hovered at the doorway. He came up and handed her a short note, which she read. "New intel indicates that Captain Brooke Oliver and Lieutenant Hyatt Smith may also be on premises. One or both of them may be working with the Chinese, so approach with caution." She looked around the room. "Take a minute to test your remotes and check your gear. We're moving in ten. Conor, you're with me."

As she led him to the ordnance supply room, Raven ticked off the items she needed: C-4 plastic explosive, digital detonators, remote triggers, smoke grenades. Then she caught him staring at her. "What's wrong?"

"I've been watching you put on lipstick and designer clothes for the last week," he said. "It's a little disconcerting to see how easily you can take command of a strike unit."

"You should see me run a press conference." She pulled a carry bag from the shelf and began filling it with the ordnance. "In a swimsuit made out of scallop shells, no less."

Conor's hand touched her shoulder. "He's still alive, Stretch."

"I know. I think I'd feel it if—" She couldn't complete the thought. She wouldn't. "Conor, this is probably going to get really ugly. Whatever happens—whatever goes down—promise me you'll get Kalen out alive."

"I will, if I can." He picked up an extra block of C-4 and stuffed it in the bag. "Then he's going to shoot me for letting you do this. You know that."

"One more thing—if I don't make it out, you tell him I love him, I've always loved him, and I would have married him. And that I'm sorry for everything." Tears stung her eyes, but she blinked them back. "Would you do that for me?"

"Yeah," he said softly. "I will."

Sean eased back from the warehouse window and rubbed the lump on the back of his head. Kameko might have looked like a little china doll, but she nearly cracked his head open.

That's what I get for kissing a sinful mouth.

He'd accessed his network of informants as soon as he'd slipped away and left her at Nine Dragon House; he discovered his old boss had been taken from the airport. The anger he'd felt had twisted into something else, thanks to Sayura's daughter, and he found himself moving in on the Dai's warehouse, a half-baked rescue attempt forming in his head.

I'll get him out, then I'll beat the hell out him, he promised himself. *The question is, how do I get him out?*

Zhihan's men were well distributed throughout the building. They were also well armed. He'd caught a glimpse of Kalen and a blond woman at one of the windows, but had to move when a guard inside decided to stand and look out at the same spot.

He studied the abandoned gas station across the street. *I wonder if they dug out the tanks or left them.*

"Hello, Irish." A feminine hand patted his cheek, and he whirled around to find Raven standing behind him. "Slumming?"

"Not as much as you, girl." He hugged her. "I suppose you've come to rescue the rock-headed bastard."

"I love the rock-headed bastard, and I've brought friends." She turned and gave a hand signal, and a familiar-looking man stepped out of the shadows. "You know Conor?"

"We've tipped a few together." He nodded at Perry. "How many friends?"

"Twelve, split three ways. I'm headed up top." Raven nodded toward the roof, then looked at the gas station across the street. "You thinking what I'm thinking?"

"If they're there, yeah, I am."

"Good." She shrugged out of her backpack. "Then here's what I want you and Con to do."

"More cars," Brooke whispered.

Kalen forced his swollen eyes to open. The beating he'd taken hadn't broken any bones, but it had been severe enough that his jaw exploded with pain as he spoke. "How many?"

"Three. Close together."

He tugged against the rope again, as he had at regular intervals for the last two hours. Brooke's fingers brushed, then clutched at his. "It's all right, Captain. We're getting out of here." He didn't tell her they'd probably be leaving in body bags.

"Sir, I—I need to apologize." They had beaten her, too, and her voice sounded muffled and thick. "Hyatt was right, you know. I got jealous of her, and it blinded me. I'm the reason we're in this mess now."

"It's all right, Brooke." He squeezed her fingers. "He fooled all of us."

"No, you don't understand. I only wanted—but, we're going to die here, because of me." She coughed, a liquid sound. "I wish Conor was around. He'd think of something funny to say." She let go of him and stiffened. "Men, getting out of the cars. Two old guys, and seven thugs."

The tong leaders and their bodyguards.

He strained against the rope and felt something give a little. By craning his neck, he was able to see the weak spot, created by sawing the rope back and forth over an exposed screw in the frame. Because they had used the same rope to tie Brooke to him, she could also exert force on it.

"Captain, start rocking your chair."

Bits of hemp snarled as they rocked and worked the rope over the screw. The motion also caused the rope to cut into Kalen's arms, but he ignored the trickles of blood. Once the tong leaders were dead, he suspected the Lotus would come down to finish them off.

He heard a soft thud overhead, and he lifted his gaze to the cloudy glass atrium at the top of the warehouse. Silent, black-garbed masked figures were dropping from it, suspended by heavy-duty cables.

"Check your twelve," he said to Brooke as two of Zhihan's men came out of the warehouse office toward them.

He felt Brooke's head fall back, then turn. "Oh, shit."

"You ready to talk?" one of the men asked, rubbing his bruised knuckles as his companion went around to face Brooke. "Or you want to bleed on me some more?"

A moment later, a figure dropped on top of the man in front of him, knocking him to the concrete floor. A swift blow to the back of the head rendered him unconscious. Behind him, he heard the thug utter a short cry before something heavy hit the ground. Then the figure straightened and pulled out a knife.

He knew who it was before she cut him free. "What the hell are you doing here?"

"I'd say I'm glad to see you, too, sweetheart"— Raven's eyes crinkled as she bent and skimmed a fingertip over his bloodied mouth—"but Christ, you're a mess." As soon as he stood, she slapped a pistol in his hand. "Here. And don't shoot anyone in black with it."

He checked the load. "You brought backup?"

"*Beaucoup* backup." She exchanged a look with the other agent, who was helping Brooke to her feet. "Captain, you okay?"

"Couple of broken ribs." Brooke gasped, but managed to stay upright. "But I can walk."

"Good, take her out through the back," Kalen told the other agent, then nodded toward the warehouse office. "Zhihan and the other tong leaders are in there. So is the Lotus."

"The Dai hired him to kill them." Raven checked her watch. "And we've got about ten seconds to get to that door before all hell breaks loose."

They ran together across the warehouse. Above them, the extraction team began dropping down from the gallery, blocking and disabling every man who tried to stop them. When they reached the door, Raven motioned him to one side.

"Wait, some of them are going to be coming out of there in"—she looked at her watch again—"five, four, three, two, one—"

An enormous blast exploded outside, shaking the entire building and shattering windows on three sides. Broken glass rained down like deadly hail.

Kalen motioned her to go flat against the wall beside the doorframe, then caught the door as it swung outward. He tripped the first man rushing out, watched the second one sprawl over him, then used the door itself to knock out the third. Raven pulled two more out and rammed their heads into the wall before nodding to him.

They went in side by side, weapons drawn and ready.

"Drop your guns. Hands where I can see them." Kalen quickly circled the table and got behind the eldest man, whom he recognized as the leader of the Hip Sing tong. "Right now, gentlemen."

Raven swiftly collected the weapons from the bodyguards, keeping her back to the wall. Kalen watched Zhihan, who stood behind his father at the head of the table.

"Forgive this intrusion," Ruiban said to the other men in Chinese, as if Kalen and Raven were mere annoyances. "My son has much to learn about the cunning of our enemies." He gestured toward a corner, where Kalen saw a beautiful black woman in a scarlet kimono standing with a tray of teacups. "But the Lotus is an excellent teacher."

Alake bowed slightly. "Thank you, Master Dai." As she straightened, she pulled a gun with a silencer out from under the tray, and fired it at Kalen.

"No!" Raven screamed, lifting and firing her own weapon at the Nigerian.

Kalen reeled back, but stayed on his feet. When she looked at him, she saw that Alake's bullet had hit him in the left bicep.

"She was the Lotus," Zhihan said, almost as if he wasn't sure. "She killed Gangi."

Alake choked something out, then clutched her abdomen and fell to the floor. A slow-spreading pool of blood seeped out from under her.

Raven looked down at the gun Zhihan still held pointed at Alake, then back at Kalen. "Are you all right?"

"Yeah." The lights abruptly went out, and there was a scuffling sound as several men tried to rush for the door. Several shots rang out over their heads. "Get down, Sarah!"

Total confusion reigned for several minutes, until
the lights came back on. Raven had two bodyguards
on the floor, her weapon poised at the head of one,
her boot on the neck of the other. The remaining
bodyguards and the two tong leaders sat cowering.

Armed agents poured into the room. "We've secured the building, Major," one of them told her.
"But two of the men escaped."

"That would be Zhihan and his father." Raven
moved slowly over to Kalen and checked his arm.
"You sure you're okay?"

"I'm fine." He walked with her to look at Alake's
body. The scarlet kimono she wore was embroidered
with delicate, pink-tipped lotuses.

Raven stared down at her. "That was a surprise."

"Tell me about it." He knelt down and examined
Alake's back. "You've got hollow-tipped rounds
loaded, right?"

"Yeah, so do you." Raven eyed the small hole.
"Which means that exit wound should be a lot
bigger."

"It would be, but neither of us killed her." He
stood up and flexed his arm. "Zhihan did."

Sean watched the flames and black smoke bil-
lowing up from the remains of the abandoned gas
station's underground storage tanks with some satisfaction. "Now that was grand work, boyo."

Conor Perry wiped some soot from his face onto
his sleeve. "Next time, give me more than thirty seconds to clear the area."

"You youngsters are wimps. Why, when I was in
Kuwait with the RA, we had to cap off this oil well—"
Sean halted his story as he saw Raven and Kalen

walking toward him. "Excuse me, Conor. I have business to attend to."

Someone had given the general a vicious beating, judging by the condition of his face, and a hole in his arm, judging by the bloodstained sleeve. Sean permitted himself a small moment of pleasure in those facts before he met Kalen's swollen, blackened eyes. "General."

"Colonel." Kalen turned to Raven. "Would you and Conor excuse us for a moment?"

Raven hesitated, then took Conor by the arm. "Come on, Perry, I'll tell you all about the fun you missed." As they walked away, she added over her shoulder, "Thank you for the explosion, Irish."

"You're welcome, darlin'." He took out a cigarette and lit it, then offered one to Kalen, who shook his head. "Did you find the swords?"

"No." Kalen glanced back at the warehouse. "The Dai and his son escaped, and presumably took the collection with them."

"Shame. I've been thinking what a nice footstool I could make myself, after I melted those fuckers down." He took a drag off the cigarette, then blew the smoke out in rings. "Won't get my chance now, I'm guessing."

"You've been AWOL for weeks." Kalen regarded him steadily. "And you walked with only one day left before your retirement date. Why?"

"Kuei-fei. I stopped her from giving you over to T'ang. Then I watched her die. I blamed you for that, General. In some ways, I still do." He dropped the cigarette and ground it out under his heel. "But I'll be taking the bulk of the blame for her from now on."

"You report back to Washington and sign those retirement papers. I'll drop the other charges against you." Kalen held out his hand. "You're a good man, Sean. I'm going to miss having you on the team."

"You're a damn good liar." He shook his hand. "Take care of yourself, General. And look after young Raven for me."

Sean turned and walked back toward the heart of Chinatown, and in the face of every woman he passed he saw only Kameko Sayura's mysterious dark eyes.

"The government has done our work for us," the Dai said with immense satisfaction as Zhihan drove down the coastal road. "With both leaders arrested and being charged, we can move to take over the other tongs and create the triad as it was meant to be."

"Gangi didn't want to control the other tongs, did he, Father?" Zhihan asked as he stared at the road ahead.

"Your brother and I disagreed about how to proceed with our plans. Gangi did not have the wisdom or insight as to how to manage our business. I do not like to speak ill of the dead, but your brother was weak, and often easily distracted by his pursuit of pleasure." The Dai sighed. "Not like you, my son."

"No, not like me at all." Zhihan increased speed as the road extended up the side of one sheer granite cliff. "You always said I should have been born first."

"It would have more convenient. But we must not dishonor your brother's memory with such talk." The old man looked out his window at the ocean below, crashing into the shoals. "You should slow down, my son. This section of the road is very hazardous."

"So are other things, Father." Zhihan gripped the wheel until his knuckles turned white. "Like hiring the Lotus to assassinate my brother. Because it was convenient."

The Dai was silent for several moments. "You are as wise as you are strong, my son. Do not let emotion make you forget your duty to me, and your family."

"Gangi was my family." Now Zhihan looked at his father, and the seething hatred inside him spilled into his voice. "And you had him murdered."

"Foolish boy, you never knew what your brother had planned." Ruiban made a cutting gesture. "Gangi went to that embassy to meet with General Grady. He planned to give him the swords, and evidence against me. I could not allow that to happen."

"So you gave him to the Lotus." Zhihan watched the orange speedometer needle creep past seventy. He slowly took one hand off the wheel and reached into his pocket. "And you lied to me about it."

"He was a traitor. He would have destroyed everything I have worked for, all I have planned for the last twenty years."

Zhihan nodded. "Where did the Lotus thrust the sword? In his heart?"

The old man made an impatient sound. "What does that matter?"

"I want to know."

"I told her to make it quick."

"Then I will do the same." Zhihan lunged sideways, the knife in his hand slashing at his father's chest. Ruiban threw up his arms, trying desperately to shield himself.

The car spun out of control, sending both men into the dashboard. Zhihan shouted an obscenity and wrenched the wheel, trying to turn out of the spin.

There was a shuddering impact as the front of the car smashed through a guardrail, then Zhihan saw the water rushing up to meet them.

He smiled. At least he had done this much. He had gotten revenge for his brother, and perhaps a little for the two FBI agents his father had ordered him to kill. "Good-bye, Father."

Ruiban screamed, and then the car hit the rocks at the bottom of the cliff and exploded.

Chapter 15

"Where is she?"

General Eckard set aside the report he was studying. "Afternoon, Kal. I thought you'd be in the hospital for a few more days."

"I got better." He strode over to the big desk. "What did you do with Sarah Ravenowitz, Billy?"

"Sit down, Kal." Eckard lifted a brow when he didn't move. "I may only have one star on you, General, but that gives me enough rank to make it an order."

Kalen dropped into the chair in front of him. "I gave your team orders to bring her directly to me after the cleanup in Chinatown. Why didn't that happen?"

"Because my orders superseded them. Sarah was brought to the military police station and turned herself in to the authorities as soon as the operation was finished. As she promised."

He was beginning to wonder if the world had turned upside down and he was the last to realize it. "Why would she do that?"

Eckard removed a page from a file in his desk and handed it to Kalen. "Here's her confession, signed day before yesterday."

The words on the paper made no sense, no matter how many times he read them. "She confessed? To what? Why?"

"Major Ravenowitz has been AWOL for eight years, Kal." The general got to his feet, and went to the window to watch a detachment of soldiers practicing for parade march by. "Maybe she couldn't live with the guilt of what she'd done anymore."

Kalen told him exactly what he thought of that.

Eckard chuckled and glanced back at him. "I didn't think you'd swallow that worm. She's quite a woman, your major."

Kalen felt like upending the desk and tossing it through the general and the window. "We've known each other long enough to dispense with the usual bullshit, Billy. Now, you want to tell me what is going on, or do I go over your head?"

"We apprehended her right after you were abducted from the airport, and she made a deal. Her freedom for your life. I gave her the men she needed to raid the warehouse and get you out. In return, she confessed to the charges and will plead no contest at her court-martial. She'll also keep the media out of it, which the army appreciates." Eckard gestured at the paper. "I dismissed the conspiracy charges and cited extenuating circumstances. She'll probably do ten years, instead of twenty."

Over his dead body. "Are they holding her at Langley?"

"Yeah, but the court-martial convenes tomorrow." Eckard gave him a sad smile. "There's nothing you can do now but let her go, son."

"I did that once," he told the general. "It was the biggest mistake I ever made in my life."

The general looked faintly alarmed. "Think about this, Kal. You're already neck-deep in fertilizer after the way this mission went down. You're not going to do your career any good, getting publicly involved with this woman."

"I'm resigning my commission."

"Why?"

"Sarah's pregnant with my kid." He turned and walked out.

The general thought about the situation as he unwrapped one of the Cuban cigars he'd appropriated during his last visit to Guantánamo. Then he chuckled as he lit the end. "Pregnant. Son of a bitch. You don't get any more involved than that."

Her cell in Oakland had been two feet wider than her cell at Langley, Raven realized as she paced the floor. She wondered what her cell in Leavenworth would be like.

At least I'll be able to see the baby once a month, after he's born.

Delivering the bad news to Honore via telephone had not sent the Frenchwoman into a paroxysm of swearing, for once. She'd wept instead. "*Cherie*, what can I do?"

"I'll need a baby-sitter in a few months. The job lasts ten years," Raven said matter-of-factly. "Would you be available?"

Honore promised to take the baby, and then she wept some more. Then she demanded to know what Kalen was going to do about her predicament.

"There's nothing he can do. You can ask him to help out with the baby-sitting." She wasn't sure how he'd feel about sharing in the care and responsibility for their child, but she would hope for the best. "Remind him that the kid isn't going to have a mom for a while, so a dad would come in handy."

"I will show *le enfant* your photos, every day," Honore promised her. "He will know he has the most beautiful *maman* in the world."

She had been treated with a mixture of contempt and awe since being transported to Langley. One female MP had shown her instantaneous resentment by shoving her every step of the long walk to her cell, while taunting her with what she'd look like after ten years of hard labor.

"You mean, like you?" Raven couldn't help saying, and nearly got knocked into a wall for the remark.

Another MP, this one a young starstruck boy, had snuck back to ask her to autograph one of her magazine covers for his girlfriend, and brought her an extra dinner tray that night. They kept her segregated from the other prisoners awaiting trial, so she had no one to talk to.

"Anyway, Garlene and I are planning to get married, soon as I make spec-four," the young MP was telling her after he came to collect her tray and lingered to tell her his life story. "She's not as pretty as you are, Major, but she's a real good cook. Almost as good as my mom."

There were worse reasons to get married. "I wish you and your fiancée every happiness, Bobby." Raven gazed at his earnest face and wondered if she'd ever been so young. And remembered a night with Kalen when she'd threatened to get pregnant and force him marry her.

I want a kid with red hair, like yours.

It was hard to do this and think of him. "Can I give you one bit of advice?"

"Sure, Major."

"Stay with her," a deep voice said from behind him. "Don't ever let her out of your sight, not for a minute."

Bobby came to attention as soon as he saw the starred uniform. "Yes, sir. Sorry, sir, I didn't hear you come in."

"I need a moment alone with this prisoner, soldier."

Bobby made a neat pivot to the right and marched off, leaving Kalen standing in front of her cell.

"You're supposed to be in the hospital." Raven nearly threw herself at the bars, then backed away. "Eckard?" He nodded. "Goddamn two-faced generals, always promising one thing and delivering another."

"I keep my promises." He walked up to the bars and curled his hands around them. "And you should have struck a better bargain for yourself."

"Sorry. I was kind of preoccupied with saving your life."

"You did, for which I am very grateful." He glanced behind her. "You didn't mention that you'd be spending ten years in prison for it."

She shrugged. "No big deal. It's what I deserve, anyway."

"What about the baby? Doesn't he deserve a mother and a father, together, happy, loving him?" He extended a hand into the cell, holding it out for her to take. "Come here to me."

"Kalen—"

"Come here." When she did, he curled his arm around her neck and tugged her toward the bars until her brow touched his. "Do you trust me?"

She nodded, and closed her eyes.

"Then I want you to do exactly what you planned tomorrow, at the court-martial. Acknowledge the validity of your confession and plead no contest. I'll take it from there."

"You can't stop this. I know you're a general, but there are some things even a Joint Chief couldn't stop. This is one of them." She frowned. "What *are* you going to try to do?"

"I can't tell you that." He lifted his head and pressed his mouth against her brow. "Sweetheart, you've got to give me absolute, blind trust, or it won't work. Can you do that for me, and you, and the baby?"

"Yes, but—"

"Good." He stepped back away from the cell. "I'll see you in court tomorrow. Oh, and one more thing." He gave her a direct look. "I am ordering you as your superior officer not to describe the events of your life since the operation in China to the present date. Ever. Do you understand that order, Major?"

"Of course I do, but—Kalen?"

He walked down the corridor without looking back.

Bobby appeared a few seconds later, looking pale and even more awed.

"Do you know who that was?" he demanded in a stage whisper. "General Grady. General Kalen Effing Grady. He's supposed to be moving up to the big table next year. Commander in chief of the whole goddamned army."

"Yep." Raven went to lie down on the hard cell bunk in her cell and stared at the dull gray ceiling. "That was him."

In the morning, the dress uniform she'd ordered arrived, and Sarah dressed carefully. If this was going to be her last public appearance, she would look her absolute best.

Bobby helped by smuggling her some of his girlfriend's cosmetics. "Garlene says she'll never use them again. She's just going to put them in a box and take them out just to look at them, you know—you being a big celebrity and all. It's just a thrill for her to have something you touched."

She took the cosmetics, which were cheap and all the wrong colors for her, and felt like crying. Then she knew how to thank him.

"Something I've touched, hmmm?" She leaned close to the bars where he was looking in, and planted a decidedly sisterly kiss on his half-open mouth. "There. Now she can stare at you."

"Uh, thanks, Major." He staggered off, still touching his mouth as if not quite sure the kiss had actually happened.

Raven used Garlene's makeup as primary colors, and quickly blended a palette that she could use on the lid of one shadow case. As she darkened her eyelids and reddened her lips, she wondered what she would look like in ten years.

Definitely not like this.

Her face required constant maintenance, the surgeon had warned her, and it had to be protected from harsh chemicals and extreme temperatures—obviously something she'd be unable to control in prison. If this plan of Kalen's didn't work, and she ended up emerging from Leavenworth after a decade, would he still want her?

He loved the way you used to look, a chilly little voice inside her said. *Maybe in ten years, it'll all equal out.*

Her MP escorts arrived in dress uniforms, indicating they'd be with her all the way into court. They cuffed her hands behind her back before she was allowed to step out of the cell, and then she had to stand still to be leg-shackled. The short chain that hung between her ankles forced her to cut her stride in half to avoid falling on her face.

This is real elegant. Some reporter from Vanity Fair *would probably pay big bucks to snap off a few exposé shots of me right now.*

As Langley was a maximum-security site, she really wasn't worried. Besides, what did it matter? She didn't care what she looked like anymore. All she wanted was to make sure that her baby was safe and that Kalen knew she loved him.

Going to prison for ten years is one heck of a way to show devotion, the tiny cold voice whined as she was led into the Judge Advocate General's building.

The MPs removed her shackles and cuffs, and she was allowed a few moments to compose herself before they escorted her into the courtroom.

It was practically empty. No one sat in the spectators' seats, and only two officers occupied the prosecution table. Her own legal counsel, a rather jaded warrant officer who had told her she was an idiot as soon as she arrived at Langley, indicated with a wave of one weary hand that she should sit beside him.

"This isn't going to take very long," he told her. "Your confession has been forwarded from Oakland as evidence, and the judge will pass sentence as soon as you enter a plea. You're sure you still want to go with no contest?"

Trust me, Sarah.

"Yes."

"Your life, Major."

The bailiff called out for them to rise as the military judge entered the courtroom, and took his position behind a large, plain table at the front. Unlike civilian court, the military didn't waste its money on interior decorating to impress.

"Special court-martial is convened by Commanding Officer, General Paul B. Nilson, United States Army Air Defense Liaison, Langley Air Force Base, Virginia, on this seventeenth day of March, 2002." The bailiff continued, reading the reduced charge of desertion, handed the file to the judge, then resumed his position.

The judge, a full bird colonel, looked over the documents. "Major Sarah J. Ravenowitz, counsel, please rise." When Raven and her attorney stood, he set down the file. "How do you plead?"

Not guilty, not guilty, not guilty! "No contest, sir."

"Are you aware, Major Ravenowitz, that by entering such a plea you will be subject to automatic conviction of these charges, and sentenced accordingly?"

Good-bye, Kalen. "Yes, sir."

"Counsel." The judge glared at her attorney. "Have you advised your client of the gravity of her situation and the consequences she now faces?"

Before her lawyer could speak, three people walked into the courtroom. Raven turned her head, and saw Kalen, Conor, and Brooke Oliver marching in.

The judge peered at them through his glasses. "Let me guess. You're here for the major?"

Kalen snapped to attention. "General Kalen Michael Grady, division commander, Central Intelligence Division. Colonel, I have evidence that will refute all charges against Major Ravenowitz."

"You do." The judge rubbed his chin. "General, this prisoner has just pleaded no contest to these charges. You're a little late."

"She had no choice but to enter that plea, sir. This is a matter of national security."

The judge didn't like hearing that. "Are you telling me she was forced to enter a plea against her will?"

"No. With the court's permission, may I address the defendant?" When the judge nodded, Kalen turned to her. "Major Ravenowitz, were you ordered by me not to reveal any details of your actions over the last seven years to anyone?"

Raven realized what he was doing, and nearly stuttered getting the words out. "Yes, sir."

Kalen faced the judge again. "As you can see, my orders were implicit, your honor. Major Ravenowitz has been obliged to remain silent, under any circumstances. Even upon pain of imprisonment by her own country."

Now the judge looked suspicious. "What could be so important, General, that this young woman could not even speak in her own defense?"

"In order for me to relay that information, sir, you will have to clear this courtroom."

"If this turns out to be some kind of joke, I will hold you in contempt of court." The judge ordered the courtroom cleared and waited until the final officer exited before gesturing for Kalen, Conor and Brooke to approach. "Take the prosecutor's desk, since he's not using it, General."

"Permission to approach, your honor." Kalen took a case from Brooke and carried it up to the judge. "These documents are eyes-only, highly sensitive, classified data. I cannot enter them into evidence, but I provide them as proof of Major Ravenowitz's duties during the time I had her declared AWOL." He gestured toward Brooke and Conor. "I've also brought witnesses, CID agents who have been in close contact and working with the major on various operations in Asia and Europe."

The judge peered inside the case. "Good Lord, there have to be a hundred thousand pages of data in here." He took out a handful and skimmed through them. "Why keep the major on AWOL status all these years, General?"

"It was the best means we had to provide her with credible cover, sir."

The judge hmphed. "Best you give me the short version of all this, or I'll be sitting here reading until my retirement kicks in."

"Yes, sir. After receiving severe facial injuries in China, Major Ravenowitz underwent reconstructive surgery to alter her appearance. Since that time, she has used a new identity to operate deep undercover for my department, with an emphasis on tracking an international assassin known as the Lotus."

Raven felt numb as she listened to Kalen outline everything she had done to track the killer, and other operations she had worked on for other countries as what he claimed was a strictly as-necessary basis.

Conor was called up to show the judge the computer files, and Raven recognized the description of some of them. *I forgot, they cracked my Judas code.*

But the most stunning moment was when Kalen requested that Brooke testify to the judge about the number of regular reports she claimed to have received from Raven over the years.

"Sir, the major and I have been in close communication every week since I joined the division," Brooke outright lied. "I have prepared some four hundred weekly reports from her transmissions personally, and have verified them for authenticity of data. Every report Major Ravenowitz has made has been of the highest standards and great value to the division's efforts against international crime."

Kalen added the pièce de résistance by crediting her with the success of the Dai operation, during which she uncovered Hyatt as the CID mole for the Chinese. "Had it not been for Major Ravenowitz's quick thinking, Captain Oliver and I would have been murdered by the tong."

"I was wondering where those bruises had come from." The judge sat back. "Very well, General, you've made your case for the major. Sit down, all of you." He turned to Raven. "Major, these people are either very dedicated officers, or very accomplished liars. Do you have anything you want to add to this?"

Unable to breathe, much less speak, Raven shook her head.

"Very well. General, you can pack up your secret documents and call everyone back in here now."

As soon as the officers of the court returned, the judge ordered everyone to rise.

"I don't question the Uniform Code of Military Justice. It is the soldier's law, and as soldiers we are required to adhere to it. However, certain extenuating circumstances exist that allow exceptions to the letter of the law. These circumstances, which will remain classified, qualify under both the 'hazardous duty' and the 'important service' exemptions as specified in article 85, paragraph 49.3C, subsection A. In serving to protect the common welfare of this country, and under standing orders not to reveal the nature of her assignment, Major Ravenowitz has been compelled to act accordingly. I hereby find the defendant not guilty of the charge of desertion. Major, you are reinstated to your full rank, retroactive to the date charges were first brought against you, and you are free to go."

Chapter 16

"You grew up in this place?"

"I was born in Japan and lived there while my mother was still alive," Meko said as she led Tara into Nine Dragon House. "But, yes, most of my childhood was spent under this roof."

"It's kinda cool, but . . . creepy, too." The teenager rubbed her arms. "I bet you're glad you're getting rid of this place for good."

Meko had listed the house with a real estate agent as soon as she'd discovered her father had left the property to her in his will. "Yes."

Yet even as she said that, her gaze strayed to one table in the front room, and the memory of the deep, passionate kiss Sean had given her there surfaced.

Wherever you are, Sean Delaney, I hope you have finally found some peace within yourself. Because I certainly haven't.

She gave Tara the tour, saving the Dragon Wall for last. As she knelt to clear away some overgrown weeds from the small blue dragon, she traced the outlines of the pearl it protected, and looked up at her young friend. "Pretty lame, huh?"

"Nah, I think it's the cutest one." Tara's dolphin bracelet jingled faintly as she gestured toward the tiles. "What's the deal with the big white basketball?"

"It's not a basketball, it's an enchanted pearl."

"You're kidding." The girl laughed. "Imagine wearing a rope of those around your neck."

"It's not that kind of pearl, it's more like a crystal ball with great magical powers." She grinned as she recalled the story she'd made up about her dragon as a child. "See, the smallest dragon here was given the pearl and told that she had to guard it and keep it safe forever. She was too small to fight the other dragons, and the pearl was too big to fit in her pocket."

"So she called out the Dragon National Guard?" Tara teased.

"No. She wrapped herself around it, and fell into a deep sleep that lasted a thousand years. And when she woke up, she had grown three times her original size, while all the other dragons had grown old and weak." Meko dusted off her hands. "From then on she had no problem fighting them off and protecting the pearl."

The teenager giggled. "That sounds like Sleeping Beauty meets Crouching Tiger, Hidden Dragon. So what happened to the dragon after she kicked all that old dragon butt?"

"I don't know," Meko admitted as she stood up. "Maybe she took their pearls and kept them for herself."

"She wouldn't do that," Tara said, sounding indignant. "She'd give them away, and then she'd be restored to her true form for being so kind—a princess."

"A dragon who turns into a princess?" Meko nodded. "I like that ending." There was a rustling sound from behind the wall, and concealing her alarm, she took Tara's hand. "Let's get out of here, huh? We've still got to get some sourdough bread for our picnic."

As Tara chattered about their plans for the day, Meko felt someone watching her from the garden. "Damn, I forgot to check the side door," she said. "Get in the car. I'll be right back."

She went around the house, wading through the hip-high weeds to get to the small labyrinth her father had built for her and her brothers as children. It should have been badly in need of trimming, just like the rest of the yard, but someone had been carefully maintaining the low hedge.

"Hello?" She looked around, almost hoping it was Sean. "Is someone there?"

There was no reply, and no more sound.

As Meko walked slowly back to the car, she glanced over her shoulder. A figure stood just inside the labyrinth hedge, but it wasn't Sean Delaney. It was an old man with white hair, stooped with age. He wore a black robe with a star on the back and carried a slightly bent stick.

Then he vanished.

Meko almost went back to the labyrinth, but decided it was only Xun, her father's gardener. That would explain why the hedges were trimmed but the rest of the lawn and gardens were in utter disarray. It was probably all the old man could do to keep the labyrinth in shape.

It didn't explain why he was wearing her father's favorite robe, though.

"Spooky place, huh?" Tara said when she got in the car.

"Why do you say that?"

"You look like you've just seen a ghost."

She started the car and pulled out of the drive. She was well down the street before she replied, "Maybe I did."

He watched her lock up the house, then followed her as she drove to a nearby bakery. They made an odd couple, the tall, lanky teenager and the petite, graceful woman, but from the way they laughed together he could tell they were enjoying themselves.

He should have stayed away, but he wanted to see her one more time. *Just this once, while she's here. To make sure she's okay.* She would never know. As far as he was concerned, she never had to see him again.

He got out of the car when they did, and shadowed them from their picnic spot to the shops of Fisherman's Wharf. He watched them feed scraps of bread to the bay otters, and peer in the window displays, and all the while he wanted nothing more than to catch up, say hello, and see how she would react.

Maybe this time, he thought as he rubbed the back of his head, *she wouldn't try to fracture my skull.*

The girl went into a bikini shop while Meko sat on a bench outside. He walked across from her, watching her as he passed. She closed her eyes and turned her face up to the sun, as if she hadn't a care in the world.

And as long as Sean Delaney stayed away from her, she wouldn't.

Kalen waited until they were outside the court and well out of earshot before he thanked Brooke and Conor for helping him.

"It was the least I could do, considering." Kalen's point man leaned over and gave Raven a kiss on the cheek. "Conor's an excellent name for a boy, you know." Then, whistling, he strolled off.

"Major." Brooke stepped in front of Raven and snapped out a sharp salute. "It has been an honor serving with you."

"You just lied your ass off for me," Raven said. "Why?"

Brooke smiled a little. "Because I owed you." She nodded to Kalen, and followed Conor.

Raven stood staring after them for a long time. "You didn't tell me you were going to perjure yourselves."

"We bent the truth."

"Kal, you just took a very open-and-shut case of desertion and twisted it into a slinky." She shook her head slowly. "If anyone finds out what you did—if that judge checks up on you—all three of you could go to jail with me."

"He won't check up me, and if he does, he'll find backup documentation for everything I said." Kalen took her arm and led her to a waiting convertible.

"What did you do, falsify every record in the CID?"

"No. I threatened to resign my commission." He opened the car door for her. "The Joint Chiefs decided I was more important than prosecuting a retiring major."

"Retiring?" She sat down and watched him circle the car to the driver's side. "I'm retiring?"

"Medical—you're pregnant, it's a totally legal out for you." He glanced at her. "Unless you'd prefer to return to duty?"

"No, I've been out of the army too long to go back. And Honore would kill me." She sat back and rubbed her fingers against her eyes. "So that's it? That's all that happens?"

"There's one more thing we have to do." He sounded almost happy. "Feel like taking a ride?"

"Sure." She had nothing to do but sit and contemplate her own outrageous good luck for the next several hours, until she emerged from this daze. "Where to?"

"You'll see."

Kalen drove from Langley out into the country, past towns and places he had taken her on long weekends when they had been lovers. Some of the trees were beginning to bud, and misty green new grass covered the fields in all directions.

"I forgot how pretty it is out here." She watched as they passed house after beautiful house. "Are we visiting someplace special?"

"We're almost there." He turned down a narrow dirt road and drove another quarter of a mile through some of the most gorgeous elm and oak trees Raven had ever seen. Squirrels were out chasing each other through the branches, and birds were everywhere.

But what took her breath away was the house that appeared at the end of the private drive. It was exactly the kind of house she'd always wanted—big, solid, built of brick and wood, with huge windows and a second story that promised a loft with a view.

"God, it's beautiful," she said as he parked and climbed out to get her door.

"It's mine."

"Trade you my apartment in Paris for it." She laughed as she walked up to the door and watched him unlock it. "When did you buy this?"

"Seven years ago." He gestured for her to go in. Outside, the house looked ideal. Inside, it could have been designed for her personally. Natural wood furniture covered with bold, jewel-toned cushions, an oversized fireplace, quilts and brass and flowers placed at strategic points through the wide front room. She walked through it, unable to blink, into a kitchen that provided the most up-to-date, efficient appliances, all in gleaming white porcelain and polished cherry wood.

"This is unreal." She moved faster, climbing the stairs to the second floor, which Kalen had made into a master bedroom. The view through the peaked window looked out over a horse pasture hemmed by a majestic circle of old oaks. On the bed was an old blue quilt sewn in a pattern of interlocking rings, and she sank down on it, touching the timeworn patches with her fingers.

"You kept my grandmother's quilt."

"It's a beautiful thing. Beautiful things are meant to be cherished."

She jerked her head up. "Do you know how much this means to me?" He nodded. "It's a dream house; you must love living here."

He shook his head. "I've never lived in it."

She couldn't have heard him correctly. "What?"

"It was a present, for you. For when you got back from China." He went to the bureau by the wall and opened a drawer. "It goes with this." He handed her a small, square velvet box.

Raven brushed the dust off the top before she opened it. Inside was a ring set with two blue topazes. "Our birthstones."

"Let me do that." He took the ring from the box and slid it onto her finger. "It's a little loose."

"I was heavier seven years ago, wasn't I?" She felt dizzy. "Kalen, why did you do all this?"

"Do you remember what you said to me before you left for China?"

I want a house, and ring, and you, naked, on my grandmother's quilt, waiting for me when I get back. "Yes, but I was just kidding, like always."

"I wasn't." He took her hands between his. "I was going to ask you to marry me when you came back from that mission. That's why I could never live here. I'd stop by on weekends, telling myself I had to work on the place, but it was just so I could think of you. Imagine you here, with me."

"What about when you found out I was still alive?"

"I still came here. Whenever I was missing you. It was as close to you as I could get." He looked around. "I tried to remember everything you said you wanted. There's a big backyard, with enough room for a football game or two. There's a stable for horses, a creek nearby where we can take our kids fishing."

"All this, for me." She couldn't quite grasp that. "Waiting for me, all this time. And you never told me."

"Now you know." He looked down at her. "So, what do you think?"

"I think you love me. I think you've always loved me and you never told me about this and I should smack you, but you have enough bruises." She went into his arms. "Why didn't you tell me, Kal?"

"I thought I had all the time in the world."

"You do now." She poked his chest with her finger. "Spill it."

"Okay." He looked out at the pasture. "I love you. I'll resign from the army to be with you. If you want to go back to Paris, I'll go with you. All I want is for us to live together, and to raise our kids together. Maybe, if you change your mind about getting married, we'll do that too."

"I don't know." She stepped out of his arms and walked over to the bed. "Things have changed—I've changed. I don't know if I can settle for less than what I really want."

"Then tell me what you want."

"A civilian position working with the CID."

"Done."

"This house."

"As long as I can live in it with you, it's yours. I'll transfer the title tomorrow."

"You can keep the title; I'd just like to live here. That's not all." She slid back on the bed and unbuttoned her jacket. "I want to retire from modeling."

"No argument there."

She gave him a droll look. "I didn't think there would be. I would like to do special appearances for Honore, once or twice a year. I owe it to her."

"Not a problem. Anything else?"

"Oh, a whole list. I want you, on this bed, right now." She tossed her jacket on the footboard and began pulling her shirttail out of her skirt. "I think the exact specification was naked, on my grandmother's quilt."

He eased down beside her and watched her hands intently. "And?"

"You have to be a father to my baby."

"I already am."

"Not just biologically. In practice, too. Four A.M. feedings, walking the floor when he's colicky—all of it. You're also going to have to buy the baseball gloves, the first car he wants, and have that man-to-man talk with him about the birds and the bees when the time comes."

"Can I negotiate on the sex talk?"

"No, but if we have a girl, I'll do it. And this ring." She held it up to the light to watch the twin stones sparkle. "It's not enough. I want another one to go with it."

He smiled slowly. "Any particular style?"

"A plain gold band will do."

He eased her back on the bed. "We'll pick it out together."

"You have to wear one just like it," she said, and breathed in deeply. "And you have to keep smelling like this forever."

"I can manage that."

"There are a few more things, but we can talk about them later. Just one more thing now."

He bent his head until his mouth was a mere whisper apart from hers. "What else?"

"You have to marry me as soon as possible. In a tux. In a church. And I get to wear Vera Wang."

"Done." He kissed her, deep and slow, then closed his arms around her. "Welcome home, Sarah."

She was home, Raven realized. Home for good, home forever. Because she was in Kalen's arms, and that was really all the home she would ever want, or ever need.

Turn the page for a look
at the last book in
Jessica Hall's thrilling trilogy—

THE
KISSING BLADES

Coming from Signet in August 2003

Kameko Sayura added a thirty thousand dollar check to the daily deposit bag thinking how lovely the custom designed emerald and gold necklace and matching hoop earrings would look on the woman who'd just bought them.

"Nice chunk of change, boss." commented her young assistant, Tara, as she finished tallying the slip. Tara was as dear to Meko as a daughter, but not even for Tara would Meko give up her practicality.

She pointed one finger at the ceiling. "It means I get the roof fixed *before* the summer rains get here."

"You're such a Scrooge." Tara pressed the back of her hand against her forehead in mock exhaustion. "After I spent two hours sweating over the hot new display, too."

"Let me see." Meko inspected the case reserved for her costume and trend pieces, where Tara had artfully arranged Meko's newest offering, lovers' cuffs, made from a pair of mink-lined enameled handcuffs. "Very nice work."

"Yes, despite her many abuses, I'm still devoted to my thankless emloyer." Tara sighed, then glanced at the wall clock. "Better get going if you want to hit the bank before it closes. Do you want me to lock up?"

Meko shouldered her purse and took out her car keys. "No, I have to finish setting that bracelet, so I'll be right back. I'm going to lock you in, though."

"Do you have time to run by the post office?" Tara produced a small trial-sample box. "You wanted to send this back to that German company."

"I'll throw it in the car and run by in the morning." Meko took the deposit bag and folded it in half before slipping it into her purse, then added, "Would you mind pulling twenty-six rubies for me before you go? Use the one carat brilliant stock that just came in."

The teenager's blue eyes widened. "You want me to match them?"

"You've got a great eye for color." Meko pursed her lips. "And, if J.Lo buys it for her mom tomorrow, you'll get ten percent extra commission." She grinned. "If that's acceptable to you, Ms. Cratchet."

"Acceptable?" Tara's voice cracked on the word. "I think I just became your slave for life."

"I've always wanted to own my own teenager." She went to the door, then recalled another errand and retrieved the duffle bag of clothes she needed to take to the cleaners from behind the counter. "Use the sorting tray on my desk, Tara, the lamp in there has the best light. And remember to wear a pair of gloves."

She made a face. "I hate gloves."

"If you become sensitized to working with metals and stones, your hands will crack and bleed every time, and you'll never be able to work as a jeweler. *Wear* the gloves." She slid on her sunglasses. "Be back in a minute."

Meko rarely left Tara alone in the store, and locking her in was simply an extra security measure. Despite their upscale location on the fringes of Beverly Hills, the store was always a potential target for robbery. With over two hundred thousand dollars of jewelry on the premises, and more in loose stones and precious metals in her workroom, Meko knew the risks. She'd even recently upgraded her state-of-the-art security system to send out a silent alarm. Still, her expensive stock took second place to Tara's personal safety.

There were only two people in line at the bank, so she was able to make the deposit quickly, and stopped on the way back to the store to drop off her dry cleaning and pick up some giant-sized lemon ices from a vendor at the park. Tara loved them, and they needed to celebrate a great sale every now and then.

As she parked in her reserved spot by the curb in front of the store, Meko eyed her reflection in the rearview mirror. "Okay, so I'm spoiling her. Sue me."

Juggling the ices while unlocking the front door took a minute, then Meko walked in. "Got a surprise for you, kiddo," she called out as she locked the door behind her. "Three guesses what it is."

There was no answer.

Too busy sorting through the rubies. Meko set the cups down by the register and wandered back toward her office. "Tara? Take a break for a minute, these things are melting all over the—"

She stopped in the open doorway and stared.

The room looked like a tornado had pushed through it—papers scattered, file drawers hanging open, and chairs overturned. But the chaos wasn't what made Meko press a shaking hand over her mouth. Someone had driven a sword into the top of her desk. The ancient blade looked brittle, and had strange markings etched into it. Markings that dripped with wet, fresh blood. And something was hanging, caught on the hilt. A broken bracelet, made of links that looked like dolphins.

Tara's bracelet.

She didn't know how long she stood there, but the sound of something ringing snapped her out of her trance. At first, she couldn't identify the muffled noise. Then she recognized the ring.

Her cell phone.

She staggered away from the office and followed the ringing until she found her purse. Her hands shook so badly that she nearly dropped the phone twice before she could switch it on. Yet as she raised it to her ear, she had a terrible feeling she knew who was calling.

"Hello?"

"Your young friend is not dead yet," a man said in heavily accented English. "Do you wish her to live?"

"What?" Meko grabbed the edge of the counter to stop the room from spinning. "Where is Tara? Is she all right? What have you done to her?"

"We want the swords."

It was several days later before Kameko was able to start her search for the swords and for Tara. She drove slowly through the valley, following the directions the gas station attendant had given her, but first she had to find Sean Delaney and convince him to help her. God knew he owed her this.

As she drove, she replayed in her mind the events that had compelled her to become a fugitive. The morning after Tara was abducted, Meko had returned to the police station. Tara's parents had been there, too, but they weren't happy to see her. Tara's father had to hold his wife back to keep her from attacking Meko.

"You bitch, what did you do with my daughter?" Rebecca Jones had screamed as Meko walked by.

The detective who had taken her statement at the store ushered Meko past the distraught couple and into an interview room, where he informed her that Tara's blood had been matched to the blood on the sword. No other evidence of a break-in, however, had been found.

Don't tell the police anything.

"Your doors weren't forced, and you claim nothing was stolen." In a gentle voice, he said, "Make it easy on yourself, Ms. Sayura. Tell me what really happened between you and Tara yesterday."

"Nothing!"

He was not convinced. "I'm sure you didn't mean to hurt her. Was it an accident? Did she threaten you?"

Bile surged in her throat. She could say nothing of the men who had done this, but she couldn't help trying to defend herself. "Why do you think I would hurt her?"

"Everyone has secrets. Like you: your father was Takeshi Sayura, one of the biggest crime bosses on the west coast. And your ex-husband is a bag man for his syndicate," the detective said. "Did Tara find out something she wasn't supposed to? Did she threaten to go to the media with it?"

"My father is dead, and I don't hear from Nick anymore." Her voice went toneless. "I have never had anything to do with their illegal activities."

"But you have to admit, this doesn't look good. A

sixteen-year-old girl suddenly disappeared from your shop, and you were the last person to see her alive."

"You're wasting your time." Frustrated beyond belief, she flung a hand at the window. "You should be out there, looking for her!"

"Oh, we are, ma'am, and we will find her—wherever you left her." He sat back in his chair. "If you tell me what happened, and where she is, maybe we can work something out with the D.A."

The D.A. couldn't save Tara. Nor could Meko. But there was one man who might be able to help her find the swords, and get Tara back.

Sean Delaney.

"I can't help you, Detective." She rose to her feet, impatient to leave. "May I go now?"

"I'm sorry, ma'am. You just don't get it, do you?" The detective sighed as he stood. "Kameko Sayura, you're under arrest for the murder of Tara Jones. You have the right to remain silent. . . ."

By the time she was released on bail two days later, Tara's parents were on all the news stations, pleading for any information that would lead to finding Tara. Kameko's photo was shown, and she was identified not as Tara's employer, but as the prime suspect in her disappearance, and the last person to see their daughter alive. Meko knew her best chance of finding Tara was with Sean Delaney—the last man on earth she wanted to ask for help, but the only man she believed could provide it—if she could find him and if he was sober.